MVFOL

RVEL UNIVERSE ULTIMATE SPIDER-MAN: WEB WARRIORS VOL. 1. Contains material originally published in magazine form as MARVEL VERSE ULTIMATE SPIDER-MAN: WEB WARRIORS #1-4. First printing 2015. ISBN# 978-0-7851-9383-8. Published by MARVEL WORLDWIDE, , a subsidiary of MARVEL ENTERTAINMENT, LLC. OFFICE OF PUBLICATION: 135 West 50th Street, New York, NY 10020. Copyright © 2014 and 5 Marvel Characters, Inc. All rights reserved. All characters featured in this issue and the distinctive names and likenesses thereof, and all ed indicia are trademarks of Marvel Characters, Inc. No similarity between any of the names, characters, persons, and/or institutions in this azine with those of any living or dead person or institution is intended, and any such similarity which may exist is purely coincidental. **Printed ne U.S.A.** ALAN FINE, EVP - Office of the President, Marvel Worldwide, Inc. and EVP & CMO Marvel Characters B.V.; DAN BUCKLEY, Publisher & ident - Print, Animation & Digital Divisions; JOE QUESADA, Chief Creative Officer; TOM BREVOORT, SVP of Publishing; DAVID BOGART, SVP of rations & Procurement, Publishing; C.B. CEBULSKI, SVP of Creator & Content Development; DAVID GABRIEL, SVP Print, Sales & Marketing; JIM EEFE, VP of Operations & Logistics; DAN CARR, Executive Director of Publishing Technology; SUSAN CRESPI, Editorial Operations Manager; ALEX ALES, Publishing Operations Manager; STAN LEE, Chairman Emeritus. For information regarding advertising in Marvel Comics or on Marvel. , please contact Niza Disla, Director of Marvel Partnerships, at ndisla@marvel.com. For Marvel subscription inquiries, please call 800-217- . **Manufactured between 1/30/2015 and 3/9/2015 by SHERIDAN BOOKS, INC., CHELSEA, MI, USA.**

87654321

MARVEL ULTIMATE SPIDER-MAN WEB-WARRIORS

BASED ON THE TV SERIES WRITTEN BY
BRIAN MICHAEL BENDIS, MAN OF ACTION,
SCOTT MOSIER, KEVIN BURKE & CHRIS "DOC" WYATT

DIRECTED BY
PHIL PIGNOTTI & TIM MALTBY

ADAPTED BY
JOE CARAMAGNA

EDITOR
SEBASTIAN GIRNER

CONSULTING EDITOR
JON MOISAN

SENIOR EDITOR
MARK PANICCIA

SPIDER-MAN CREATED BY STAN LEE & STEVE DITKO

Collection Editor: **Alex Starbuck**
Assistant Editor: **Sarah Brunstad**
Editors, Special Projects: **Jennifer Grünwald & Mark D. Beazley**
Senior Editor, Special Projects: **Jeff Youngquist**
SVP Print, Sales & Marketing: **David Gabriel**
Head of Marvel Television: **Jeph Loeb**
Book Designer: **Joe Frontirre**

Editor In Chief: **Axel Alonso**
Chief Creative Officer: **Joe Quesada**
Publisher: **Dan Buckley**
Executive Producer: **Alan Fine**

SPECIAL THANKS TO PRODUCT FACTORY

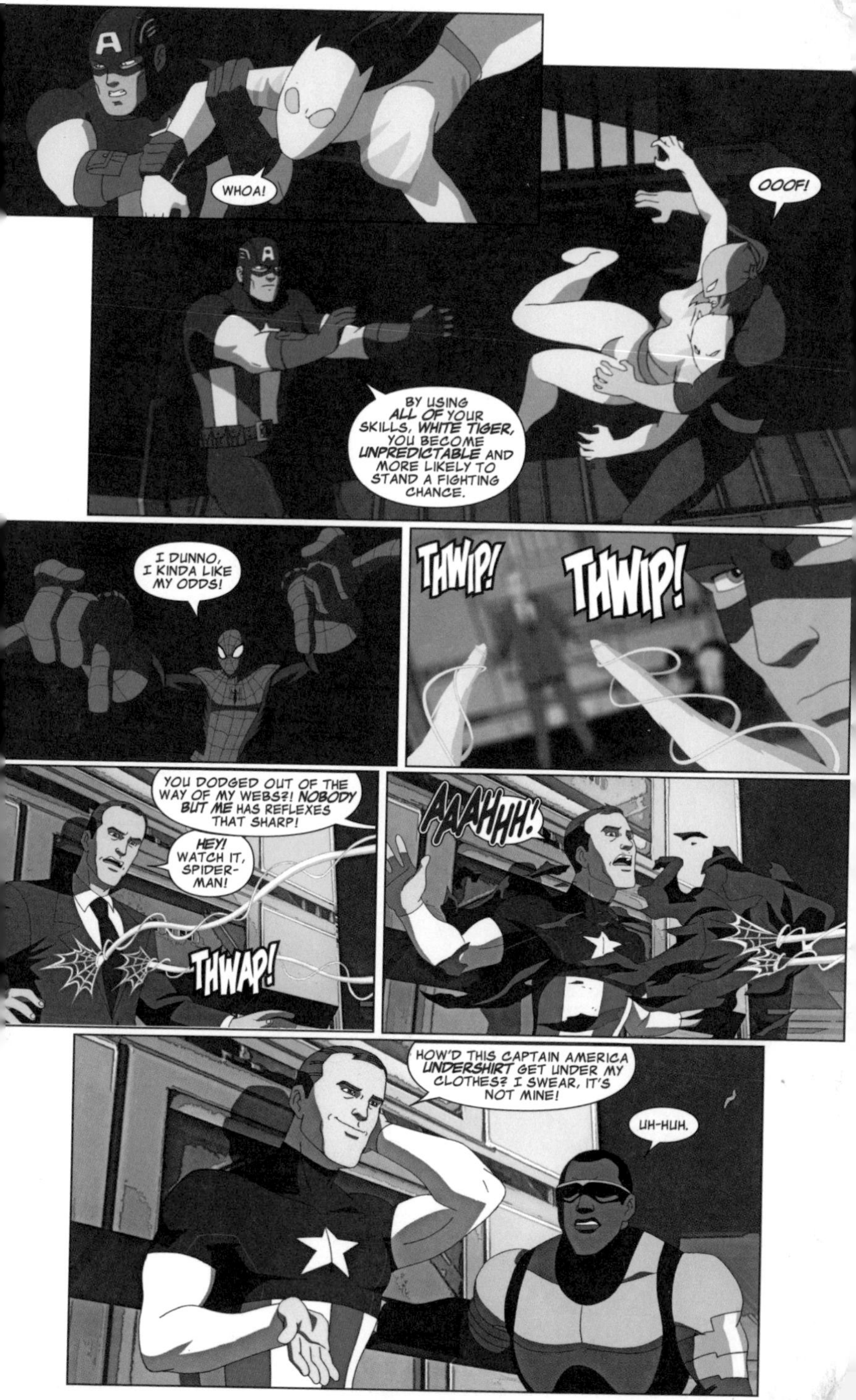

WHOA!
OOOF!
BY USING ALL OF YOUR SKILLS, WHITE TIGER, YOU BECOME UNPREDICTABLE AND MORE LIKELY TO STAND A FIGHTING CHANCE.
I DUNNO, I KINDA LIKE MY ODDS!
THWIP!
THWIP!
YOU DODGED OUT OF THE WAY OF MY WEBS?! NOBODY BUT ME HAS REFLEXES THAT SHARP!
HEY! WATCH IT, SPIDER-MAN!
THWAP!
AAAHHH!
HOW'D THIS CAPTAIN AMERICA UNDERSHIRT GET UNDER MY CLOTHES? I SWEAR, IT'S NOT MINE!
UH-HUH.

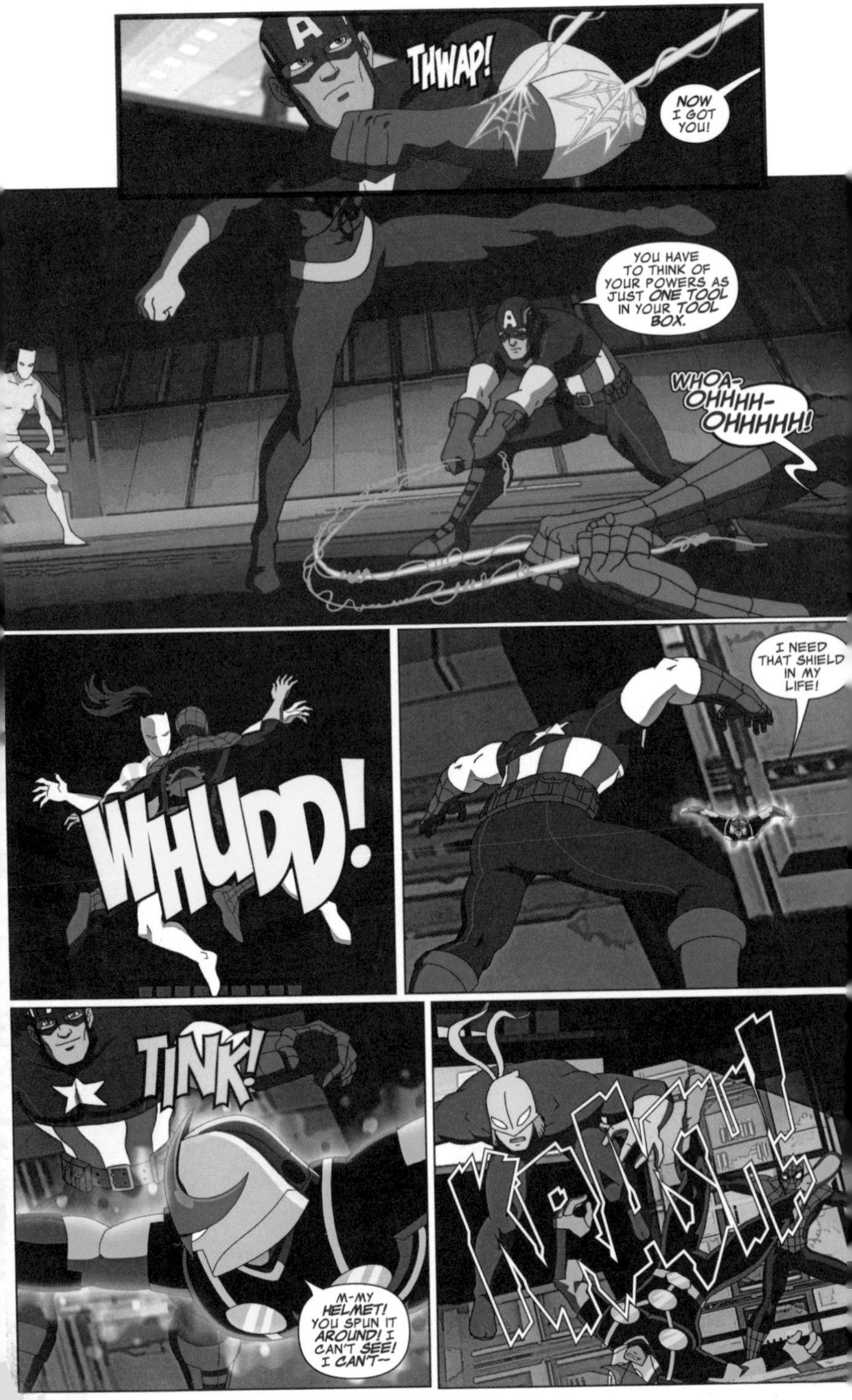
THWAP!
NOW I GOT YOU!
YOU HAVE TO THINK OF YOUR POWERS AS JUST ONE TOOL IN YOUR TOOL BOX.
WHOA-OHHHH-OHHHHH!
WHUDD!
I NEED THAT SHIELD IN MY LIFE!
TINK!
M-MY HELMET! YOU SPUN IT AROUND! I CAN'T SEE! I CAN'T--

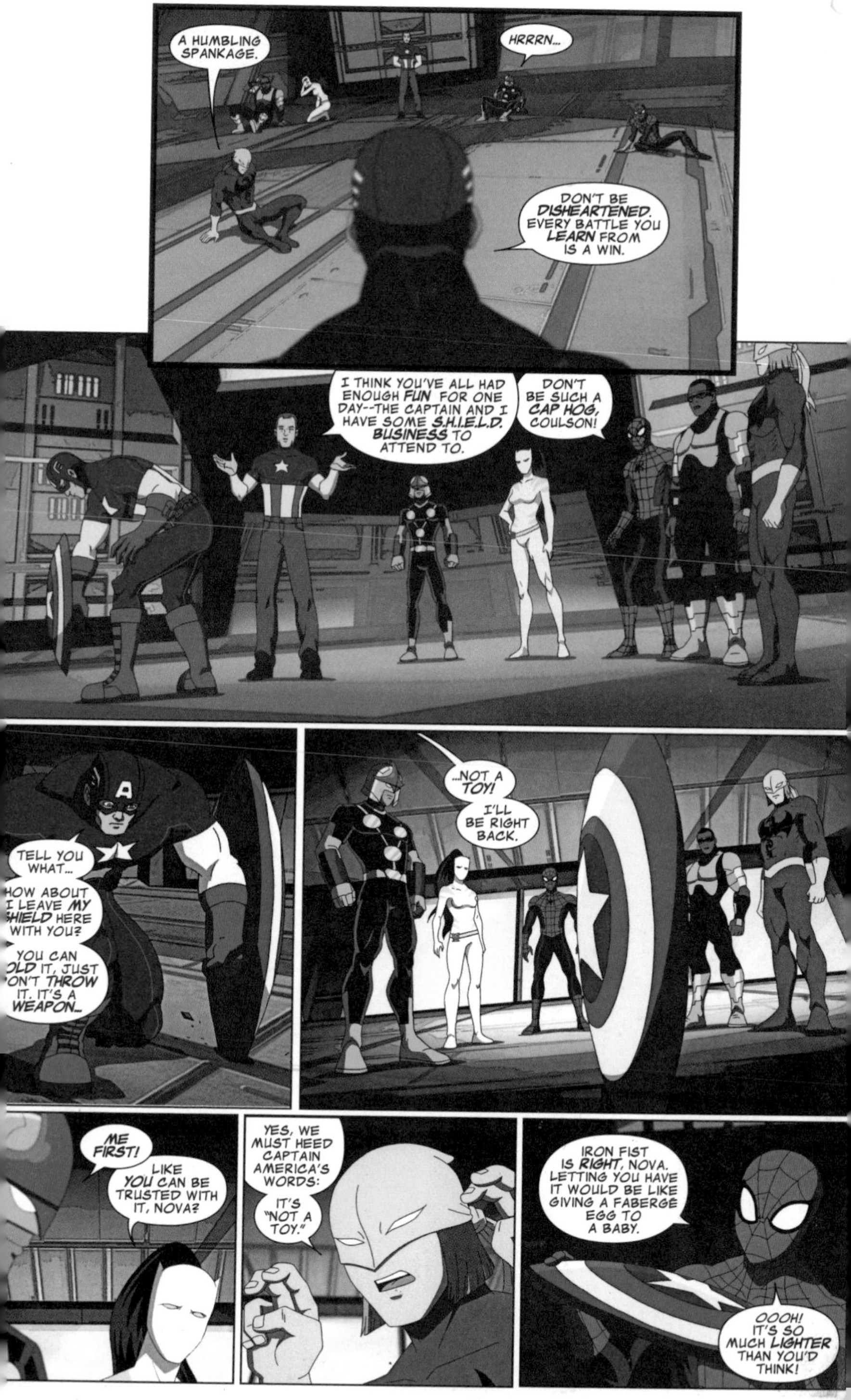
A HUMBLING SPANKAGE.
HRRRN...
DON'T BE *DISHEARTENED*. EVERY BATTLE YOU *LEARN* FROM IS A WIN.
I THINK YOU'VE ALL HAD ENOUGH *FUN* FOR ONE DAY--THE CAPTAIN AND I HAVE SOME *S.H.I.E.L.D. BUSINESS* TO ATTEND TO.
DON'T BE SUCH A *CAP HOG*, COULSON!
TELL YOU WHAT...
HOW ABOUT I LEAVE *MY SHIELD* HERE WITH YOU?
YOU CAN OLD IT, JUST ON'T *THROW* IT. IT'S A *WEAPON*...
...NOT A *TOY!*
I'LL BE RIGHT BACK.
ME FIRST!
LIKE *YOU* CAN BE TRUSTED WITH IT, NOVA?
YES, WE MUST HEED CAPTAIN AMERICA'S WORDS:
IT'S "NOT A TOY."
IRON FIST IS *RIGHT*, NOVA. LETTING YOU HAVE IT WOULD BE LIKE GIVING A FABERGE EGG TO A BABY.
OOOH! IT'S SO MUCH *LIGHTER* THAN YOU'D THINK!

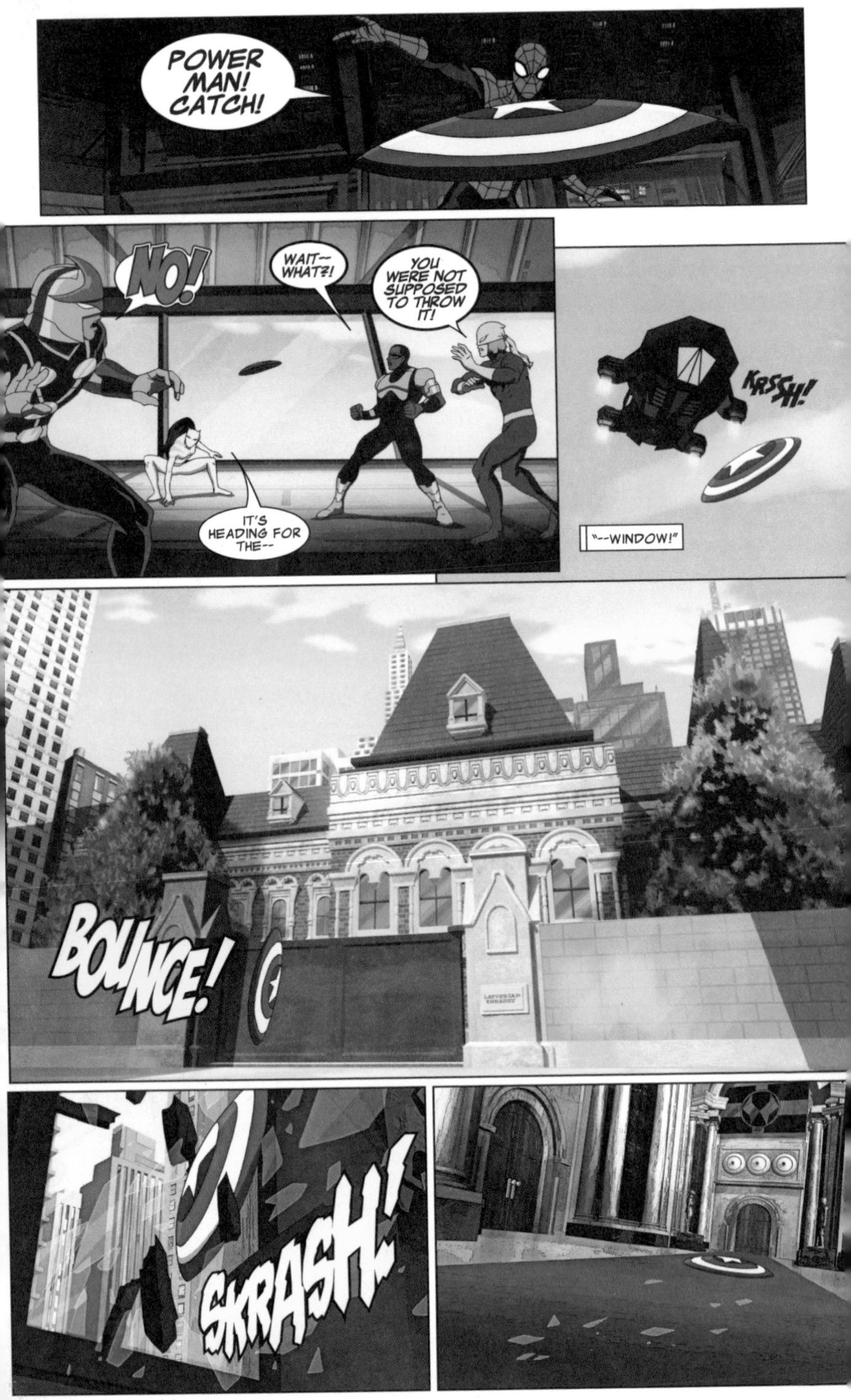

POWER MAN! CATCH!
NO!
WAIT-- WHAT?!
YOU WERE NOT SUPPOSED TO THROW IT!
IT'S HEADING FOR THE--
KRSSH!
"--WINDOW!"
BOUNCE!
SKRASH!

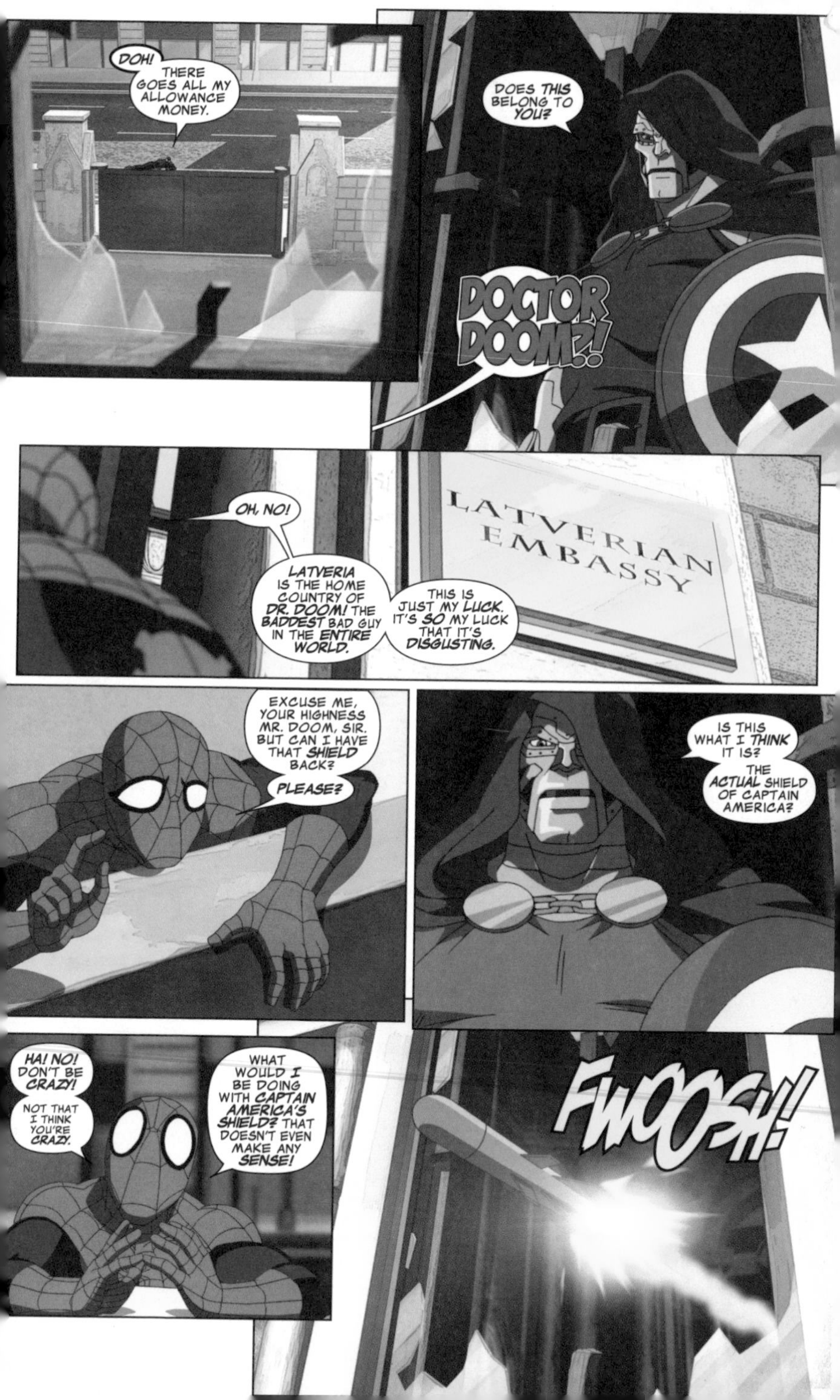
DOH! THERE GOES ALL MY ALLOWANCE MONEY.
DOES THIS BELONG TO YOU?
DOCTOR DOOM?!
OH, NO!
LATVERIA IS THE HOME COUNTRY OF DR. DOOM! THE BADDEST BAD GUY IN THE ENTIRE WORLD.
THIS IS JUST MY LUCK. IT'S SO MY LUCK THAT IT'S DISGUSTING.
LATVERIAN EMBASSY
EXCUSE ME, YOUR HIGHNESS MR. DOOM, SIR. BUT CAN I HAVE THAT SHIELD BACK?
PLEASE?
IS THIS WHAT I THINK IT IS?
THE ACTUAL SHIELD OF CAPTAIN AMERICA?
HA! NO! DON'T BE CRAZY!
NOT THAT I THINK YOU'RE CRAZY.
WHAT WOULD I BE DOING WITH CAPTAIN AMERICA'S SHIELD? THAT DOESN'T EVEN MAKE ANY SENSE!
FWOOSH!

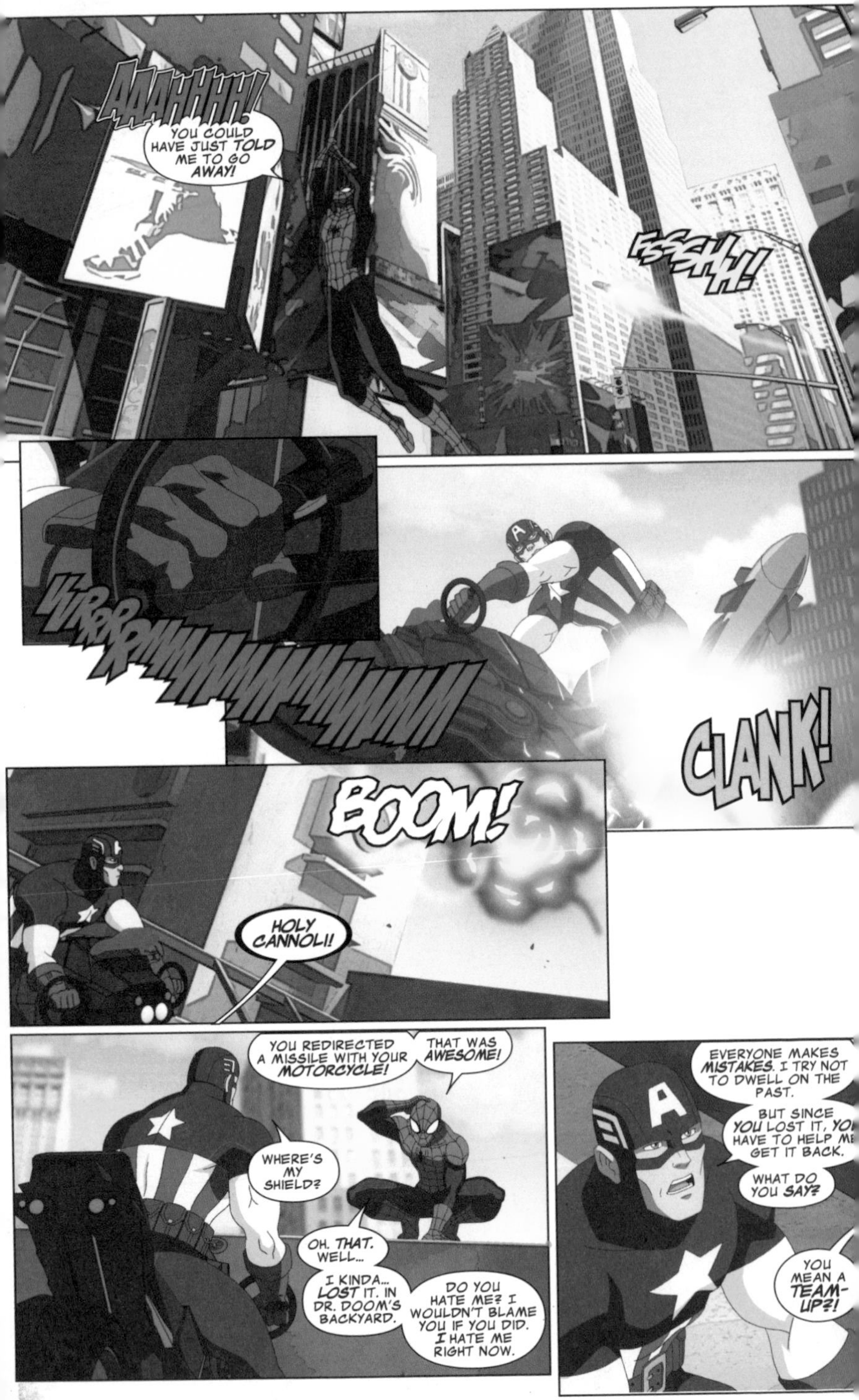
AAAHHHH!
YOU COULD HAVE JUST TOLD ME TO GO AWAY!
FSSSHH!
VVRRRRMMMMMMMMMMMMMMMMMM
CLANK!
BOOM!
HOLY CANNOLI!
YOU REDIRECTED A MISSILE WITH YOUR MOTORCYCLE!
THAT WAS AWESOME!
WHERE'S MY SHIELD?
OH. THAT. WELL...
I KINDA... LOST IT. IN DR. DOOM'S BACKYARD.
DO YOU HATE ME? I WOULDN'T BLAME YOU IF YOU DID. I HATE ME RIGHT NOW.
EVERYONE MAKES MISTAKES. I TRY NOT TO DWELL ON THE PAST.
BUT SINCE YOU LOST IT, YOU HAVE TO HELP ME GET IT BACK.
WHAT DO YOU SAY?
YOU MEAN A TEAM-UP?!

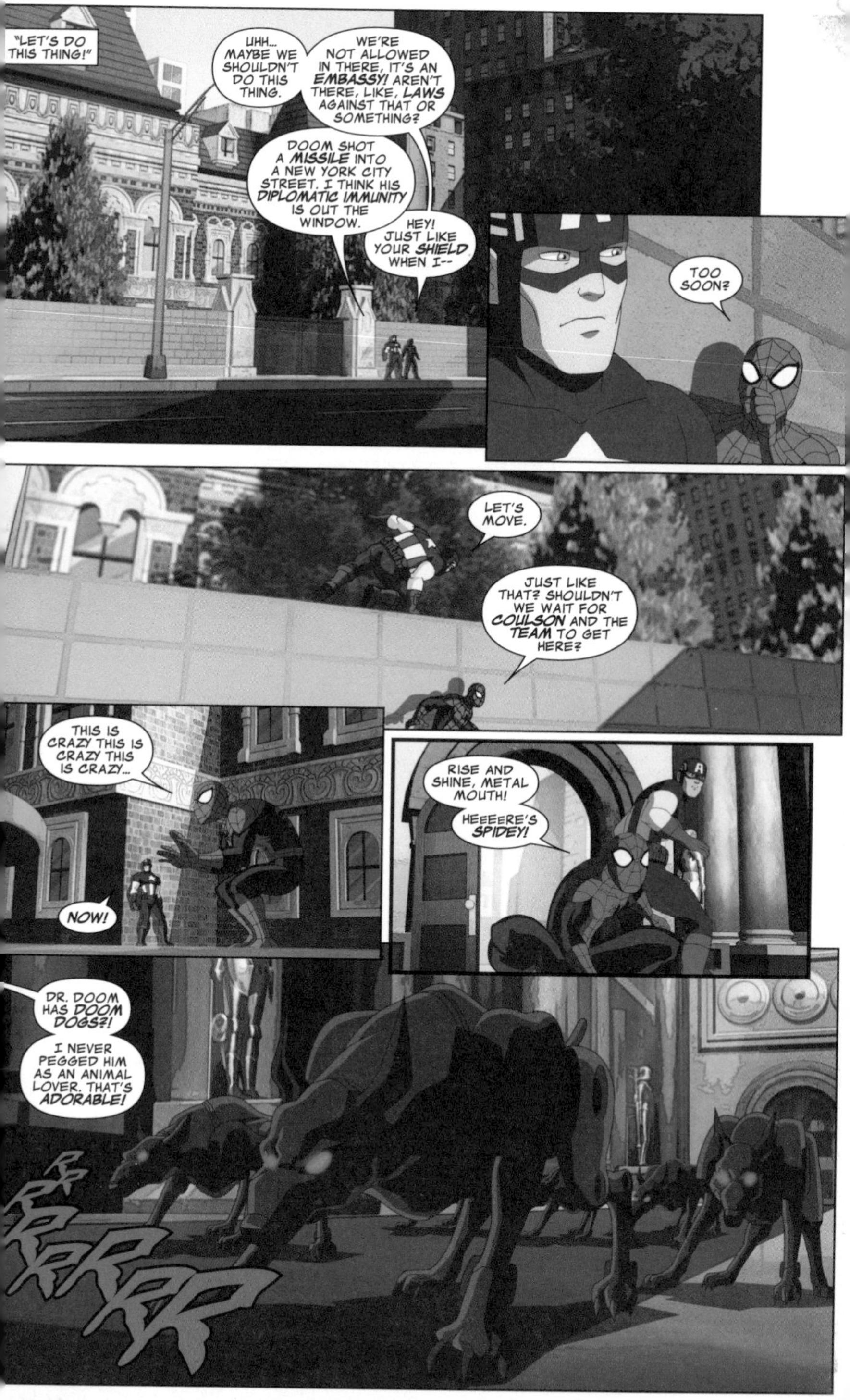
"LET'S DO THIS THING!"
UHH... MAYBE WE SHOULDN'T DO THIS THING.
WE'RE NOT ALLOWED IN THERE, IT'S AN EMBASSY! AREN'T THERE, LIKE, LAWS AGAINST THAT OR SOMETHING?
DOOM SHOT A MISSILE INTO A NEW YORK CITY STREET. I THINK HIS DIPLOMATIC IMMUNITY IS OUT THE WINDOW.
HEY! JUST LIKE YOUR SHIELD WHEN I--
TOO SOON?
LET'S MOVE.
JUST LIKE THAT? SHOULDN'T WE WAIT FOR COULSON AND THE TEAM TO GET HERE?
THIS IS CRAZY THIS IS CRAZY THIS IS CRAZY...
NOW!
RISE AND SHINE, METAL MOUTH!
HEEEERE'S SPIDEY!
DR. DOOM HAS DOOM DOGS?!
I NEVER PEGGED HIM AS AN ANIMAL LOVER. THAT'S ADORABLE!
RRRRRRR

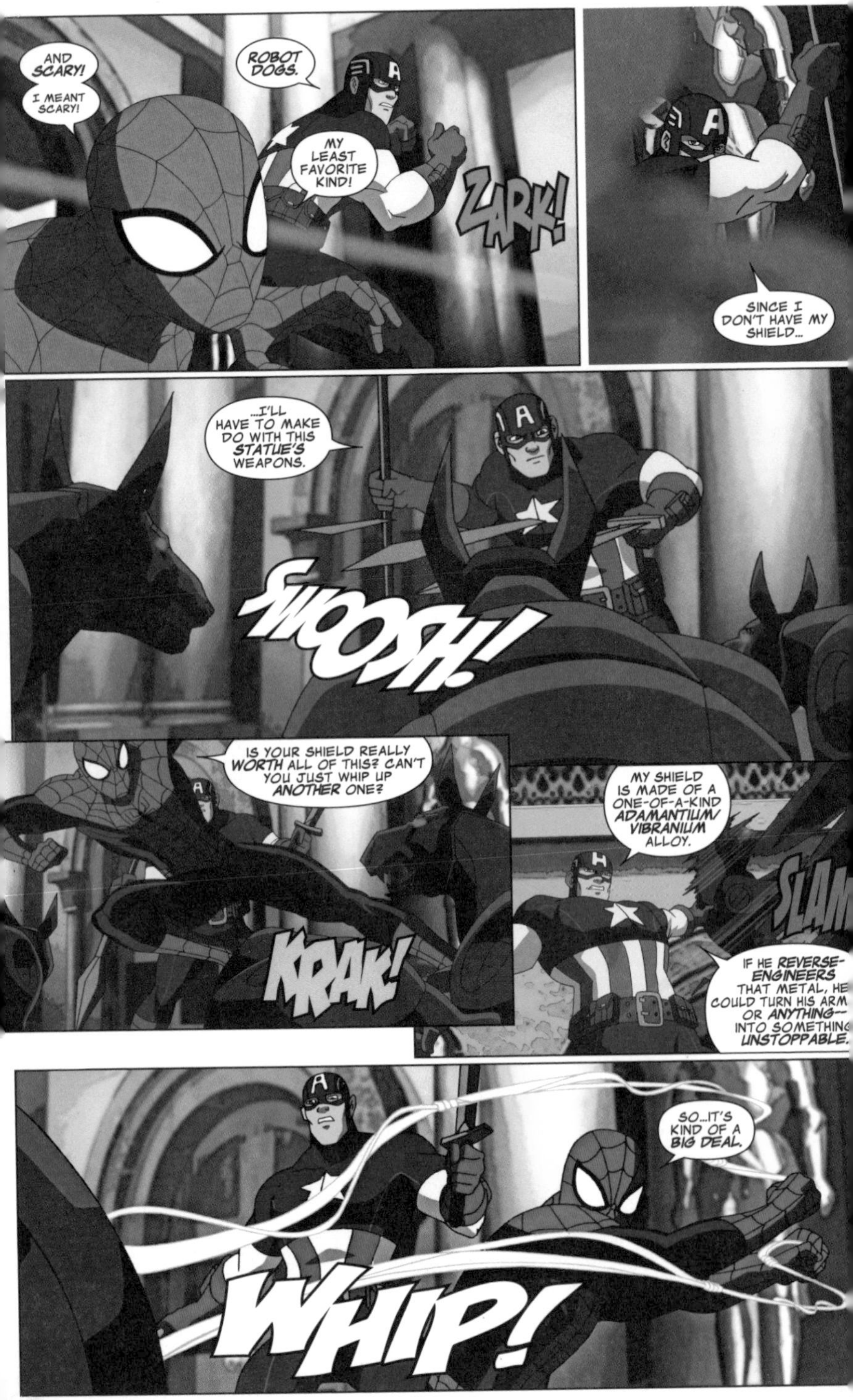

AND SCARY!
I MEANT SCARY!
ROBOT DOGS.
MY LEAST FAVORITE KIND!
ZARK!
SINCE I DON'T HAVE MY SHIELD...
...I'LL HAVE TO MAKE DO WITH THIS STATUE'S WEAPONS.
SWOOSH!
IS YOUR SHIELD REALLY WORTH ALL OF THIS? CAN'T YOU JUST WHIP UP ANOTHER ONE?
KRAK!
MY SHIELD IS MADE OF A ONE-OF-A-KIND ADAMANTIUM/ VIBRANIUM ALLOY.
SLAM
IF HE REVERSE-ENGINEERS THAT METAL, HE COULD TURN HIS ARM OR ANYTHING-- INTO SOMETHING UNSTOPPABLE.
SO...IT'S KIND OF A BIG DEAL.
WHIP!

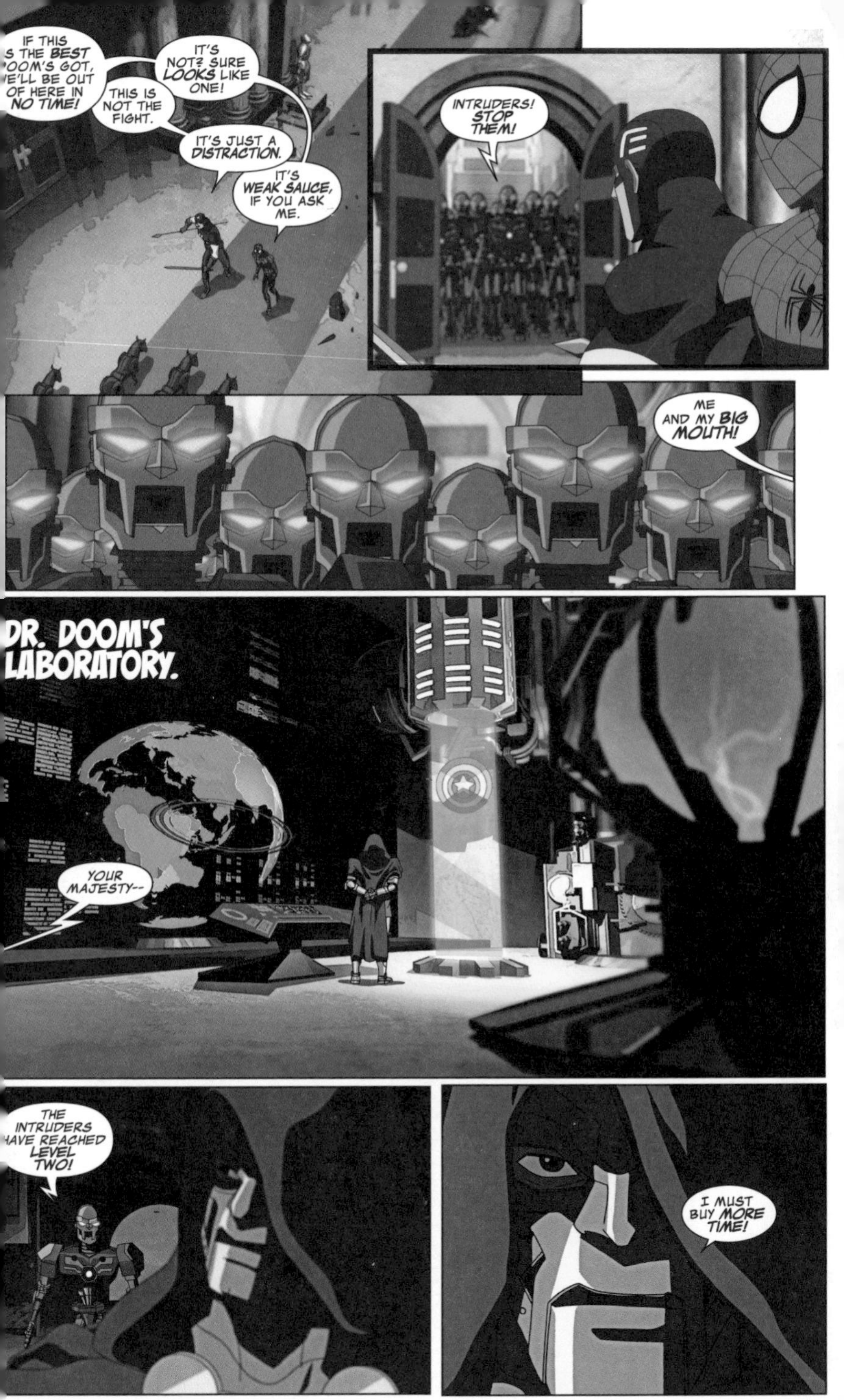

IF THIS S THE BEST OOM'S GOT, E'LL BE OUT OF HERE IN NO TIME!
IT'S NOT? SURE LOOKS LIKE ONE!
THIS IS NOT THE FIGHT.
IT'S JUST A DISTRACTION.
IT'S WEAK SAUCE, IF YOU ASK ME.
INTRUDERS! STOP THEM!
ME AND MY BIG MOUTH!
DR. DOOM'S LABORATORY.
YOUR MAJESTY--
THE INTRUDERS AVE REACHED LEVEL TWO!
I MUST BUY MORE TIME!

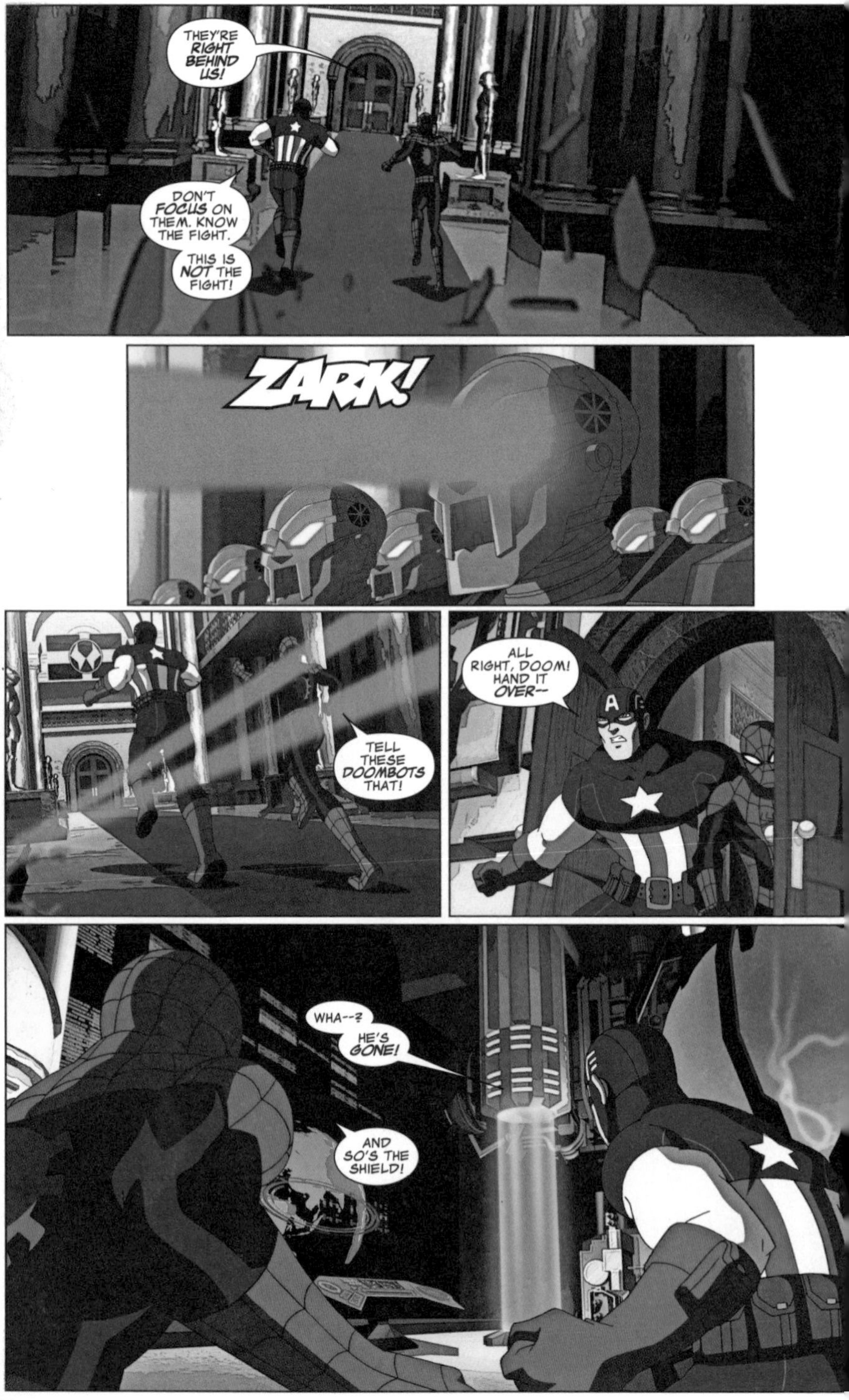
THEY'RE RIGHT BEHIND US!
DON'T FOCUS ON THEM. KNOW THE FIGHT.
THIS IS NOT THE FIGHT!
ZARK!
TELL THESE DOOMBOTS THAT!
ALL RIGHT, DOOM! HAND IT OVER--
WHA--?
HE'S GONE!
AND SO'S THE SHIELD!

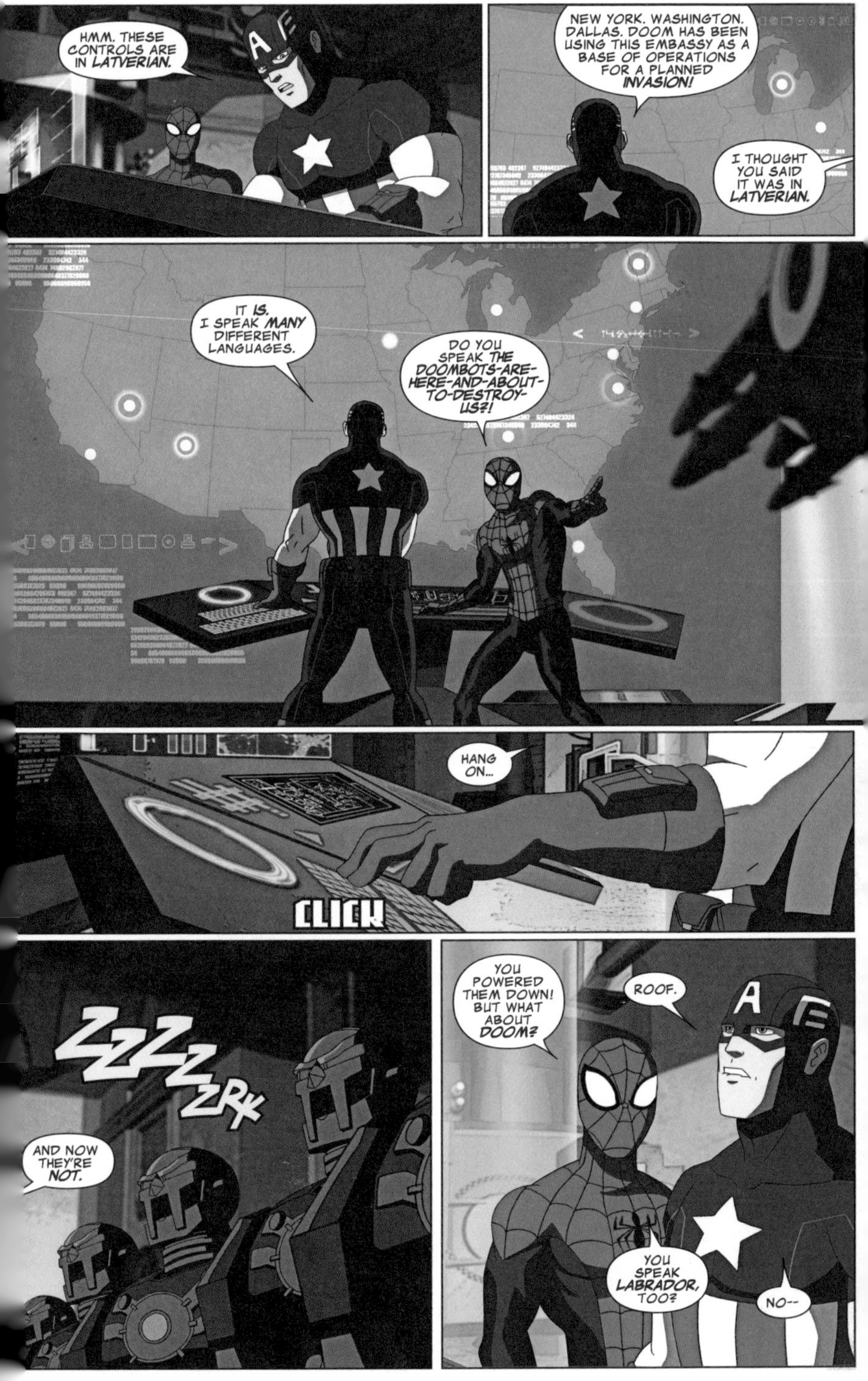

HMM. THESE CONTROLS ARE IN LATVERIAN.
NEW YORK. WASHINGTON. DALLAS. DOOM HAS BEEN USING THIS EMBASSY AS A BASE OF OPERATIONS FOR A PLANNED INVASION!
I THOUGHT YOU SAID IT WAS IN LATVERIAN.
IT IS. I SPEAK MANY DIFFERENT LANGUAGES.
DO YOU SPEAK THE DOOMBOTS-ARE-HERE-AND-ABOUT-TO-DESTROY-US?!
HANG ON...
CLICK
ZZZZZRK
AND NOW THEY'RE NOT.
YOU POWERED THEM DOWN! BUT WHAT ABOUT DOOM?
ROOF.
YOU SPEAK LABRADOR, TOO?
NO--

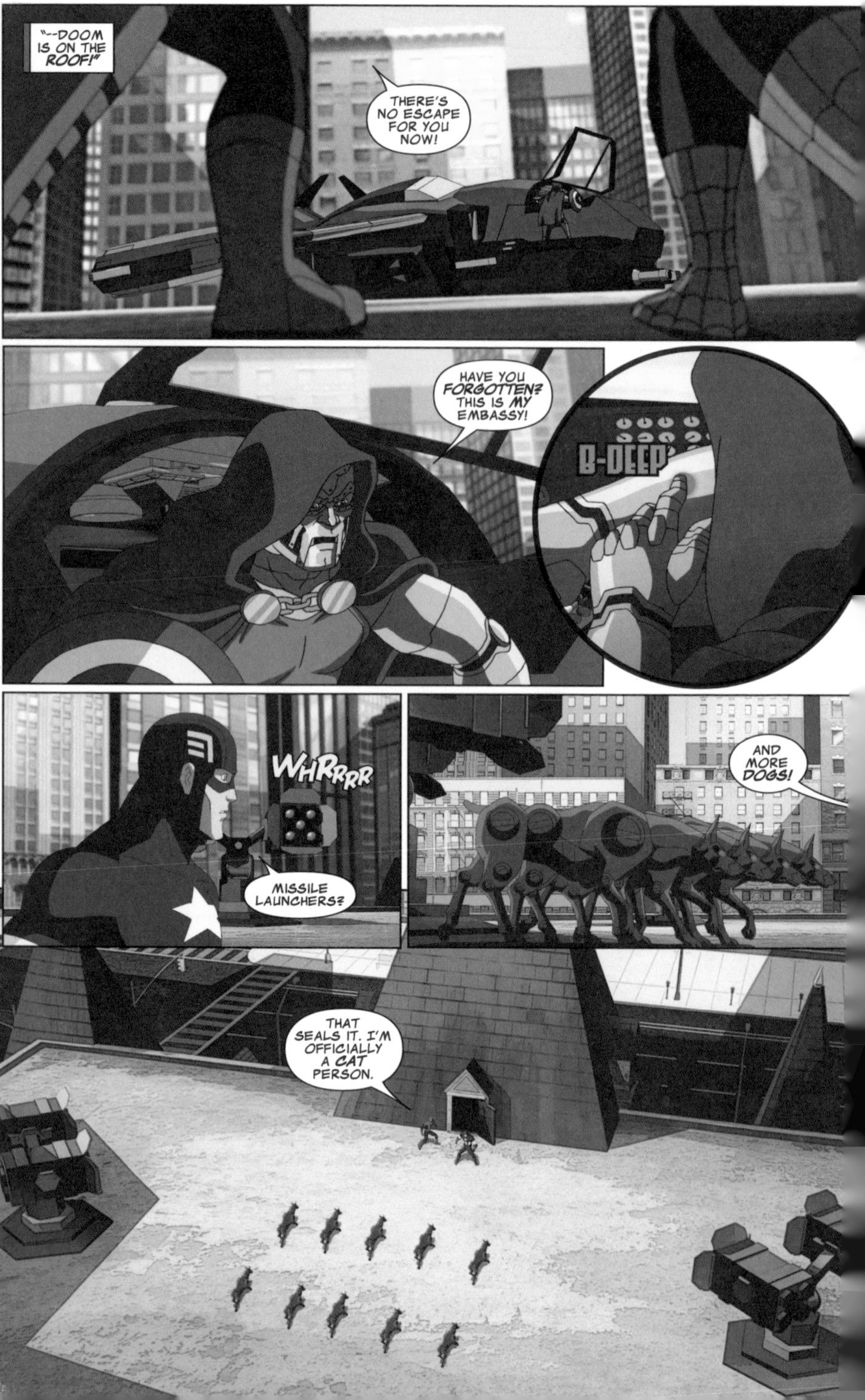
"--DOOM IS ON THE ROOF!"
THERE'S NO ESCAPE FOR YOU NOW!
HAVE YOU FORGOTTEN? THIS IS MY EMBASSY!
B-DEEP
WHRRRR
MISSILE LAUNCHERS?
AND MORE DOGS!
THAT SEALS IT. I'M OFFICIALLY A CAT PERSON.

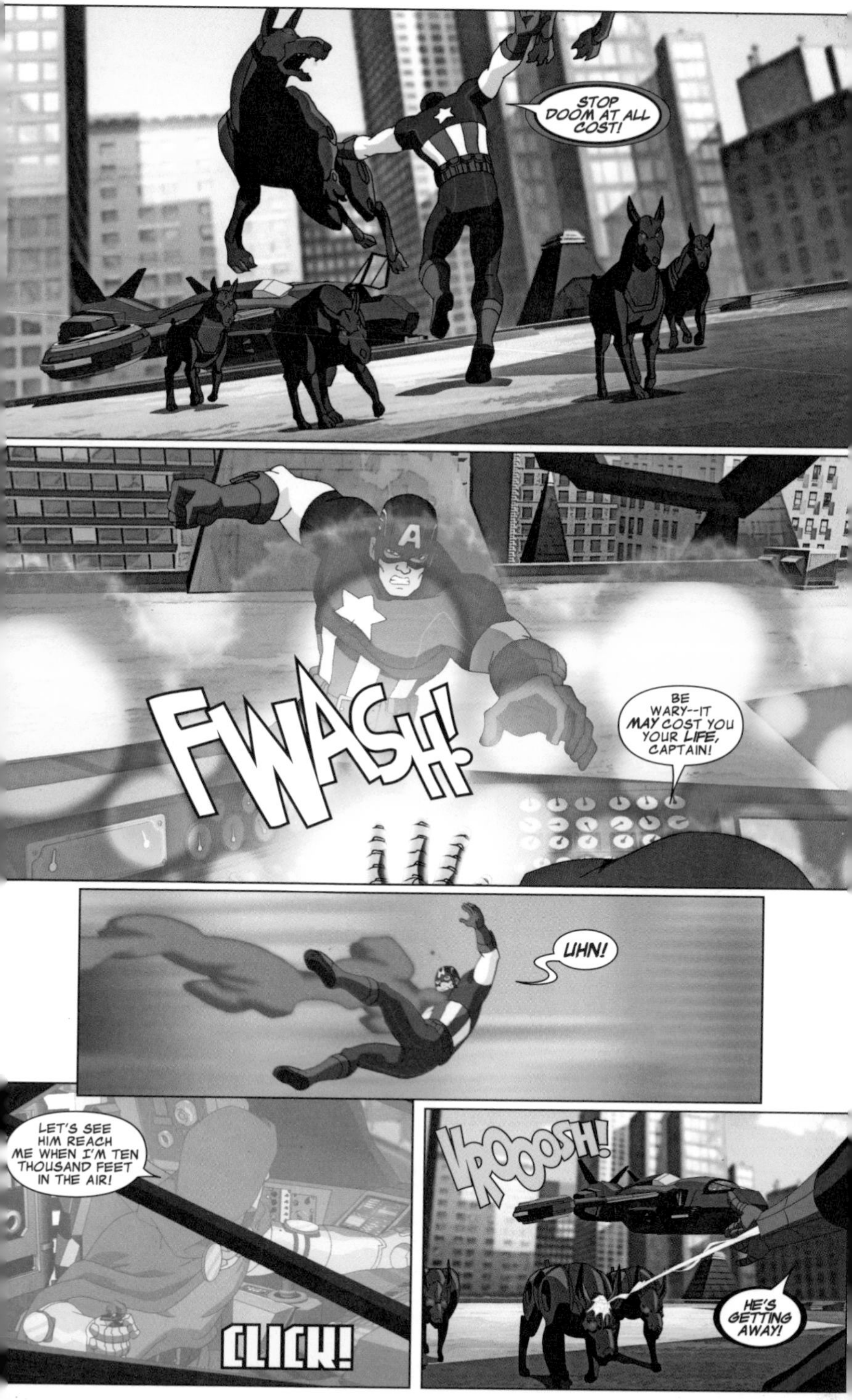
STOP DOOM AT ALL COST!
FWASH!
BE WARY--IT MAY COST YOU YOUR LIFE, CAPTAIN!
UHN!
LET'S SEE HIM REACH ME WHEN I'M TEN THOUSAND FEET IN THE AIR!
CLICK!
VROOOSH!
HE'S GETTING AWAY!

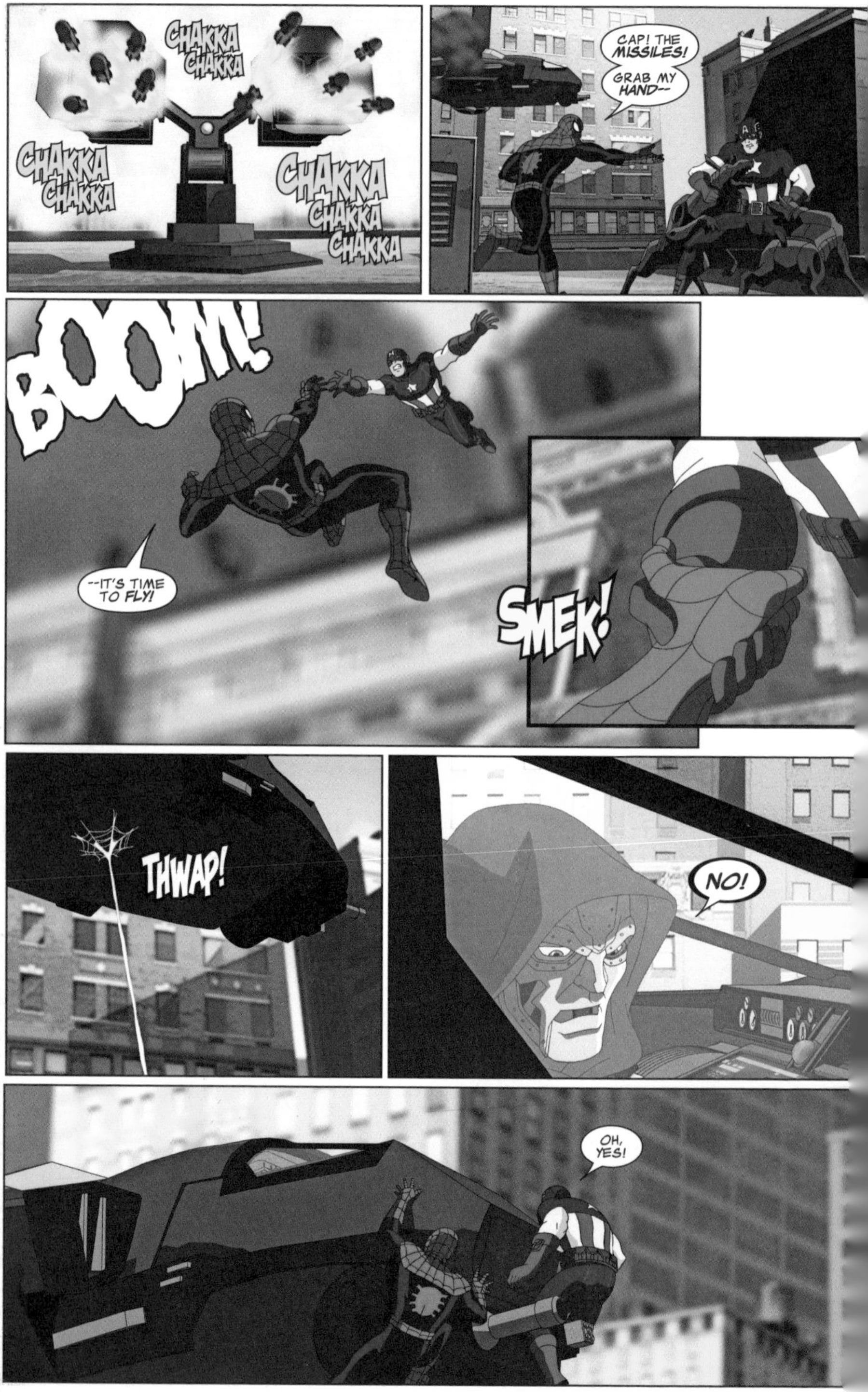
CHAKKA CHAKKA
CHAKKA CHAKKA
CHAKKA CHAKKA CHAKKA
CAP! THE MISSILES!
GRAB MY HAND--
BOOM!
--IT'S TIME TO FLY!
SMEK!
THWAP!
NO!
OH, YES!

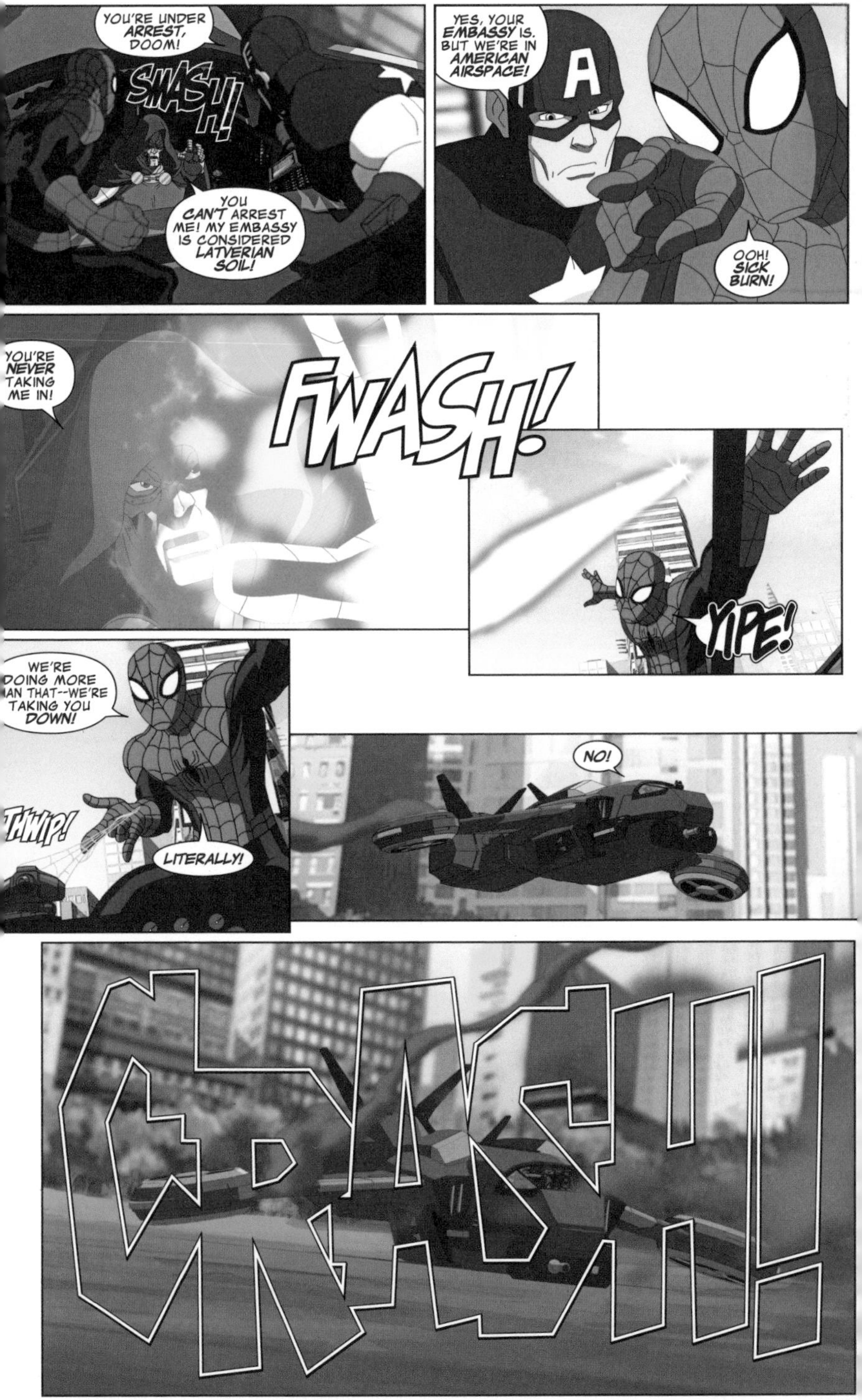

YOU'RE UNDER ARREST, DOOM!
SWASH!
YOU CAN'T ARREST ME! MY EMBASSY IS CONSIDERED LATVERIAN SOIL!
YES, YOUR EMBASSY IS. BUT WE'RE IN AMERICAN AIRSPACE!
OOH! SICK BURN!
YOU'RE NEVER TAKING ME IN!
FWASH!
YIPE!
WE'RE DOING MORE THAN THAT--WE'RE TAKING YOU DOWN!
THWIP!
LITERALLY!
NO!
CHASH!

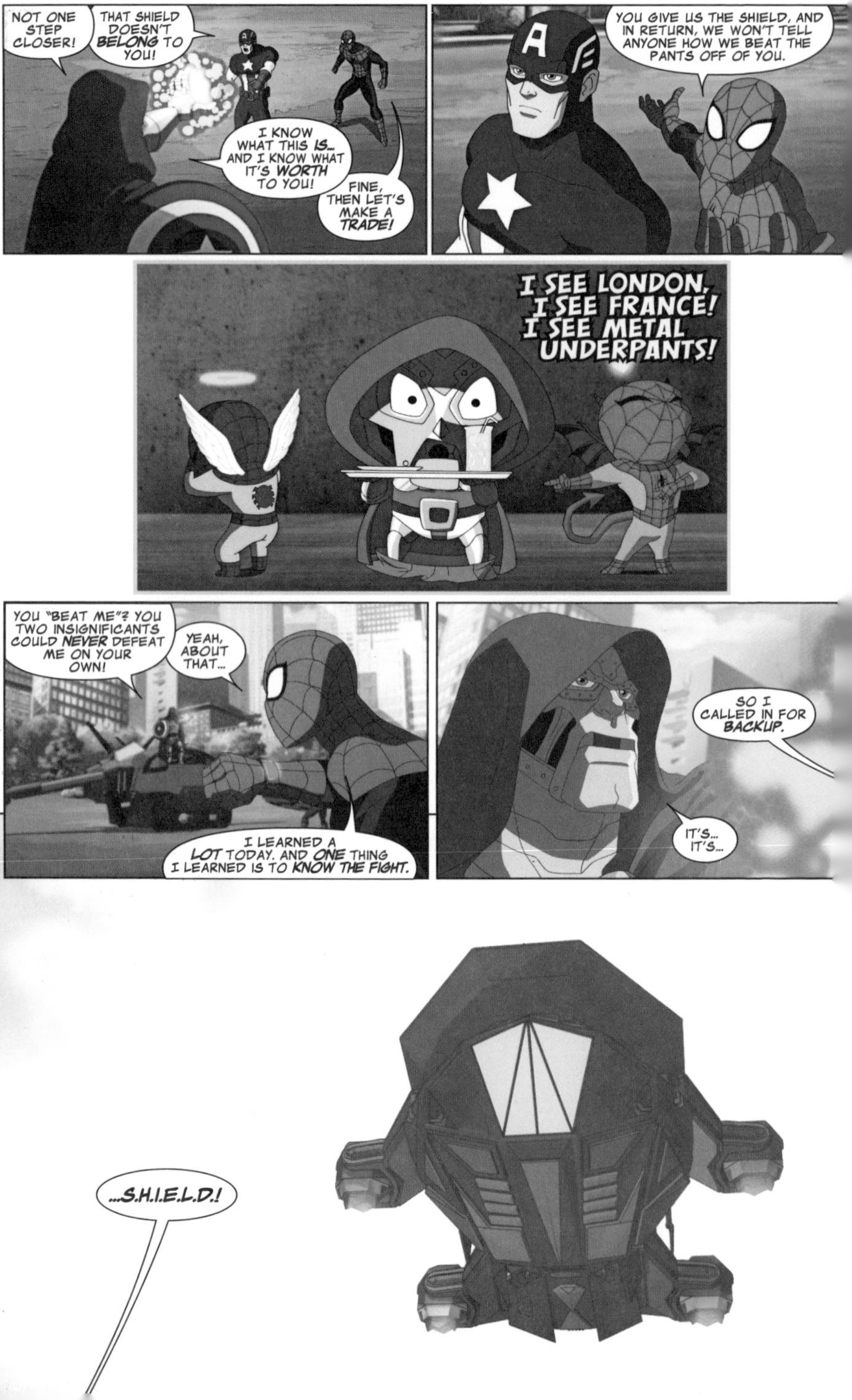
NOT ONE STEP CLOSER!
THAT SHIELD DOESN'T BELONG TO YOU!
I KNOW WHAT THIS IS... AND I KNOW WHAT IT'S WORTH TO YOU!
FINE, THEN LET'S MAKE A TRADE!
YOU GIVE US THE SHIELD, AND IN RETURN, WE WON'T TELL ANYONE HOW WE BEAT THE PANTS OFF OF YOU.
I SEE LONDON, I SEE FRANCE! I SEE METAL UNDERPANTS!
YOU "BEAT ME"? YOU TWO INSIGNIFICANTS COULD NEVER DEFEAT ME ON YOUR OWN!
YEAH, ABOUT THAT...
I LEARNED A LOT TODAY. AND ONE THING I LEARNED IS TO KNOW THE FIGHT.
SO I CALLED IN FOR BACKUP.
IT'S... IT'S...
...S.H.I.E.L.D.!

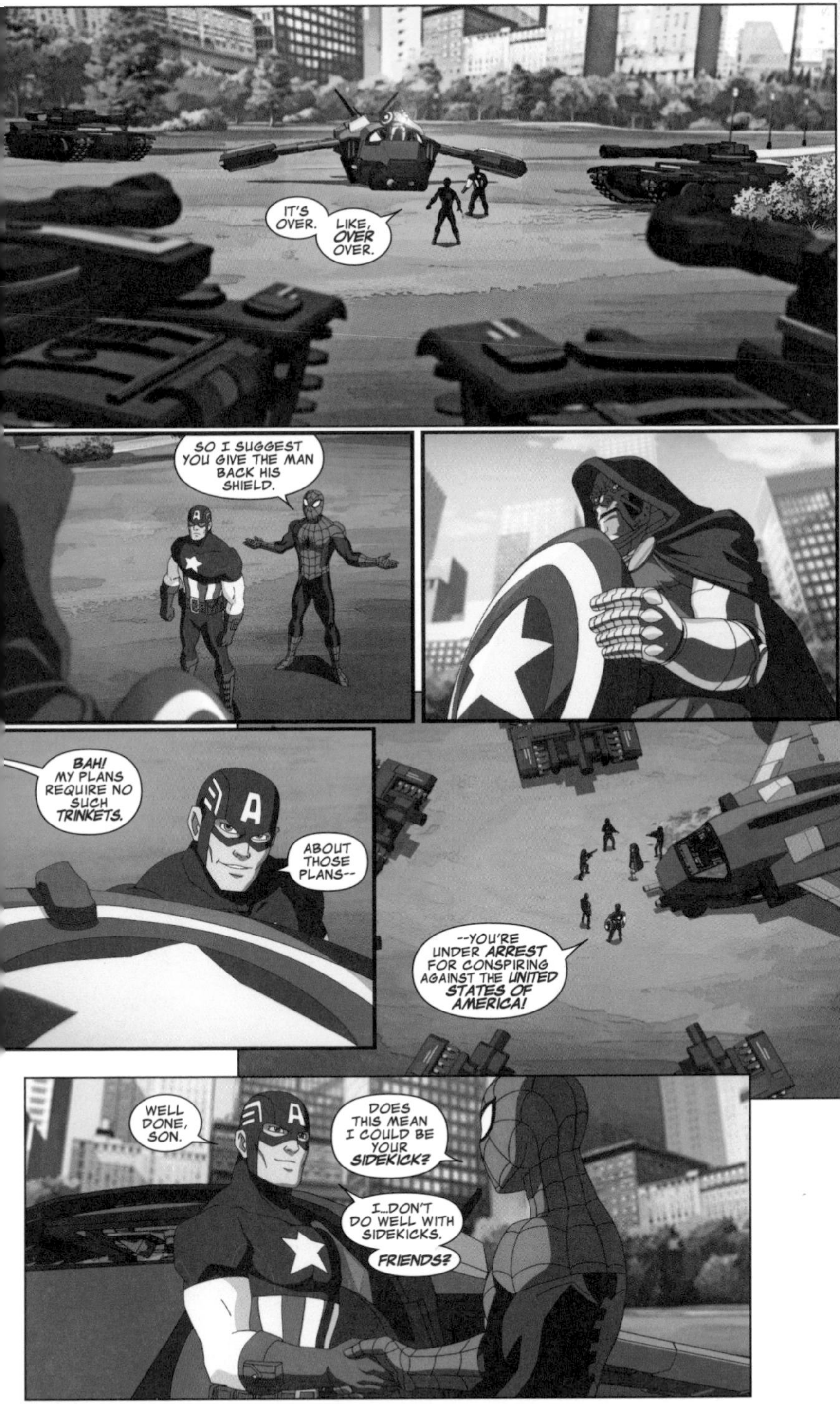
IT'S OVER.
LIKE, OVER OVER.
SO I SUGGEST YOU GIVE THE MAN BACK HIS SHIELD.
BAH! MY PLANS REQUIRE NO SUCH TRINKETS.
ABOUT THOSE PLANS--
--YOU'RE UNDER ARREST FOR CONSPIRING AGAINST THE UNITED STATES OF AMERICA!
WELL DONE, SON.
DOES THIS MEAN I COULD BE YOUR SIDEKICK?
I...DON'T DO WELL WITH SIDEKICKS.
FRIENDS?

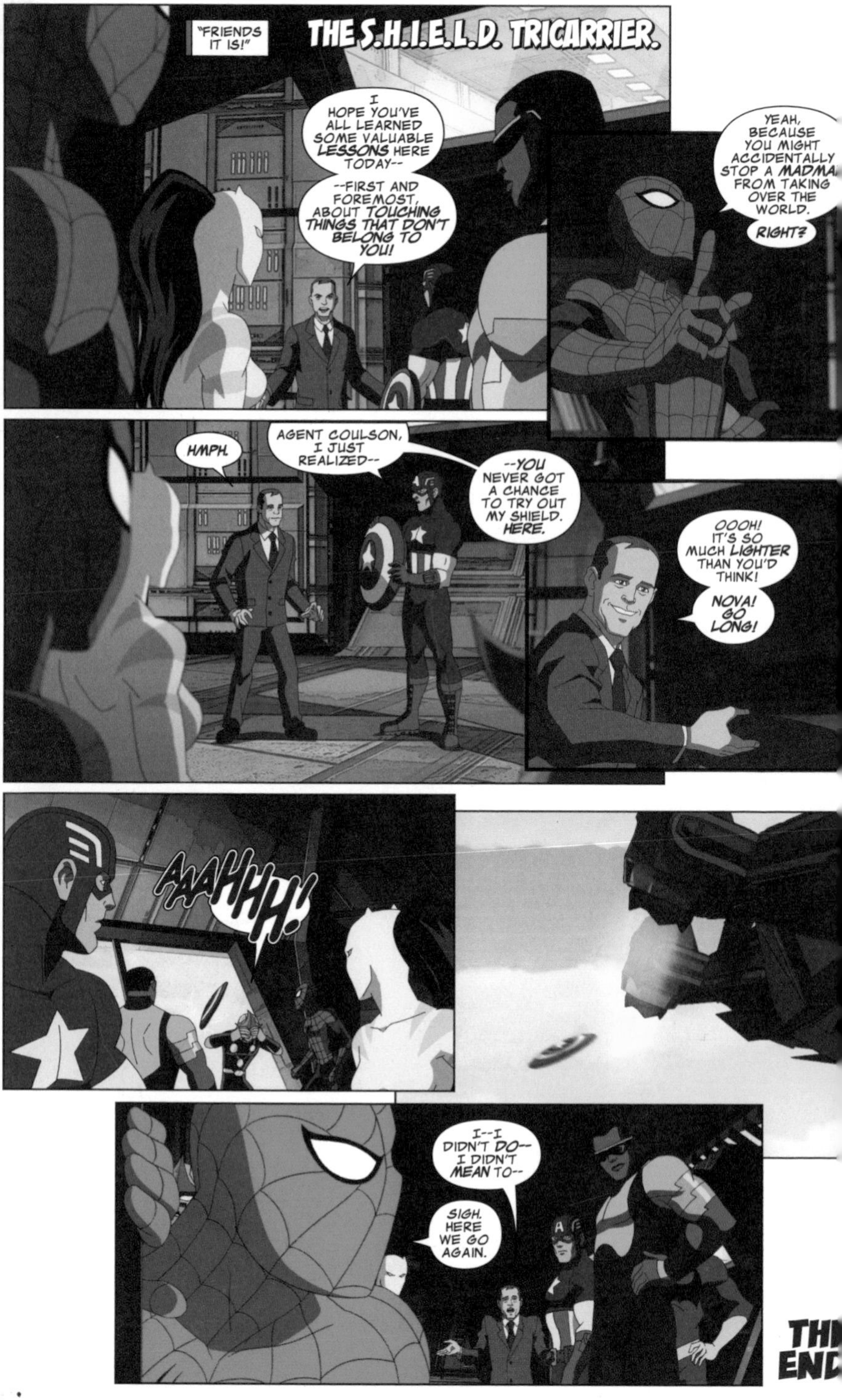
"FRIENDS IT IS!"
THE S.H.I.E.L.D. TRICARRIER.
I HOPE YOU'VE ALL LEARNED SOME VALUABLE LESSONS HERE TODAY--
--FIRST AND FOREMOST, ABOUT TOUCHING THINGS THAT DON'T BELONG TO YOU!
YEAH, BECAUSE YOU MIGHT ACCIDENTALLY STOP A MADMA
FROM TAKING OVER THE WORLD.
RIGHT?
HMPH.
AGENT COULSON, I JUST REALIZED--
--YOU NEVER GOT A CHANCE TO TRY OUT MY SHIELD. HERE.
OOOH! IT'S SO MUCH LIGHTER THAN YOU'D THINK!
NOVA! GO LONG!
AAAHHHH!
I--I DIDN'T DO-- I DIDN'T MEAN TO--
SIGH. HERE WE GO AGAIN.
TH
END

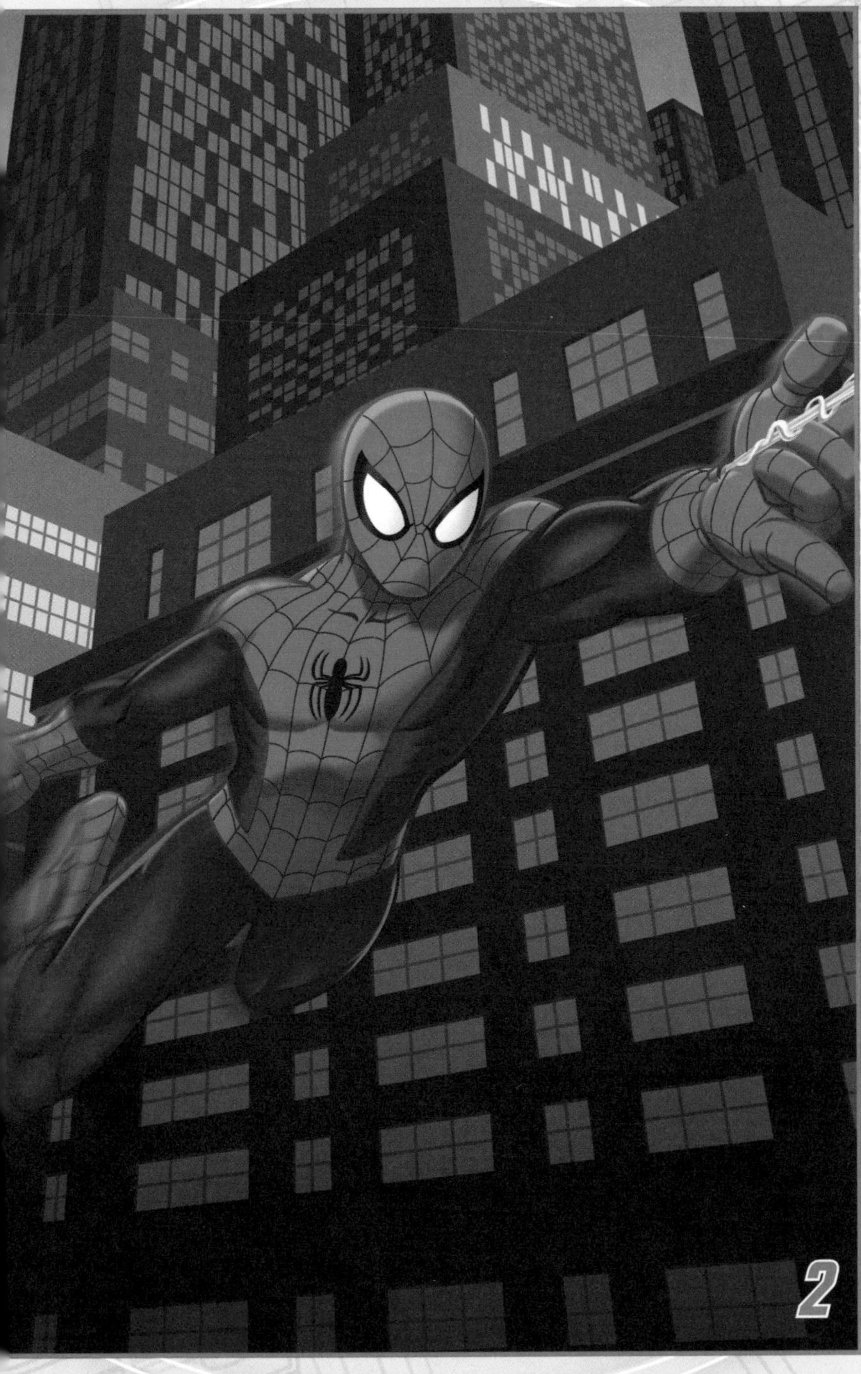
2

Based on "Hawkeye"

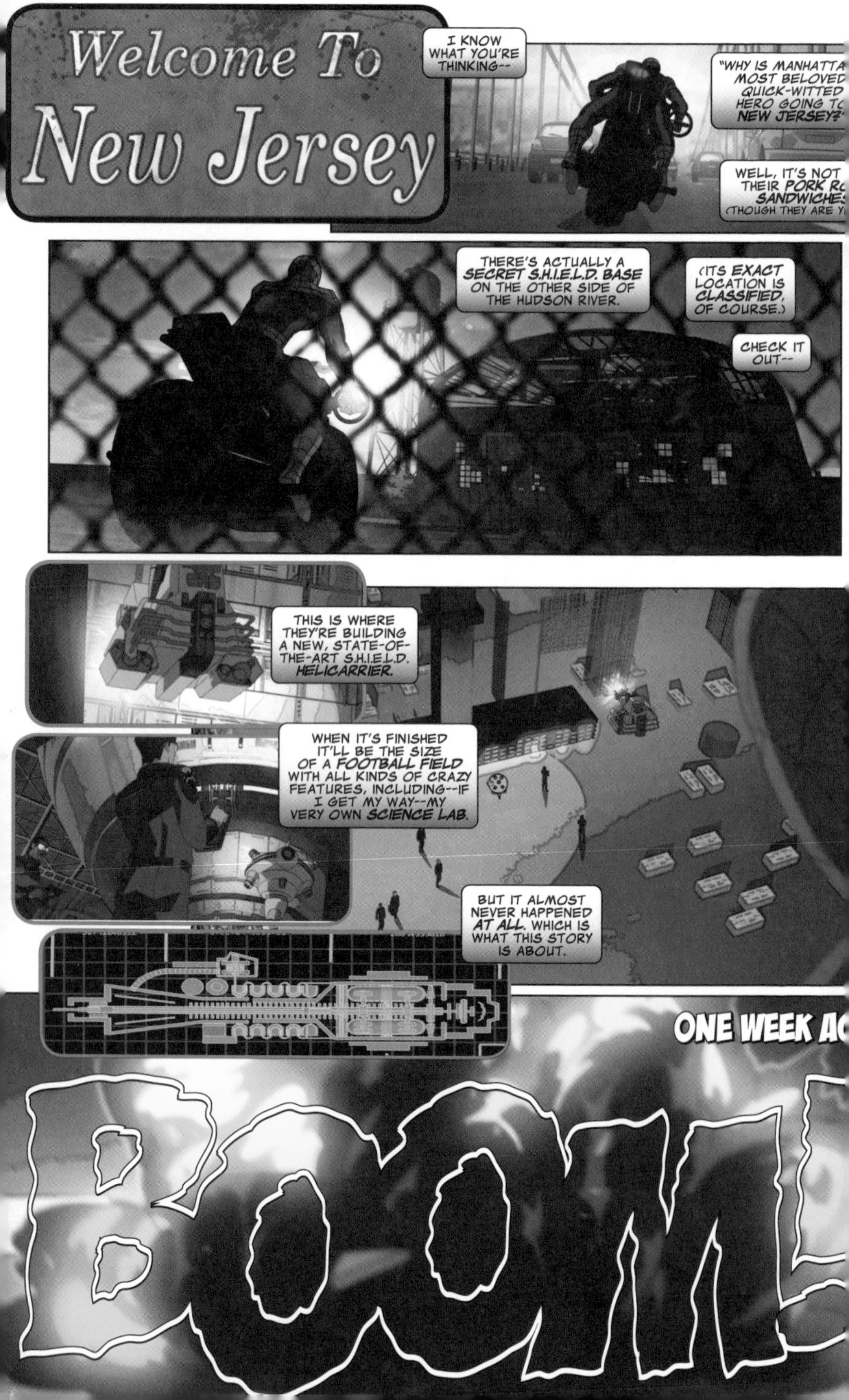

Welcome To New Jersey
I KNOW WHAT YOU'RE THINKING--
"WHY IS MANHATTA MOST BELOVED QUICK-WITTED HERO GOING TO NEW JERSEY?"
WELL, IT'S NOT THEIR PORK R SANDWICHES (THOUGH THEY ARE Y
THERE'S ACTUALLY A SECRET S.H.I.E.L.D. BASE ON THE OTHER SIDE OF THE HUDSON RIVER.
(ITS EXACT LOCATION IS CLASSIFIED, OF COURSE.)
CHECK IT OUT--
THIS IS WHERE THEY'RE BUILDING A NEW, STATE-OF-THE-ART S.H.I.E.L.D. HELICARRIER.
WHEN IT'S FINISHED IT'LL BE THE SIZE OF A FOOTBALL FIELD WITH ALL KINDS OF CRAZY FEATURES, INCLUDING--IF I GET MY WAY--MY VERY OWN SCIENCE LAB.
BUT IT ALMOST NEVER HAPPENED AT ALL. WHICH IS WHAT THIS STORY IS ABOUT.
ONE WEEK AG
BOOM!

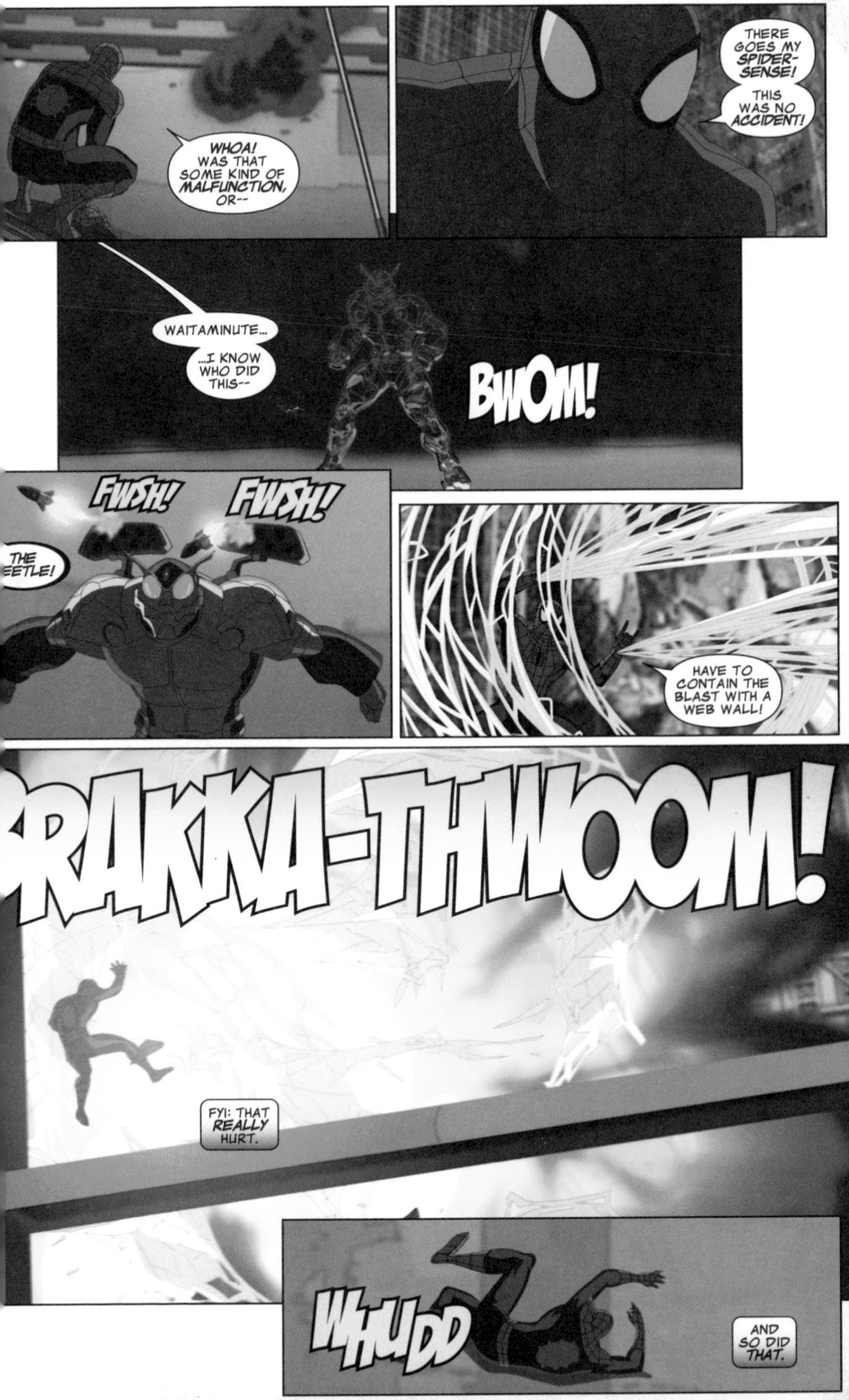
WHOA! WAS THAT SOME KIND OF MALFUNCTION, OR--
THERE GOES MY SPIDER-SENSE!
THIS WAS NO ACCIDENT!
WAITAMINUTE...
...I KNOW WHO DID THIS--
BWOM!
FWSH!
FWSH!
THE EETLE!
HAVE TO CONTAIN THE BLAST WITH A WEB WALL!
RAKKA-THWOOM!
FYI: THAT REALLY HURT.
WHUDD
AND SO DID THAT.

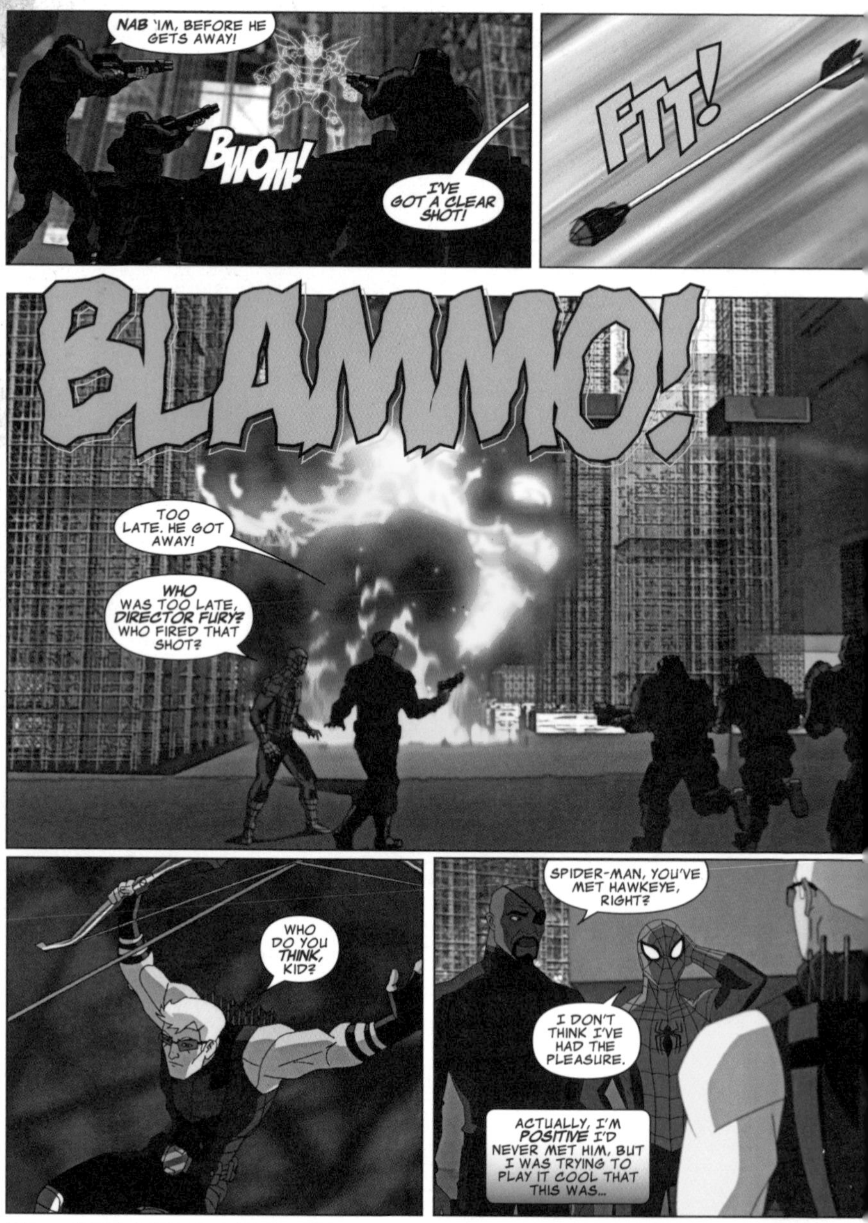
NAB 'IM, BEFORE HE GETS AWAY!
BWOM!
I'VE GOT A CLEAR SHOT!
FTT!
BLAMMO!
TOO LATE. HE GOT AWAY!
WHO WAS TOO LATE, DIRECTOR FURY? WHO FIRED THAT SHOT?
WHO DO YOU THINK, KID?
SPIDER-MAN, YOU'VE MET HAWKEYE, RIGHT?
I DON'T THINK I'VE HAD THE PLEASURE.
ACTUALLY, I'M POSITIVE I'D NEVER MET HIM, BUT I WAS TRYING TO PLAY IT COOL THAT THIS WAS...

"...THAT TIME I TEAMED UP WITH HAWKEYE!'

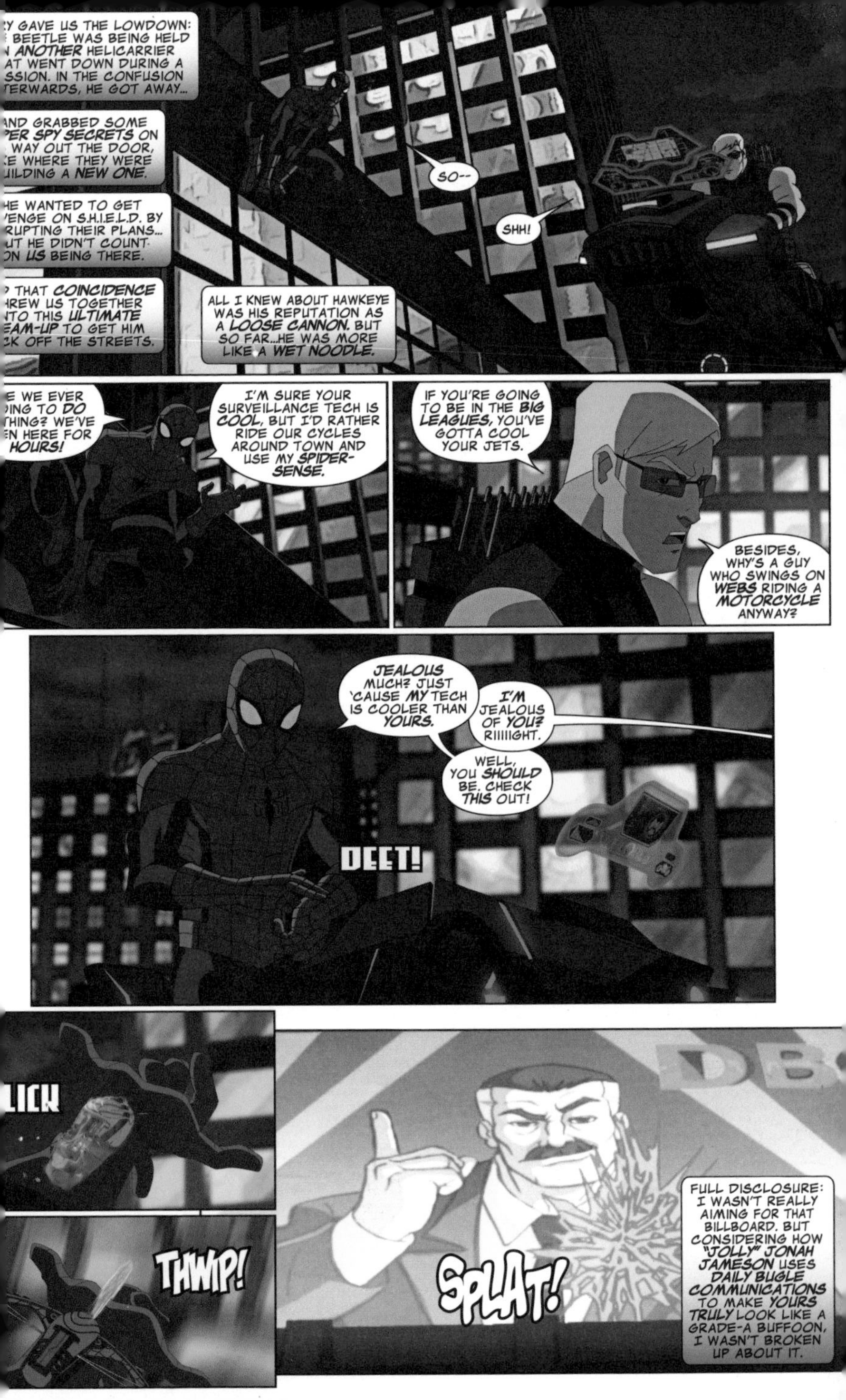

Y GAVE US THE LOWDOWN: BEETLE WAS BEING HELD N ANOTHER HELICARRIER AT WENT DOWN DURING A SSION. IN THE CONFUSION TERWARDS, HE GOT AWAY...
AND GRABBED SOME PER SPY SECRETS ON WAY OUT THE DOOR, E WHERE THEY WERE UILDING A NEW ONE.
HE WANTED TO GET VENGE ON S.H.I.E.L.D. BY RUPTING THEIR PLANS... UT HE DIDN'T COUNT ON US BEING THERE.
THAT COINCIDENCE HREW US TOGETHER NTO THIS ULTIMATE EAM-UP TO GET HIM CK OFF THE STREETS.
SO--
SHH!
ALL I KNEW ABOUT HAWKEYE WAS HIS REPUTATION AS A LOOSE CANNON. BUT SO FAR...HE WAS MORE LIKE A WET NOODLE.
E WE EVER OING TO DO THING? WE'VE EN HERE FOR HOURS!
I'M SURE YOUR SURVEILLANCE TECH IS COOL, BUT I'D RATHER RIDE OUR CYCLES AROUND TOWN AND USE MY SPIDER-SENSE.
IF YOU'RE GOING TO BE IN THE BIG LEAGUES, YOU'VE GOTTA COOL YOUR JETS.
BESIDES, WHY'S A GUY WHO SWINGS ON WEBS RIDING A MOTORCYCLE ANYWAY?
JEALOUS MUCH? JUST 'CAUSE MY TECH IS COOLER THAN YOURS.
I'M JEALOUS OF YOU? RIIIIIGHT.
WELL, YOU SHOULD BE. CHECK THIS OUT!
DEET!
LICK
THWIP!
SPLAT!
FULL DISCLOSURE: I WASN'T REALLY AIMING FOR THAT BILLBOARD. BUT CONSIDERING HOW "JOLLY" JONAH JAMESON USES DAILY BUGLE COMMUNICATIONS TO MAKE YOURS TRULY LOOK LIKE A GRADE-A BUFFOON, I WASN'T BROKEN UP ABOUT IT.

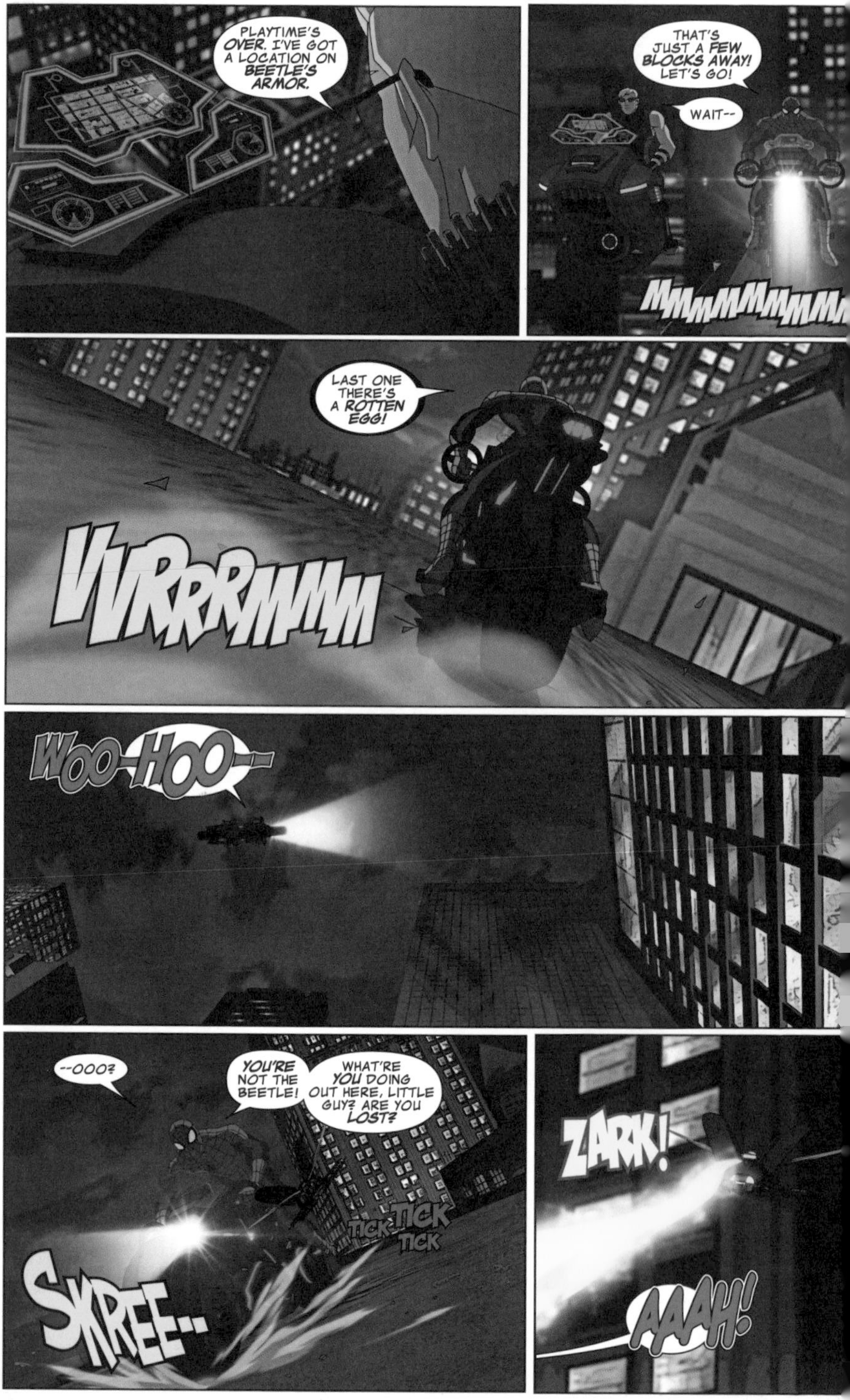
PLAYTIME'S OVER. I'VE GOT A LOCATION ON BEETLE'S ARMOR.
THAT'S JUST A FEW BLOCKS AWAY! LET'S GO!
WAIT--
MMMMMMMMMMMMM
LAST ONE THERE'S A ROTTEN EGG!
VVRRRMMMM
WOO-HOO-
--OOO?
YOU'RE NOT THE BEETLE!
WHAT'RE YOU DOING OUT HERE, LITTLE GUY? ARE YOU LOST?
TICK TICK TICK
SKREE..
ZARK!
AAAH!

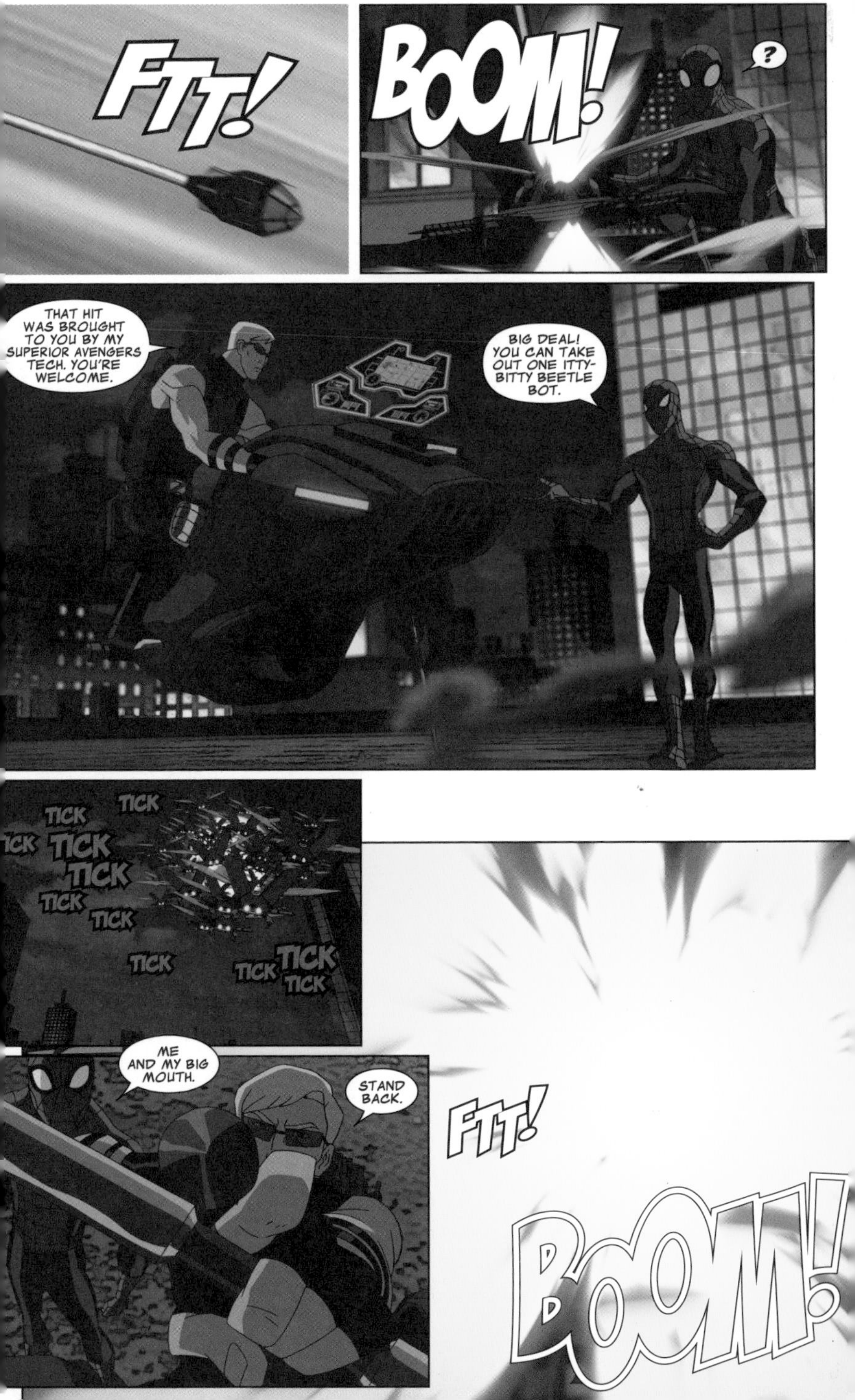
FTT!
BOOM!
?
THAT HIT WAS BROUGHT TO YOU BY MY SUPERIOR AVENGERS TECH. YOU'RE WELCOME.
BIG DEAL! YOU CAN TAKE OUT ONE ITTY-BITTY BEETLE BOT.
TICK TICK TICK TICK TICK TICK TICK TICK TICK TICK
ME AND MY BIG MOUTH.
STAND BACK.
FTT!
BOOM!

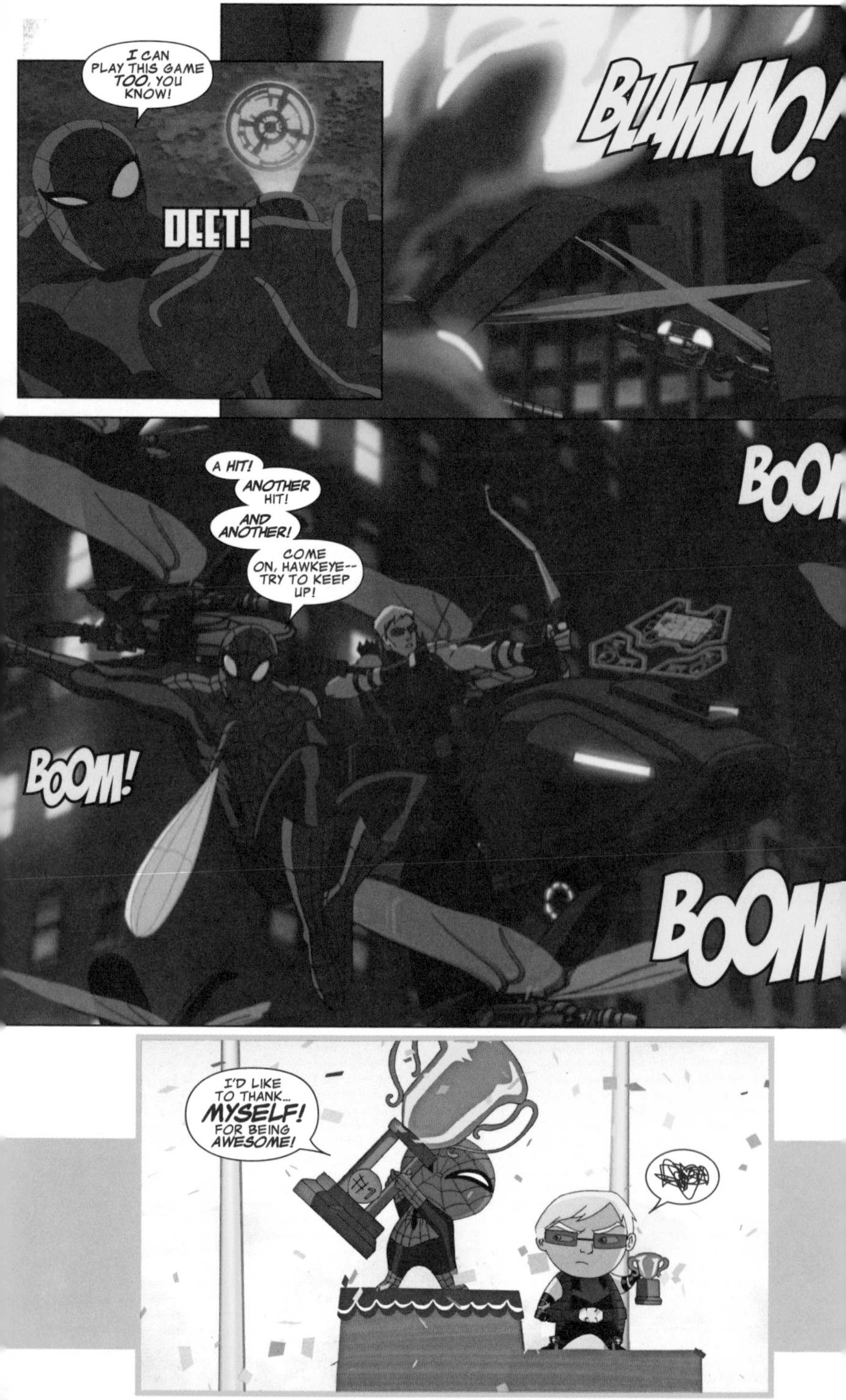
I CAN PLAY THIS GAME TOO, YOU KNOW!
DEET!
BLAMMO!
A HIT!
ANOTHER HIT!
AND ANOTHER!
COME ON, HAWKEYE-- TRY TO KEEP UP!
BOOM!
BOOM!
I'D LIKE TO THANK... MYSELF! FOR BEING AWESOME!
#1

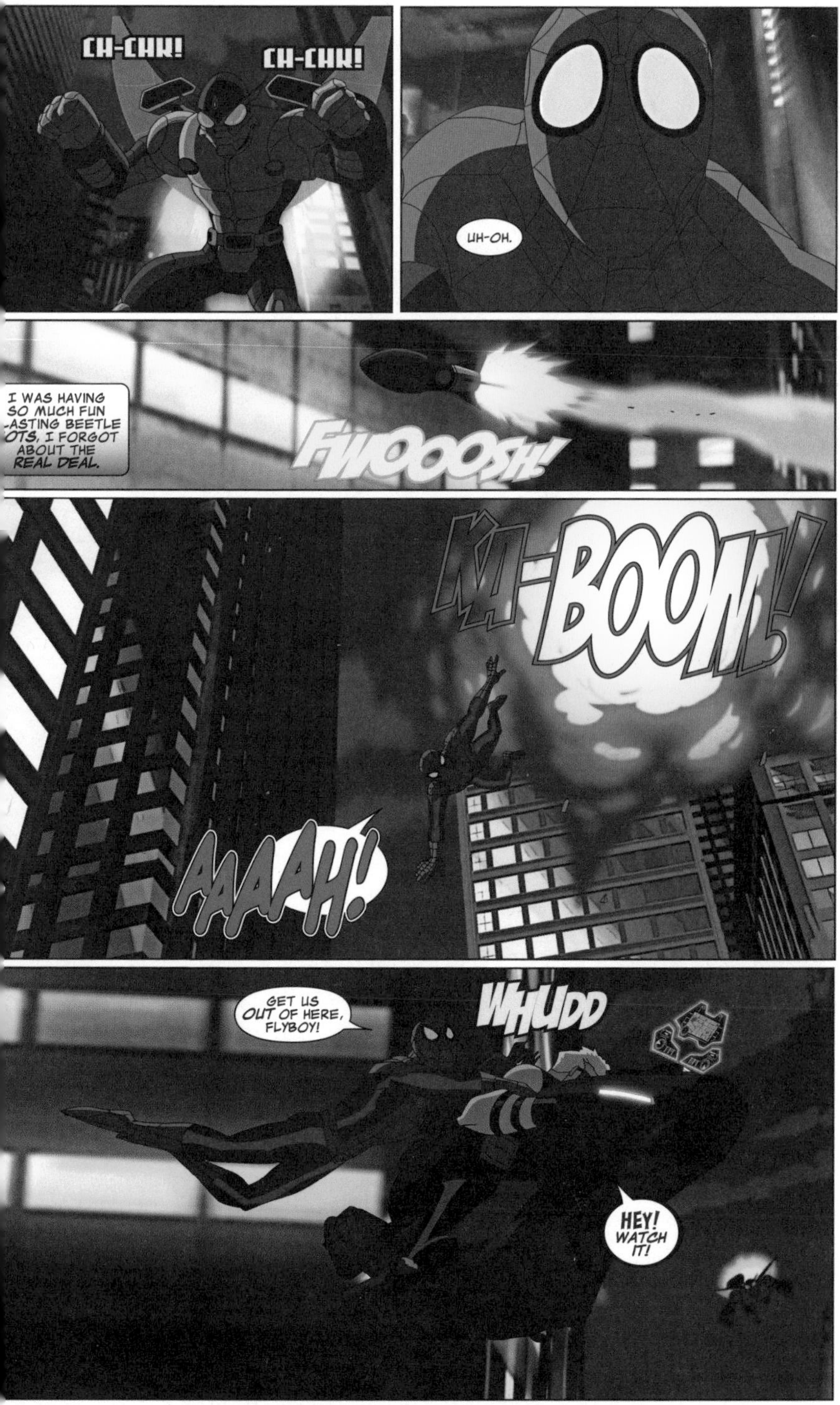
CH-CHK!
CH-CHK!
UH-OH.
I WAS HAVING SO MUCH FUN -ASTING BEETLE OTS, I FORGOT ABOUT THE REAL DEAL.
FWOOOOSH!
KA-BOOM!
AAAAH!
GET US OUT OF HERE, FLYBOY!
WHUDD
HEY! WATCH IT!

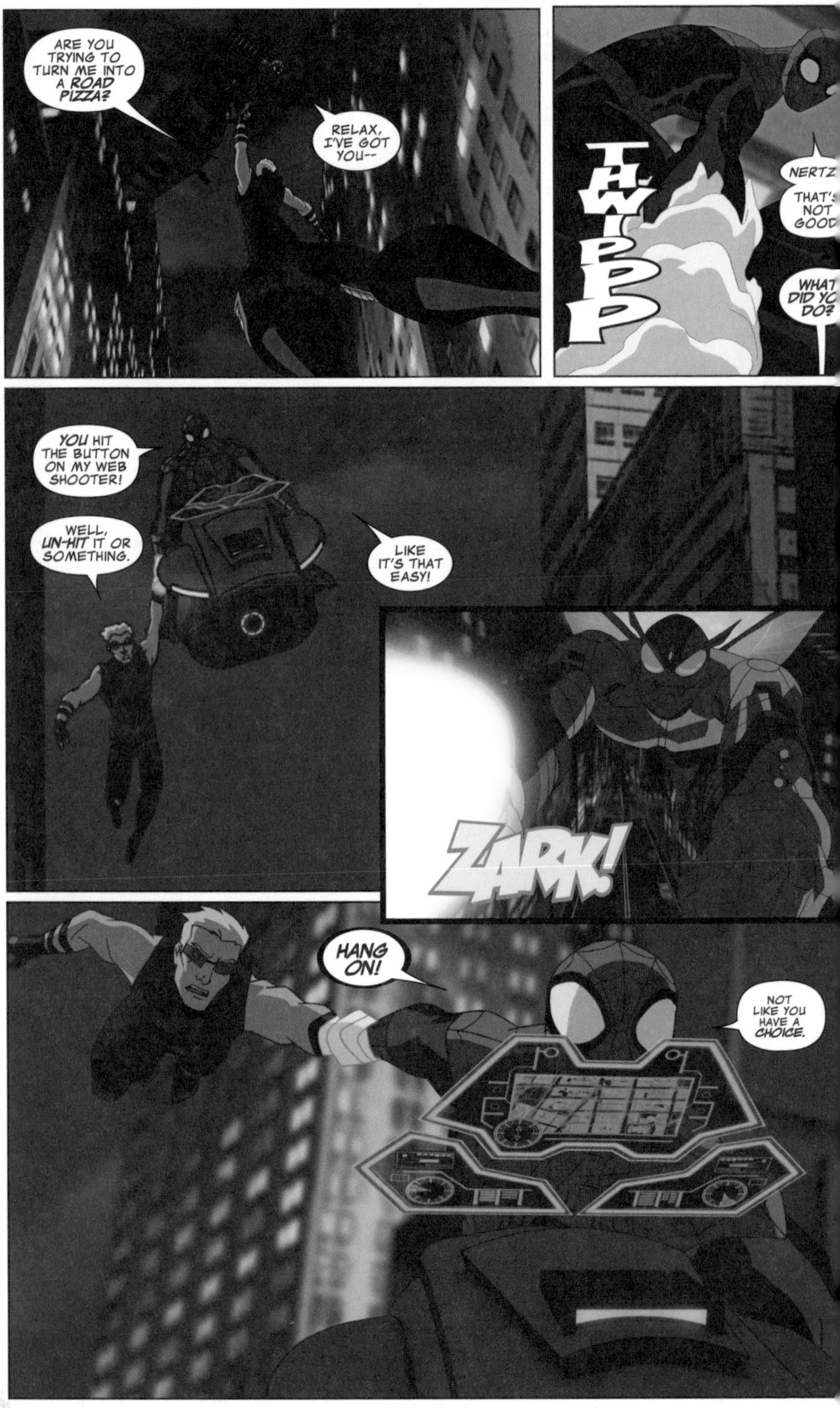
ARE YOU TRYING TO TURN ME INTO A ROAD PIZZA?
RELAX, I'VE GOT YOU--
THWIPPP
NERTZ
THAT'S NOT GOOD
WHAT DID YO DO?
YOU HIT THE BUTTON ON MY WEB SHOOTER!
WELL, UN-HIT IT OR SOMETHING.
LIKE IT'S THAT EASY!
ZARK!
HANG ON!
NOT LIKE YOU HAVE A CHOICE.

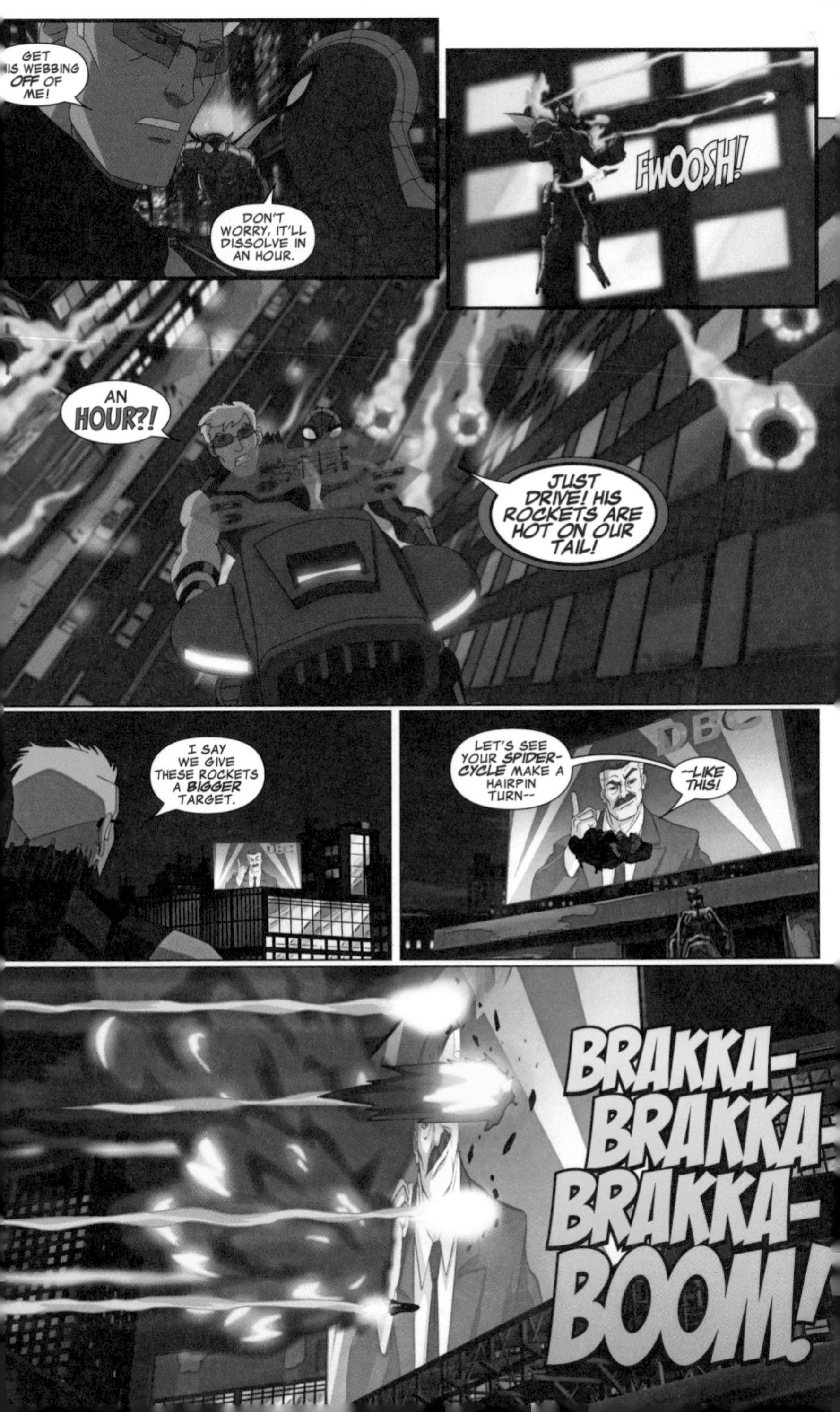
GET IS WEBBING OFF OF ME!
DON'T WORRY, IT'LL DISSOLVE IN AN HOUR.
FWOOSH!
AN HOUR?!
JUST DRIVE! HIS ROCKETS ARE HOT ON OUR TAIL!
I SAY WE GIVE THESE ROCKETS A BIGGER TARGET.
LET'S SEE YOUR SPIDER-CYCLE MAKE A HAIRPIN TURN--
--LIKE THIS!
BRAKKA-BRAKKA-BRAKKA-BOOM!

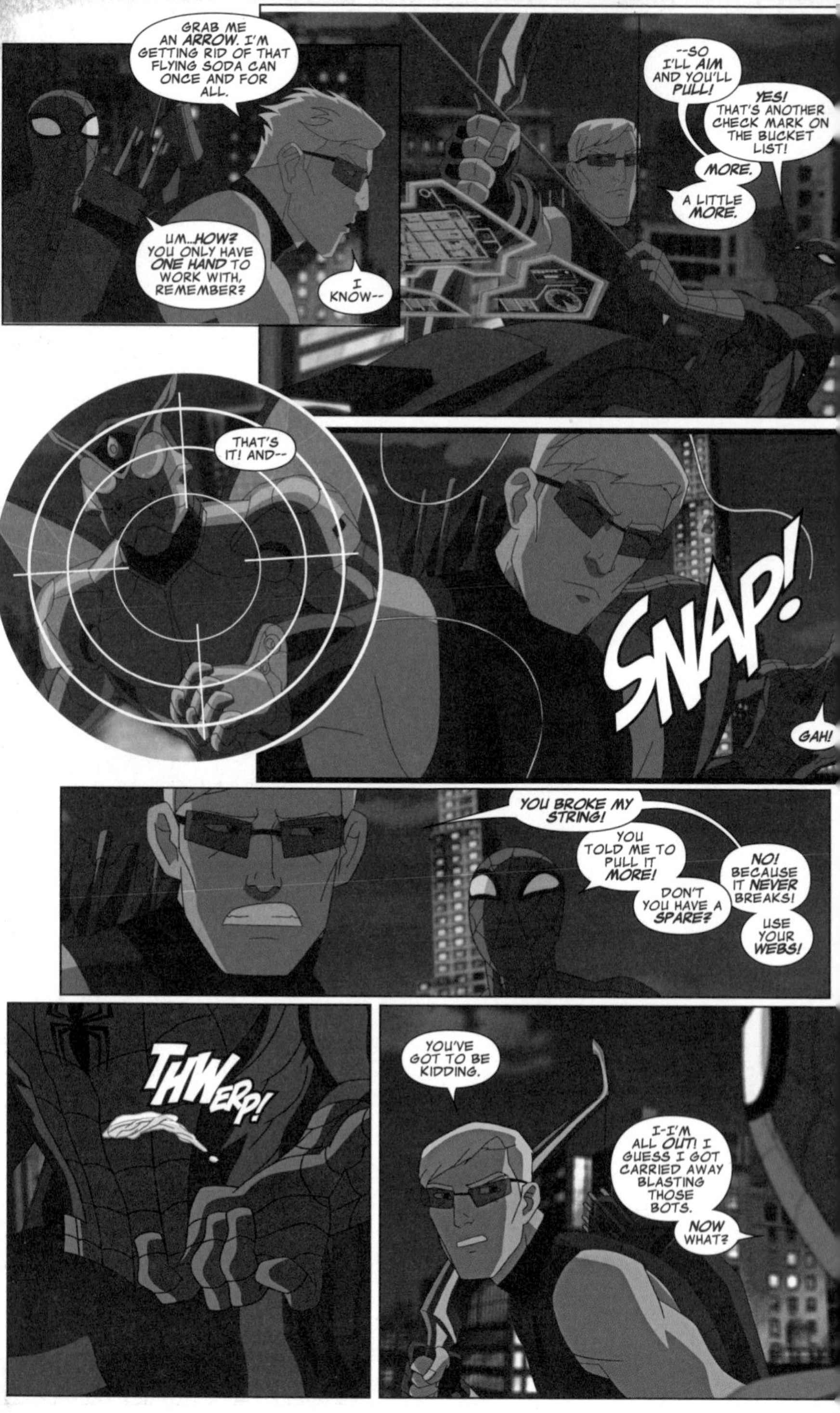
GRAB ME AN ARROW. I'M GETTING RID OF THAT FLYING SODA CAN ONCE AND FOR ALL.
UM...HOW? YOU ONLY HAVE ONE HAND TO WORK WITH, REMEMBER?
I KNOW--
--SO I'LL AIM AND YOU'LL PULL!
YES! THAT'S ANOTHER CHECK MARK ON THE BUCKET LIST!
MORE.
A LITTLE MORE.
THAT'S IT! AND--
SNAP!
GAH!
YOU BROKE MY STRING!
YOU TOLD ME TO PULL IT MORE!
NO! BECAUSE IT NEVER BREAKS!
DON'T YOU HAVE A SPARE?
USE YOUR WEBS!
THWERP!
YOU'VE GOT TO BE KIDDING.
I-I'M ALL OUT! I GUESS I GOT CARRIED AWAY BLASTING THOSE BOTS.
NOW WHAT?

ZARK! ZARK!

ZARK! ZARK!

BOMM!

MY BOW!

THAT DOES IT!

WHAT ARE YOU GONNA DO?!

KLUDD

USE THE LAST TOOL IN OUR TOOLBOX!

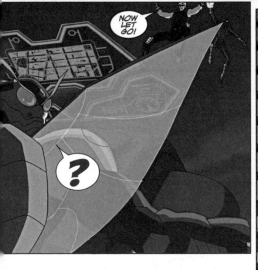

NOW LET GO!

?

KRRRMMS

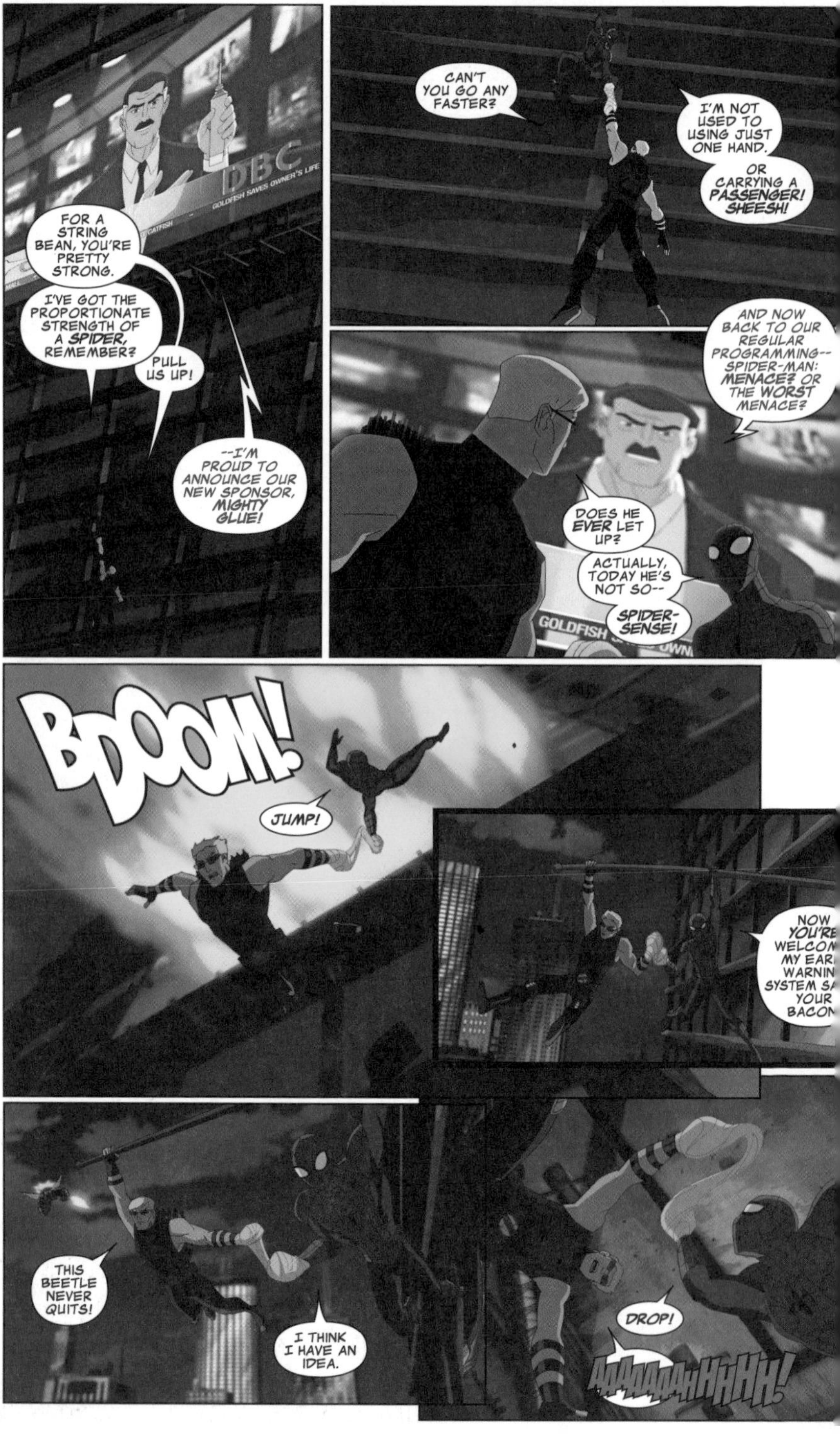
DBC
GOLDFISH SAVES OWNER'S LIFE
CATFISH
FOR A STRING BEAN, YOU'RE PRETTY STRONG.
I'VE GOT THE PROPORTIONATE STRENGTH OF A SPIDER, REMEMBER?
PULL US UP!
--I'M PROUD TO ANNOUNCE OUR NEW SPONSOR, MIGHTY GLUE!
CAN'T YOU GO ANY FASTER?
I'M NOT USED TO USING JUST ONE HAND.
OR CARRYING A PASSENGER! SHEESH!
AND NOW BACK TO OUR REGULAR PROGRAMMING-- SPIDER-MAN: MENACE? OR THE WORST MENACE?
DOES HE EVER LET UP?
ACTUALLY, TODAY HE'S NOT SO--
SPIDER-SENSE!
GOLDFISH
BDOOM!
JUMP!
THIS BEETLE NEVER QUITS!
I THINK I HAVE AN IDEA.
DROP!
AAAAAAAHHHHH!

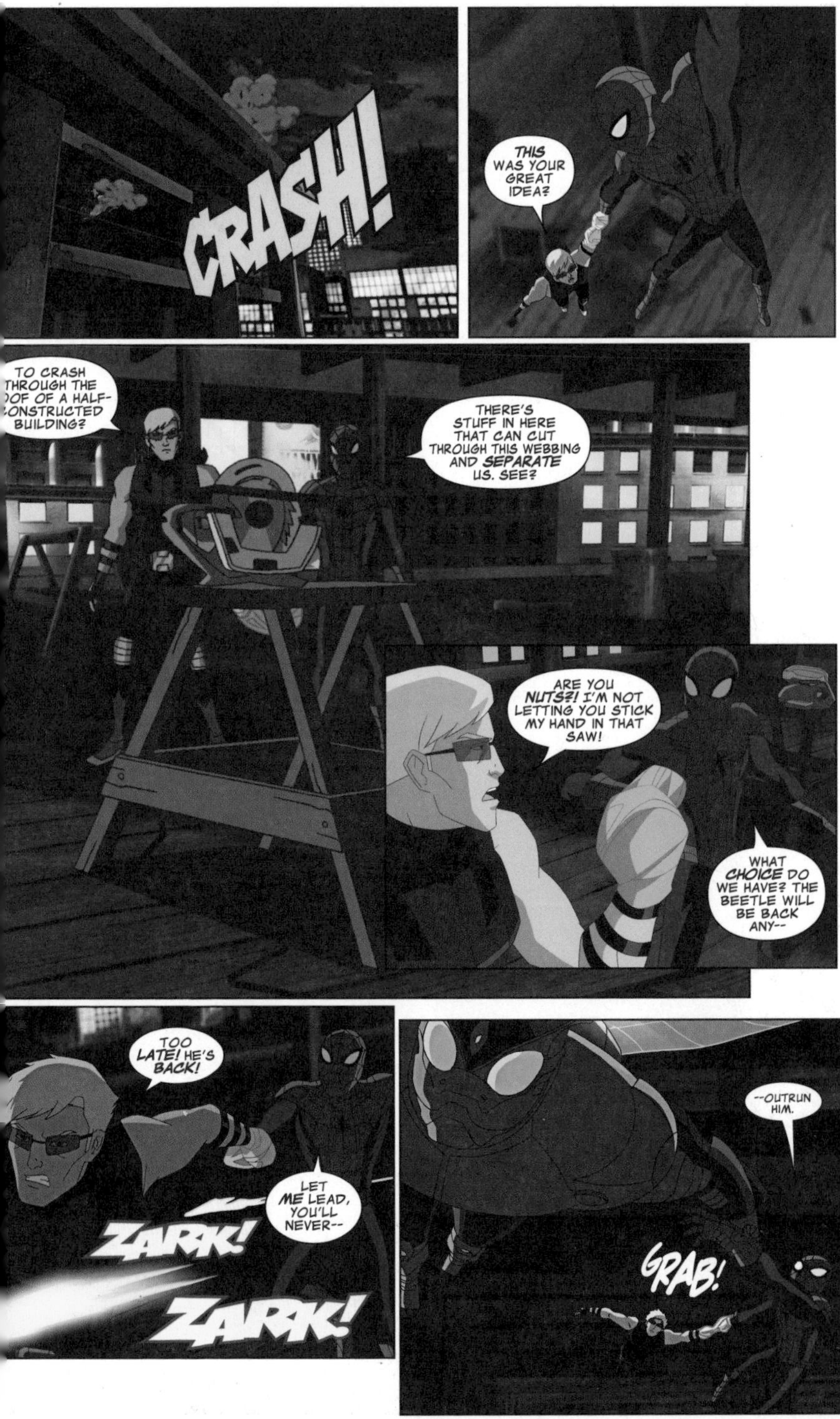
CRASH!
THIS WAS YOUR GREAT IDEA?
TO CRASH THROUGH THE ROOF OF A HALF-CONSTRUCTED BUILDING?
THERE'S STUFF IN HERE THAT CAN CUT THROUGH THIS WEBBING AND SEPARATE US. SEE?
ARE YOU NUTS?! I'M NOT LETTING YOU STICK MY HAND IN THAT SAW!
WHAT CHOICE DO WE HAVE? THE BEETLE WILL BE BACK ANY--
TOO LATE! HE'S BACK!
LET ME LEAD, YOU'LL NEVER--
ZARK!
ZARK!
--OUTRUN HIM.
GRAB!

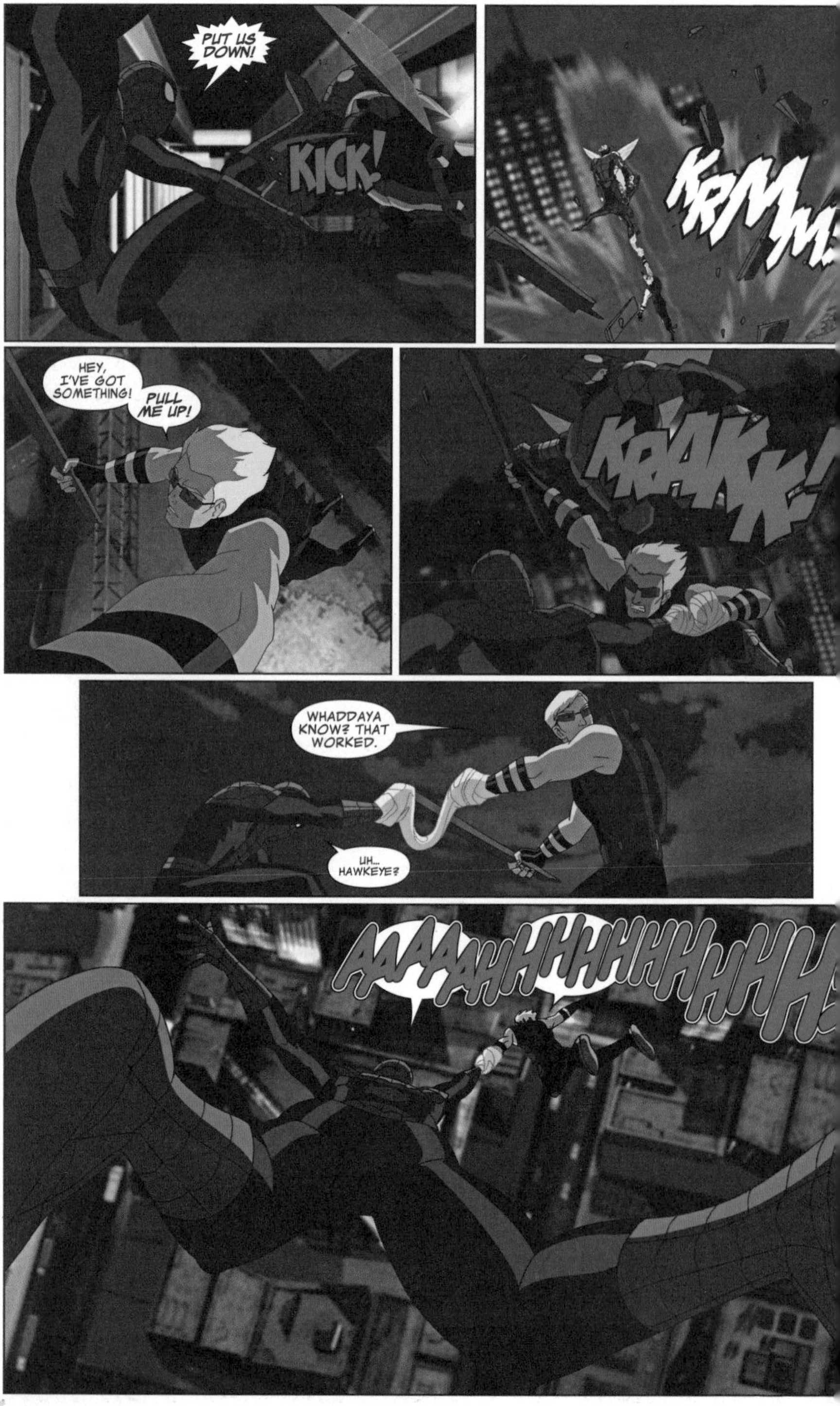
PUT US DOWN!
KICK!
KRMMM
HEY, I'VE GOT SOMETHING!
PULL ME UP!
KRAKK!
WHADDAYA KNOW? THAT WORKED.
UH... HAWKEYE?
AAAAAHHHHHHHHHHHHH

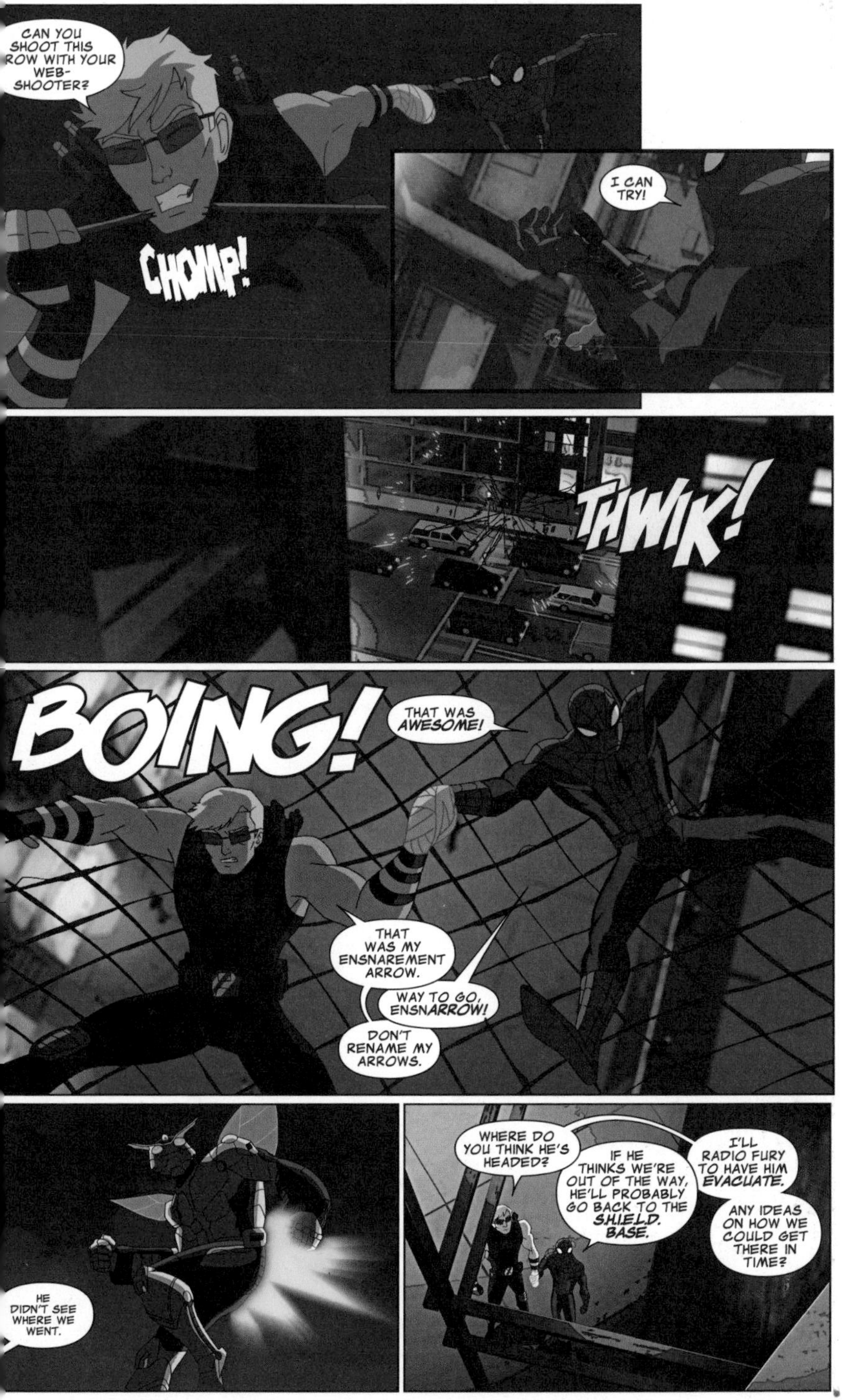

CAN YOU SHOOT THIS ROW WITH YOUR WEB-SHOOTER?
CHOMP!
I CAN TRY!
THWIK!
BOING!
THAT WAS AWESOME!
THAT WAS MY ENSNAREMENT ARROW.
WAY TO GO, ENSNARROW!
DON'T RENAME MY ARROWS.
HE DIDN'T SEE WHERE WE WENT.
WHERE DO YOU THINK HE'S HEADED?
IF HE THINKS WE'RE OUT OF THE WAY, HE'LL PROBABLY GO BACK TO THE S.H.I.E.L.D. BASE.
I'LL RADIO FURY TO HAVE HIM EVACUATE.
ANY IDEAS ON HOW WE COULD GET THERE IN TIME?

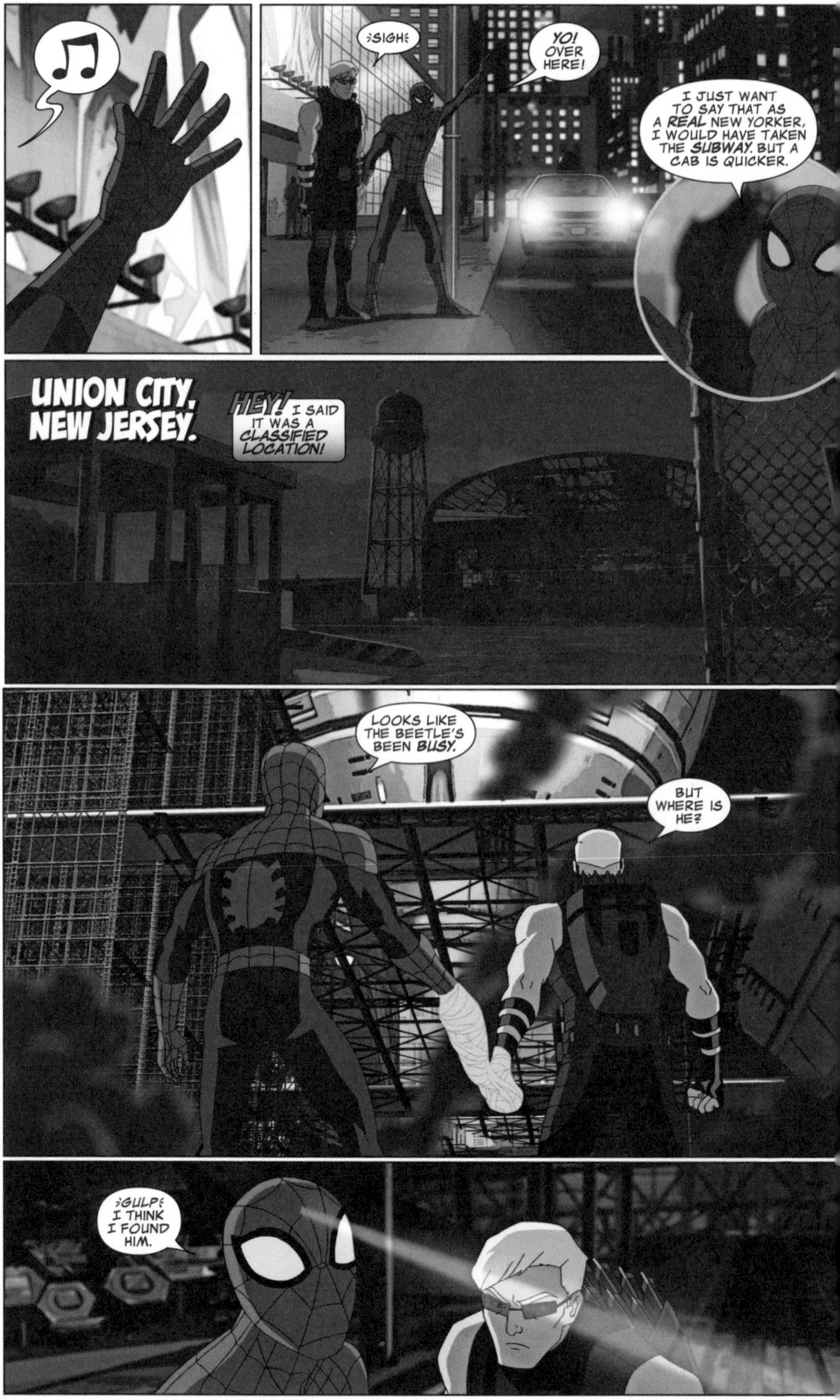
♫
:SIGH:
YO! OVER HERE!
I JUST WANT TO SAY THAT AS A REAL NEW YORKER, I WOULD HAVE TAKEN THE SUBWAY. BUT A CAB IS QUICKER.
UNION CITY, NEW JERSEY.
HEY! I SAID IT WAS A CLASSIFIED LOCATION!
LOOKS LIKE THE BEETLE'S BEEN BUSY.
BUT WHERE IS HE?
:GULP: I THINK I FOUND HIM.

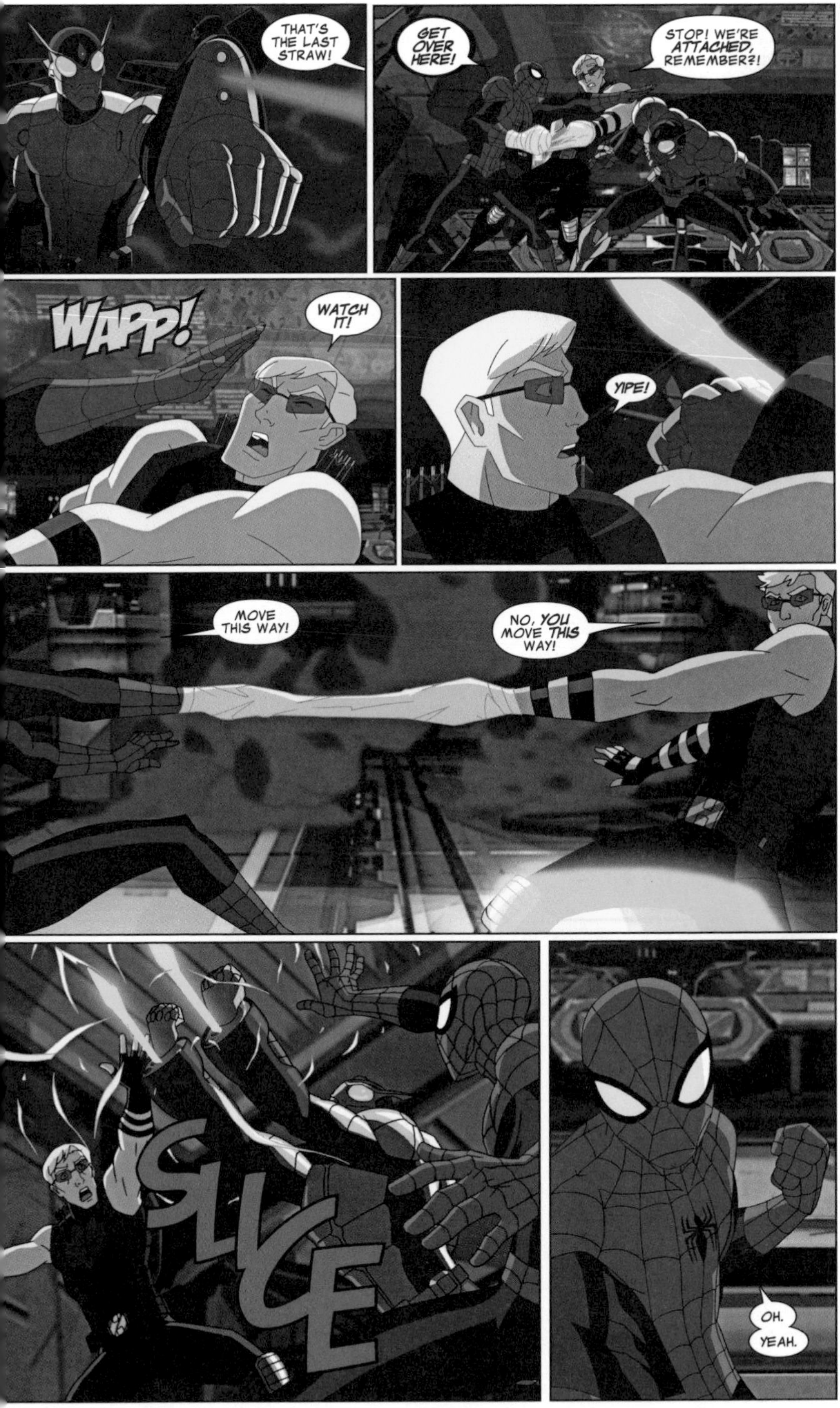
THAT'S THE LAST STRAW!
GET OVER HERE!
STOP! WE'RE ATTACHED, REMEMBER?!
WAPP!
WATCH IT!
YIPE!
MOVE THIS WAY!
NO, YOU MOVE THIS WAY!
SLICE
OH.
YEAH.

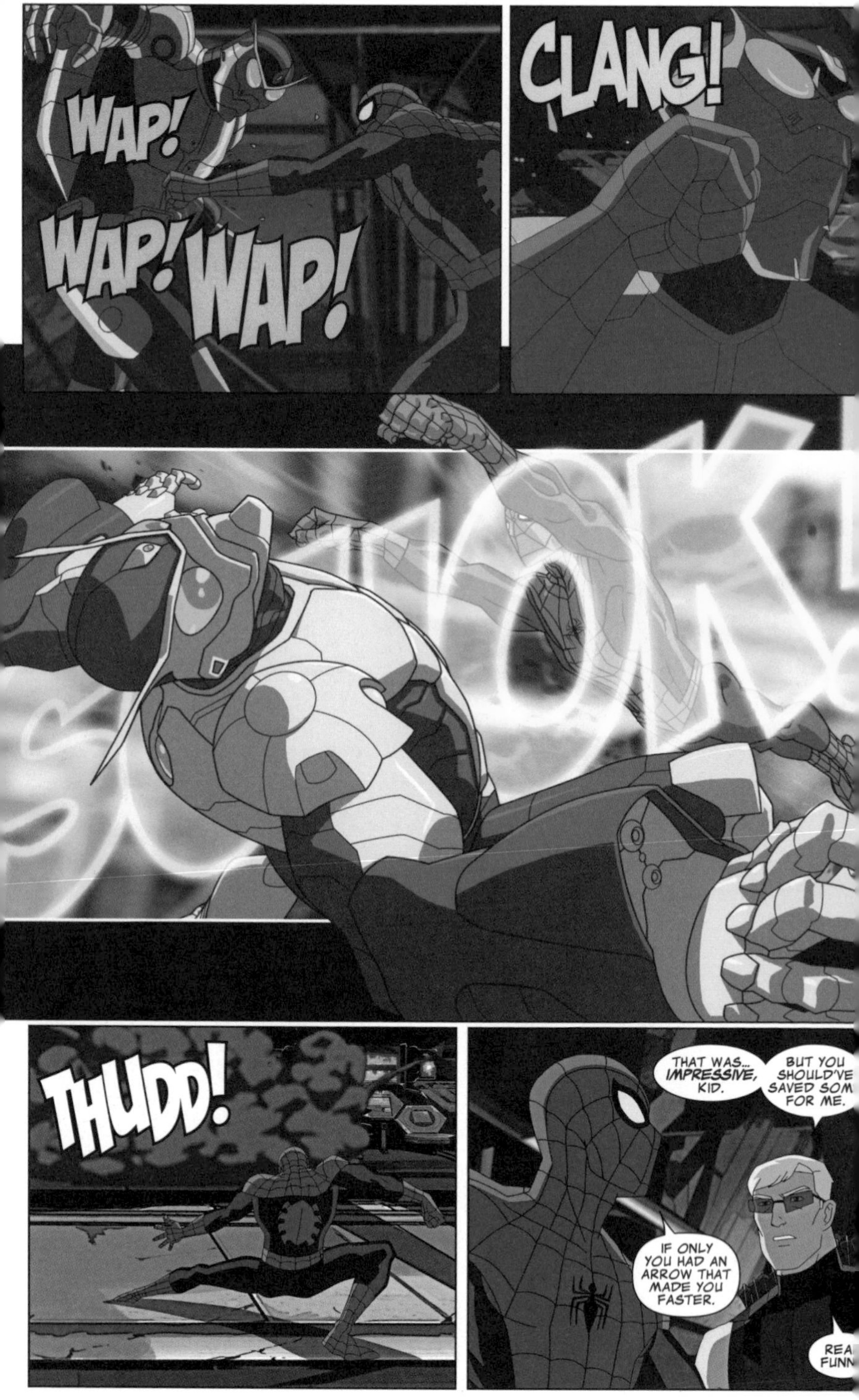

WAP!
WAP! WAP!
CLANG!
THUDD!
THAT WAS... IMPRESSIVE, KID.
BUT YOU SHOULD'VE SAVED SOM FOR ME.
IF ONLY YOU HAD AN ARROW THAT MADE YOU FASTER.
REA FUNN

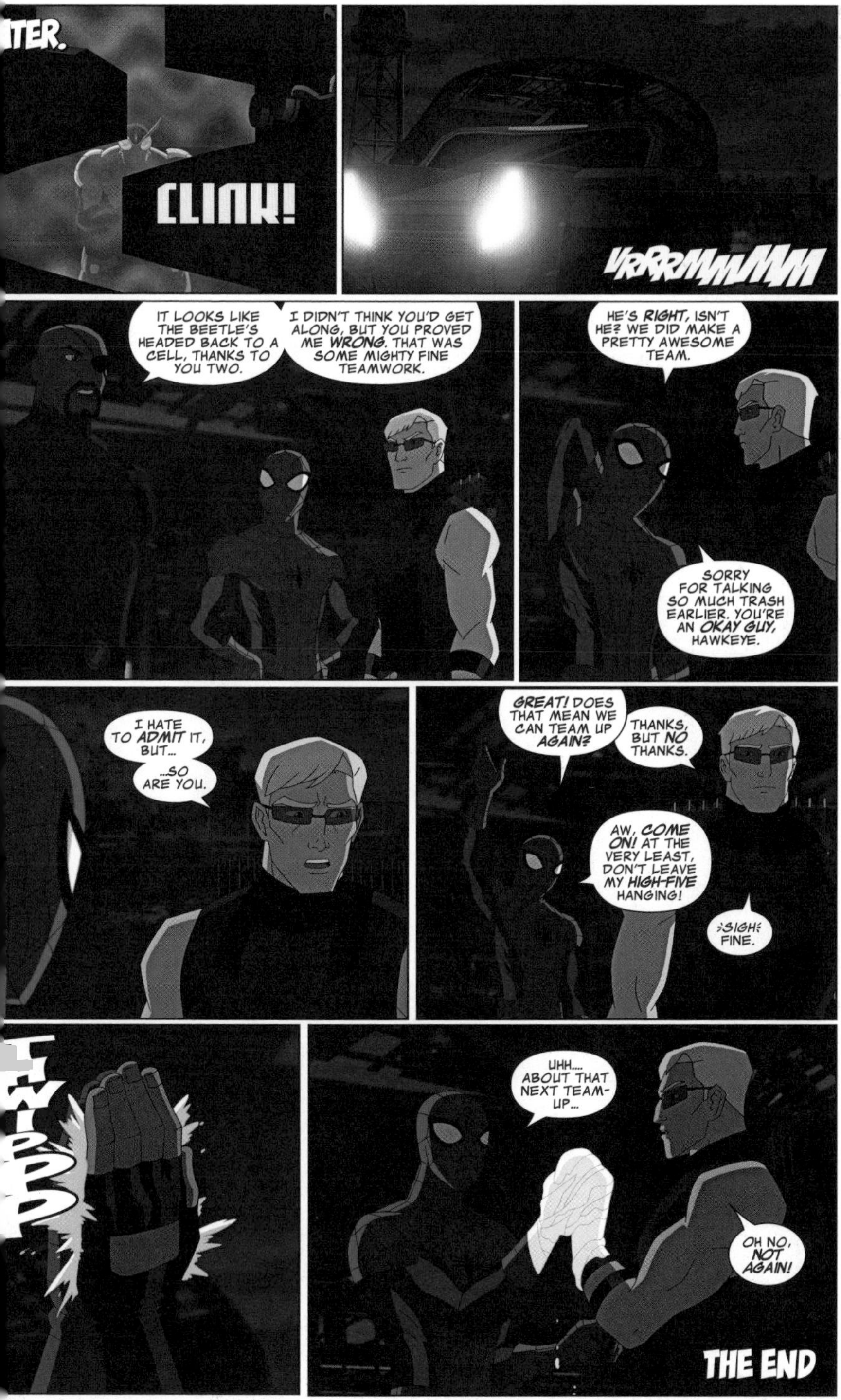
CLINK!
IT LOOKS LIKE THE BEETLE'S HEADED BACK TO A CELL, THANKS TO YOU TWO.
I DIDN'T THINK YOU'D GET ALONG, BUT YOU PROVED ME WRONG. THAT WAS SOME MIGHTY FINE TEAMWORK.
HE'S RIGHT, ISN'T HE? WE DID MAKE A PRETTY AWESOME TEAM.
SORRY FOR TALKING SO MUCH TRASH EARLIER. YOU'RE AN OKAY GUY, HAWKEYE.
I HATE TO ADMIT IT, BUT...
...SO ARE YOU.
GREAT! DOES THAT MEAN WE CAN TEAM UP AGAIN?
THANKS, BUT NO THANKS.
AW, COME ON! AT THE VERY LEAST, DON'T LEAVE MY HIGH-FIVE HANGING!
SIGH FINE.
UHH.... ABOUT THAT NEXT TEAM-UP...
OH NO, NOT AGAIN!
THE END

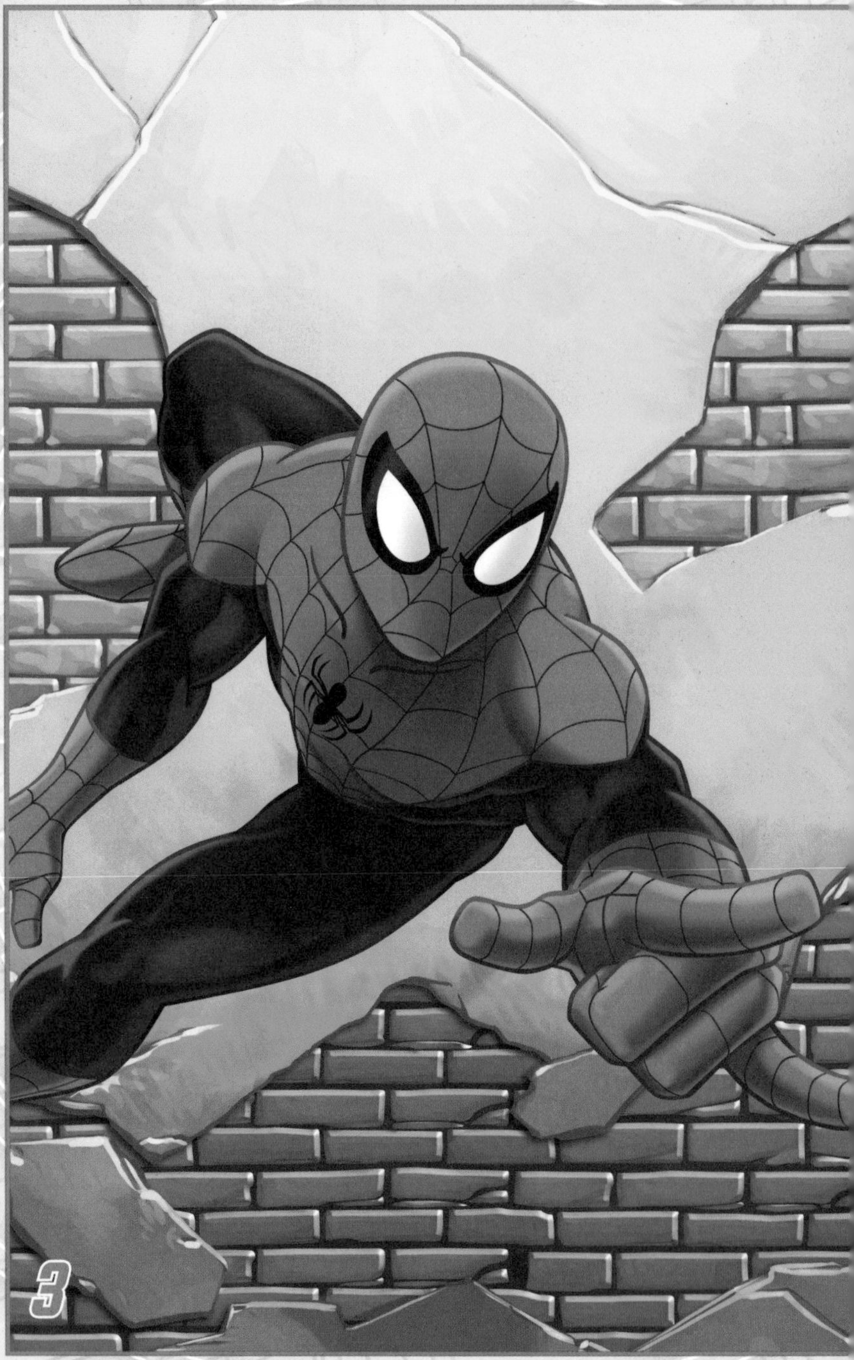
3

Based on "Swarm"

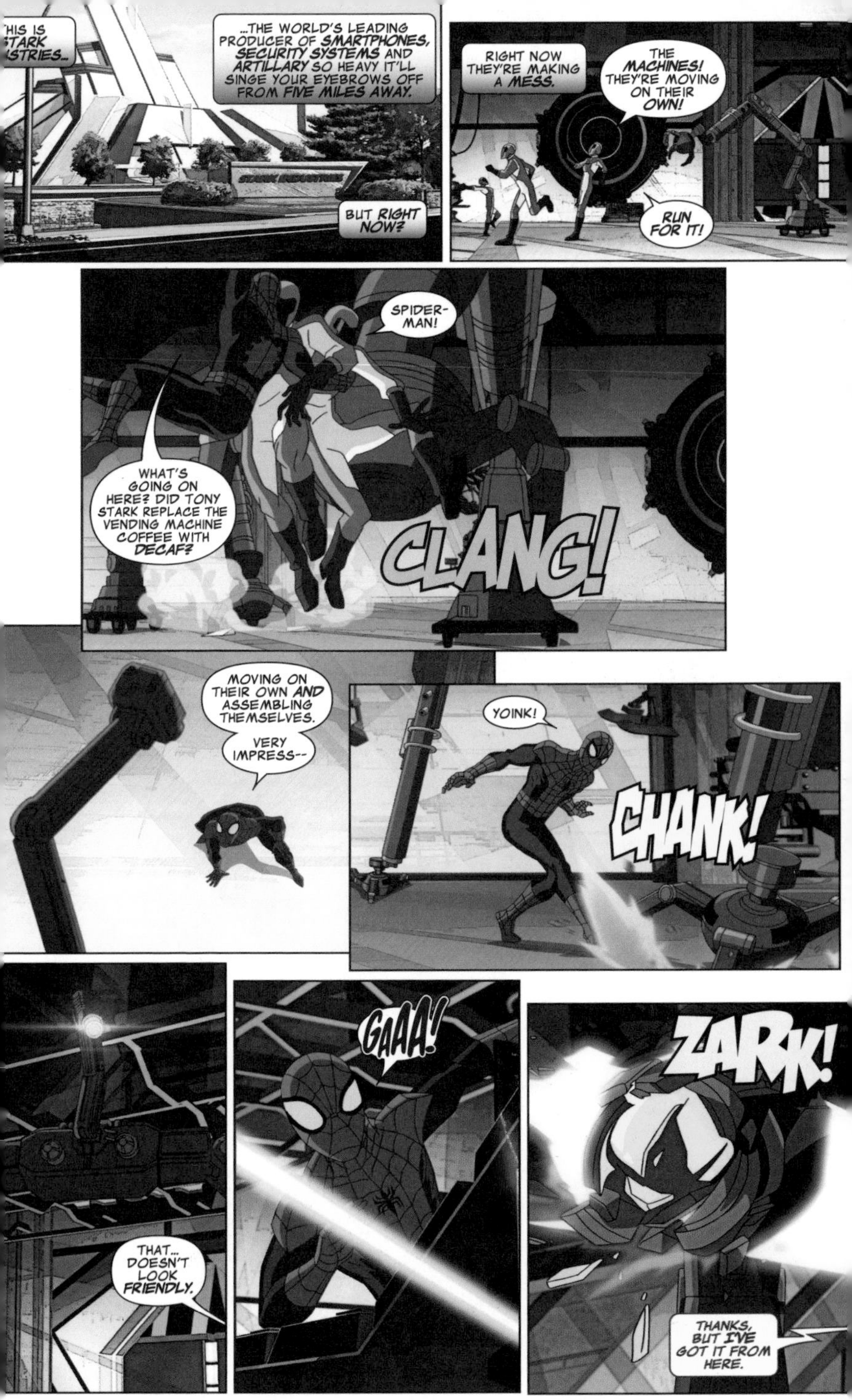

THIS IS STARK INDUSTRIES...
...THE WORLD'S LEADING PRODUCER OF SMARTPHONES, SECURITY SYSTEMS AND ARTILLARY SO HEAVY IT'LL SINGE YOUR EYEBROWS OFF FROM FIVE MILES AWAY.
STARK INDUSTRIES
BUT RIGHT NOW?
RIGHT NOW THEY'RE MAKING A MESS.
THE MACHINES! THEY'RE MOVING ON THEIR OWN!
RUN FOR IT!
SPIDER-MAN!
WHAT'S GOING ON HERE? DID TONY STARK REPLACE THE VENDING MACHINE COFFEE WITH DECAF?
CLANG!
MOVING ON THEIR OWN AND ASSEMBLING THEMSELVES.
VERY IMPRESS--
YOINK!
CHANK!
THAT... DOESN'T LOOK FRIENDLY.
GAAA!
ZARK!
THANKS, BUT I'VE GOT IT FROM HERE.

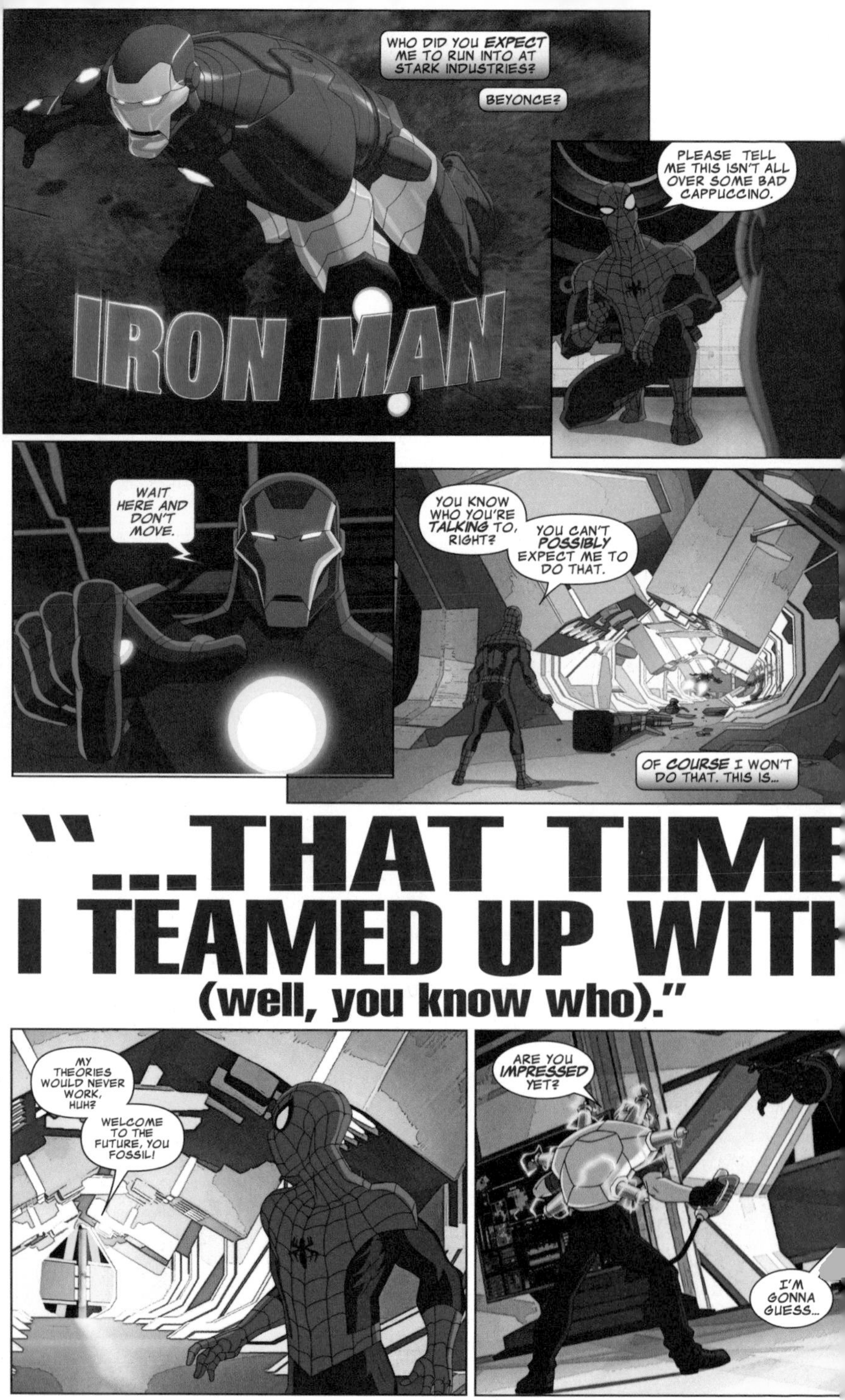
WHO DID YOU EXPECT ME TO RUN INTO AT STARK INDUSTRIES?
BEYONCE?
IRON MAN
PLEASE TELL ME THIS ISN'T ALL OVER SOME BAD CAPPUCCINO.
WAIT HERE AND DON'T MOVE.
YOU KNOW WHO YOU'RE TALKING TO, RIGHT?
YOU CAN'T POSSIBLY EXPECT ME TO DO THAT.
OF COURSE I WON'T DO THAT. THIS IS...
"...THAT TIME I TEAMED UP WITH
(well, you know who)."
MY THEORIES WOULD NEVER WORK, HUH?
WELCOME TO THE FUTURE, YOU FOSSIL!
ARE YOU IMPRESSED YET?
I'M GONNA GUESS...

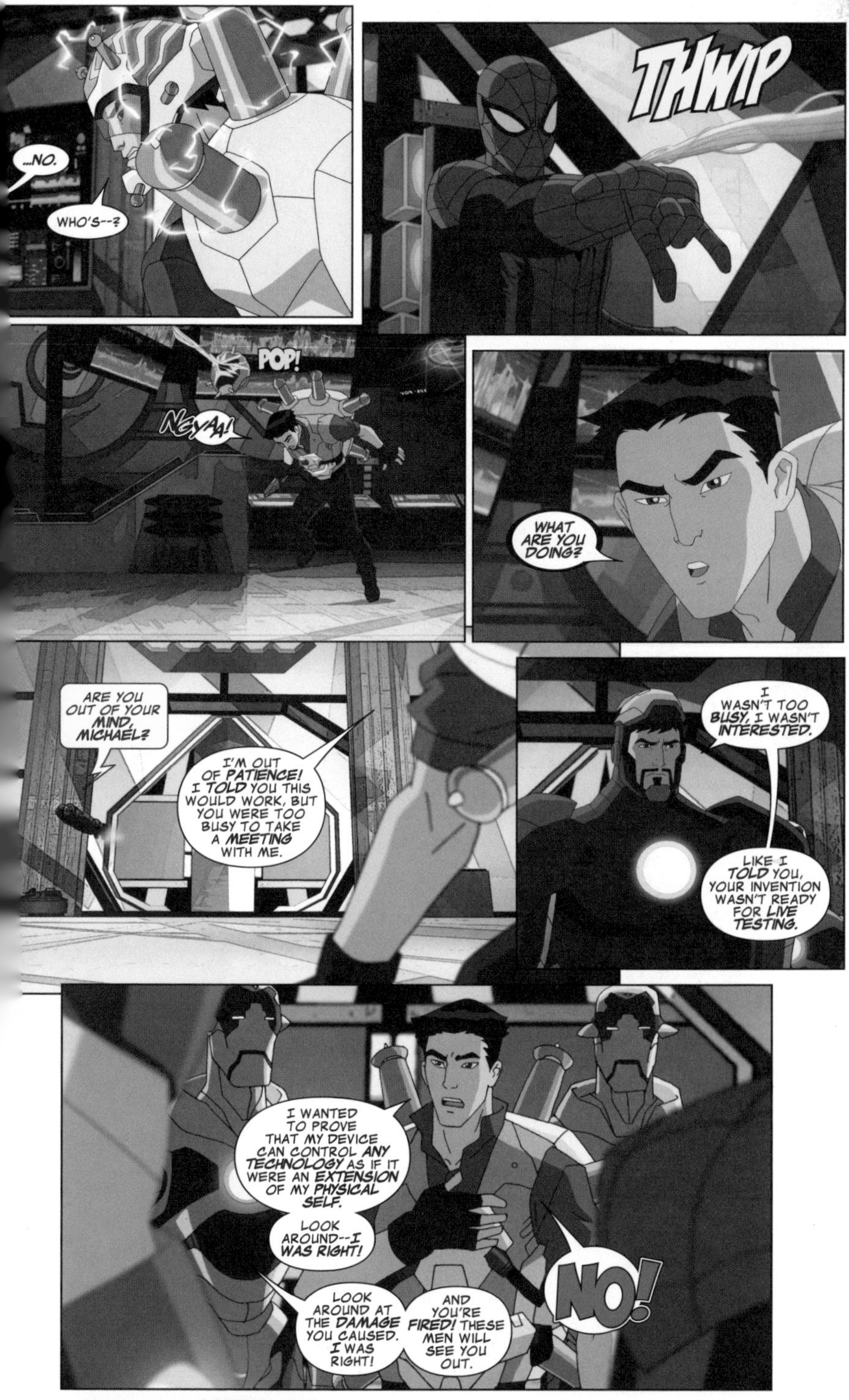
...NO.
WHO'S--?
THWIP
POP!
NGYAA!
WHAT ARE YOU DOING?
ARE YOU OUT OF YOUR MIND, MICHAEL?
I'M OUT OF PATIENCE! I TOLD YOU THIS WOULD WORK, BUT YOU WERE TOO BUSY TO TAKE A MEETING WITH ME.
I WASN'T TOO BUSY, I WASN'T INTERESTED.
LIKE I TOLD YOU, YOUR INVENTION WASN'T READY FOR LIVE TESTING.
I WANTED TO PROVE THAT MY DEVICE CAN CONTROL ANY TECHNOLOGY AS IF IT WERE AN EXTENSION OF MY PHYSICAL SELF.
LOOK AROUND--I WAS RIGHT!
NO!
LOOK AROUND AT THE DAMAGE YOU CAUSED. I WAS RIGHT!
AND YOU'RE FIRED! THESE MEN WILL SEE YOU OUT.

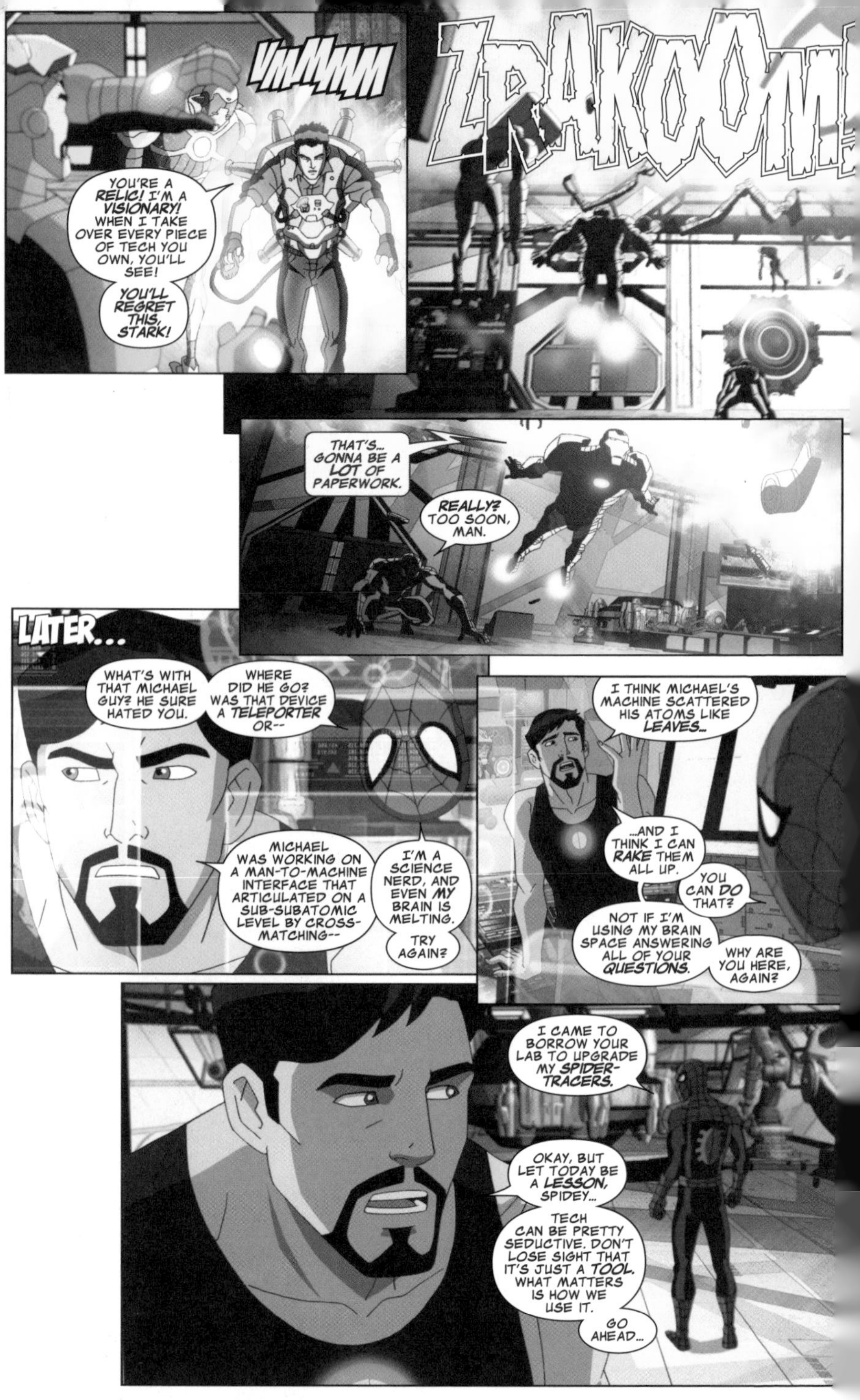
VMMMMM
YOU'RE A RELIC! I'M A VISIONARY! WHEN I TAKE OVER EVERY PIECE OF TECH YOU OWN, YOU'LL SEE!
YOU'LL REGRET THIS, STARK!
ZRAKOOM!
THAT'S... GONNA BE A LOT OF PAPERWORK.
REALLY? TOO SOON, MAN.
LATER...
WHAT'S WITH THAT MICHAEL GUY? HE SURE HATED YOU.
WHERE DID HE GO? WAS THAT DEVICE A TELEPORTER OR--
MICHAEL WAS WORKING ON A MAN-TO-MACHINE INTERFACE THAT ARTICULATED ON A SUB-SUBATOMIC LEVEL BY CROSS-MATCHING--
I'M A SCIENCE NERD, AND EVEN MY BRAIN IS MELTING.
TRY AGAIN?
I THINK MICHAEL'S MACHINE SCATTERED HIS ATOMS LIKE LEAVES...
...AND I THINK I CAN RAKE THEM ALL UP.
YOU CAN DO THAT?
NOT IF I'M USING MY BRAIN SPACE ANSWERING ALL OF YOUR QUESTIONS.
WHY ARE YOU HERE, AGAIN?
I CAME TO BORROW YOUR LAB TO UPGRADE MY SPIDER-TRACERS.
OKAY, BUT LET TODAY BE A LESSON, SPIDEY...
TECH CAN BE PRETTY SEDUCTIVE. DON'T LOSE SIGHT THAT IT'S JUST A TOOL. WHAT MATTERS IS HOW WE USE IT.
GO AHEAD...

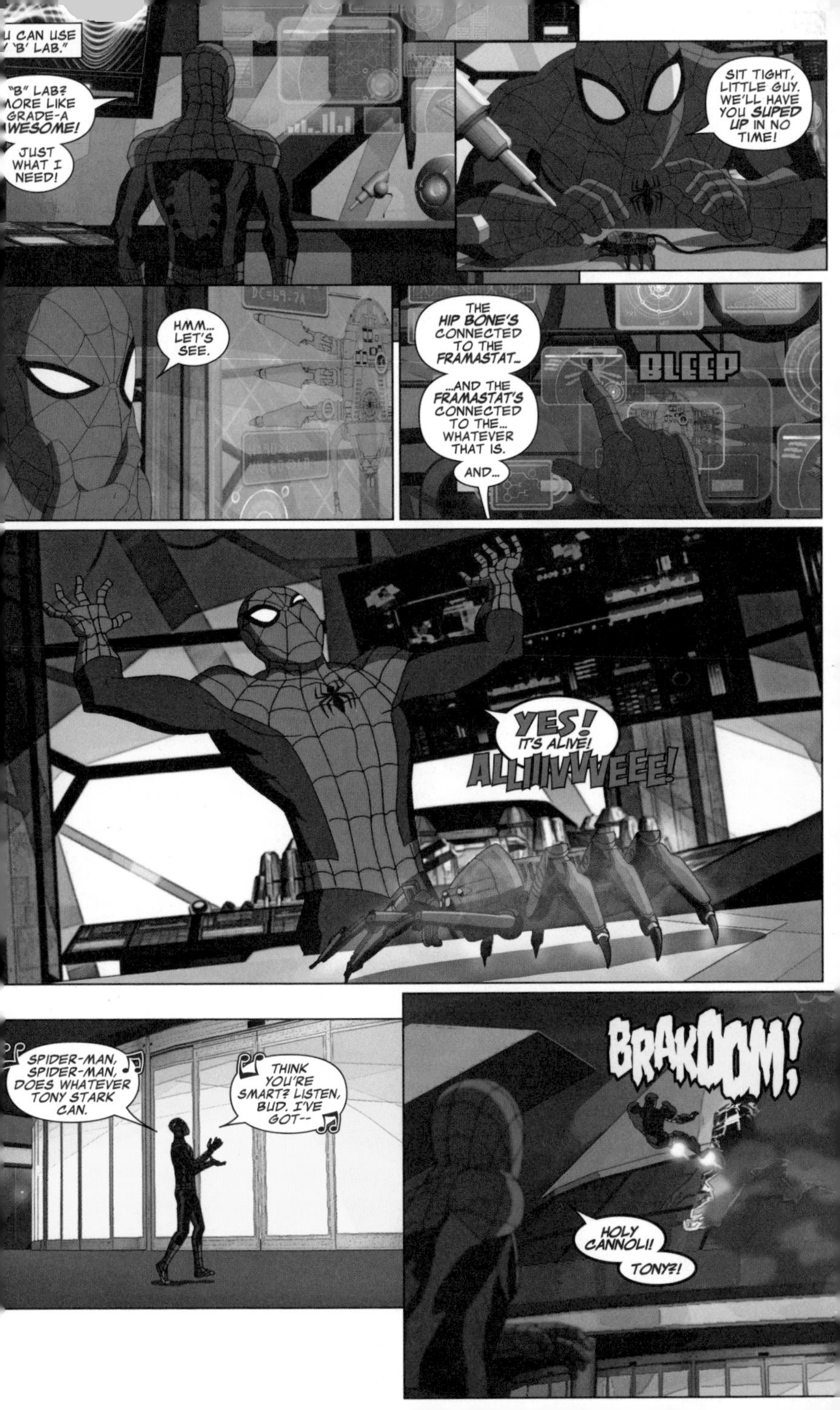
U CAN USE
'B' LAB."
"B" LAB?
MORE LIKE
GRADE-A
WESOME!
JUST WHAT I NEED!
SIT TIGHT, LITTLE GUY. WE'LL HAVE YOU SUPED UP IN NO TIME!
HMM... LET'S SEE.
THE HIP BONE'S CONNECTED TO THE FRAMASTAT...
...AND THE FRAMASTAT'S CONNECTED TO THE... WHATEVER THAT IS.
AND...
BLEEP
YES! IT'S ALIVE! ALLIIIVVVEEE!
SPIDER-MAN, SPIDER-MAN, DOES WHATEVER TONY STARK CAN.
THINK YOU'RE SMART? LISTEN, BUD. I'VE GOT--
BRAKOOM!
HOLY CANNOLI!
TONY?!

THESE... THINGS--THIS ISN'T MY TECH! IT'S--

YOU! YOU DID THIS!

I ONLY MADE ONE OF THEM!

BAD SPIDER-TRACERS! BAD! LEAVE MY FRIEND ALONE!

THEY'RE SELF-REPLICATING--

--AND USING MY ARMOR FOR MATERIAL! I HAVE TO GET THEM OFF BEFORE THEY DESTROY IT!

I HAVE AN ID BUT I'LL NE MY SPIDER CYCLE!

DO YOU TRUST ME?

VRRRRRRRMMMMM

OF COURSE NOT!

THWAP!

TOO BAD!

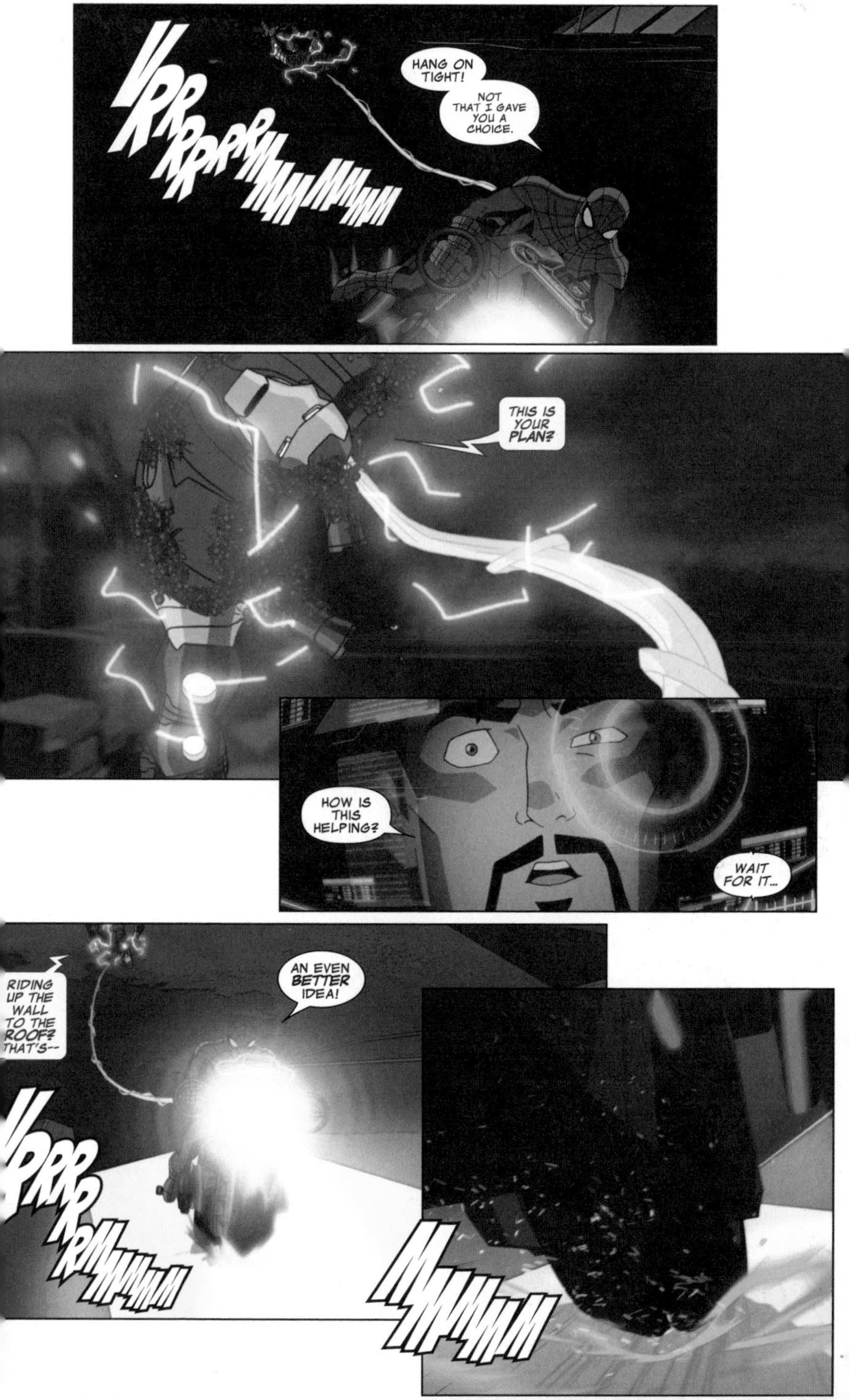

VRRRRRRMMMMMMMMMM
HANG ON TIGHT!
NOT THAT I GAVE YOU A CHOICE.
THIS IS YOUR PLAN?
HOW IS THIS HELPING?
WAIT FOR IT...
RIDING UP THE WALL TO THE ROOF? THAT'S--
AN EVEN BETTER IDEA!
VRRRRMMMMMMMMMMMMMMM

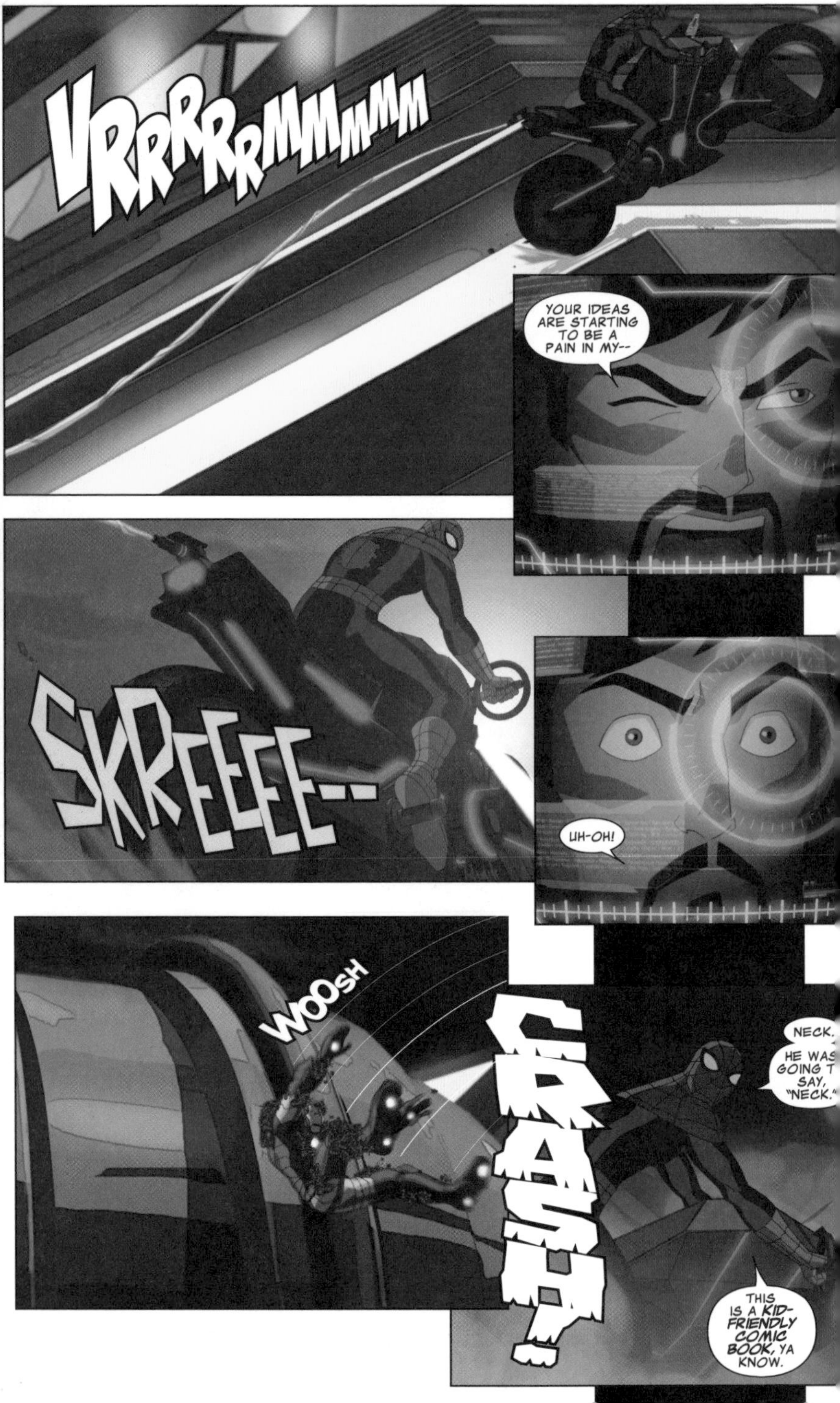
VRRRRRMMMMMM
YOUR IDEAS ARE STARTING TO BE A PAIN IN MY--
SKREEEEE--
UH-OH!
WOOSH
CRASH!
NECK.
HE WAS GOING T SAY, "NECK."
THIS IS A KID-FRIENDLY COMIC BOOK, YA KNOW.

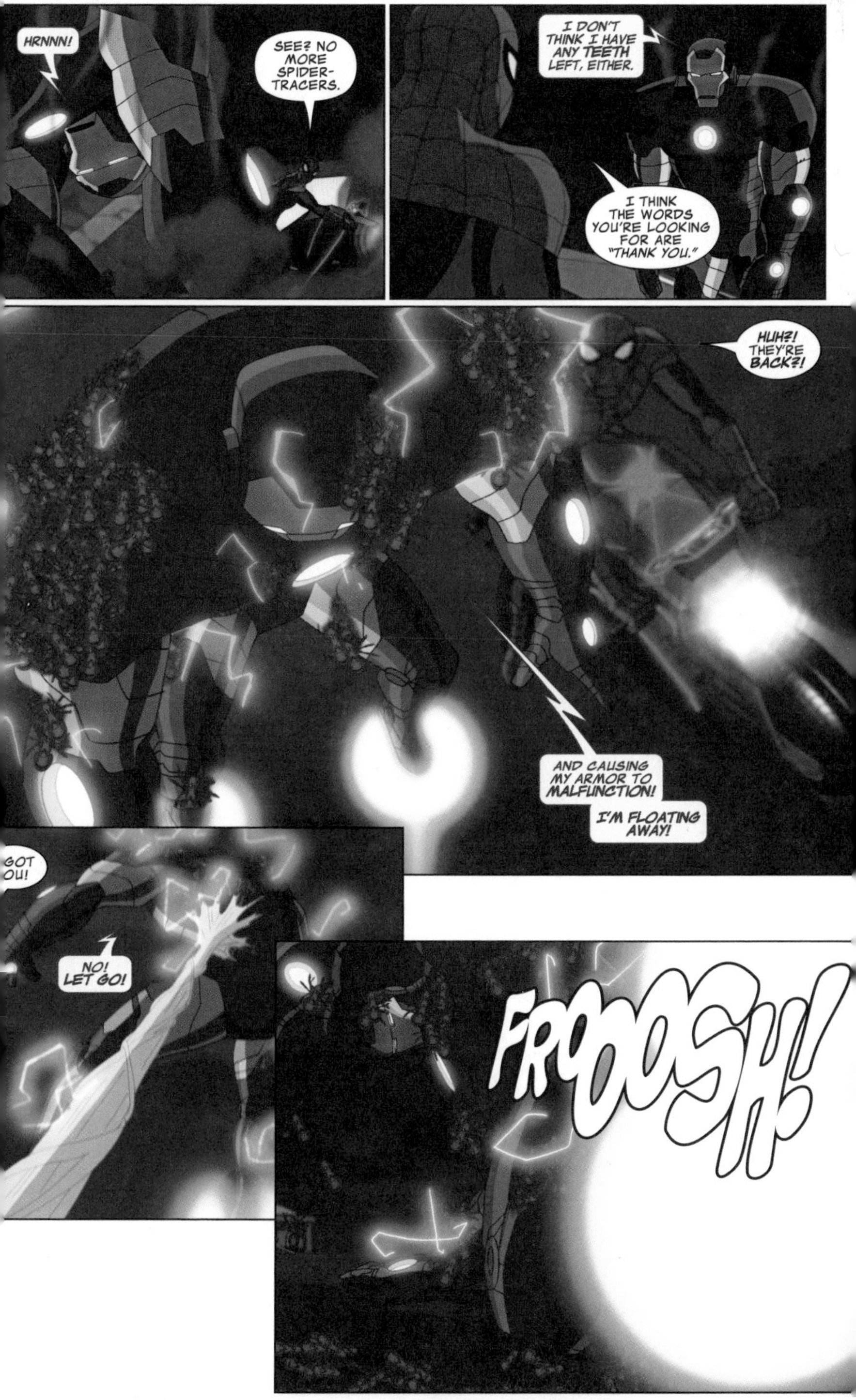
HRNNN!
SEE? NO MORE SPIDER-TRACERS.
I DON'T THINK I HAVE ANY TEETH LEFT, EITHER.
I THINK THE WORDS YOU'RE LOOKING FOR ARE "THANK YOU."
HUH?! THEY'RE BACK?!
AND CAUSING MY ARMOR TO MALFUNCTION!
I'M FLOATING AWAY!
NO! LET GO!
FROOOSH!

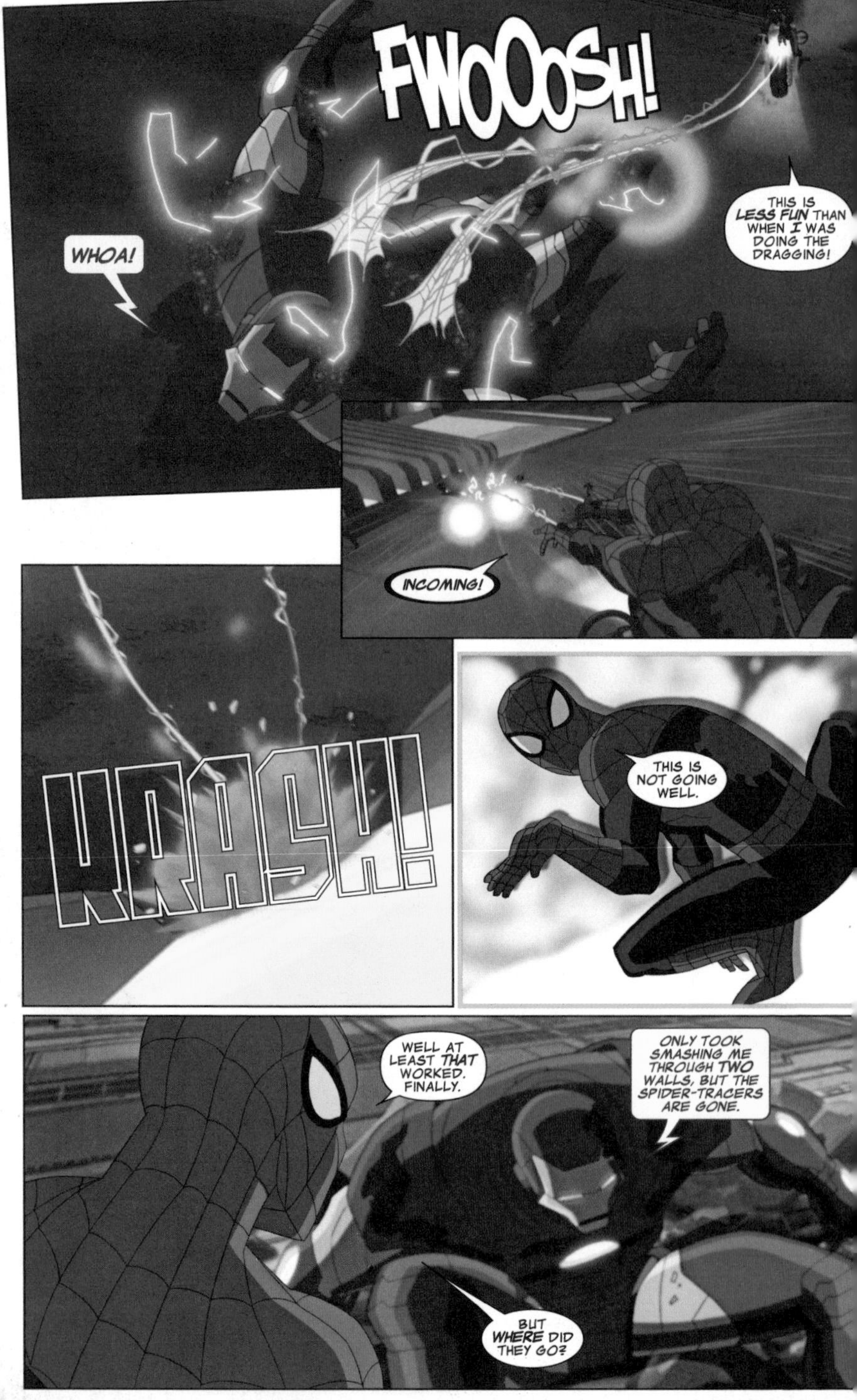

FWOOOSH!
WHOA!
THIS IS LESS FUN THAN WHEN I WAS DOING THE DRAGGING!
INCOMING!
KRASH!
THIS IS NOT GOING WELL.
WELL AT LEAST THAT WORKED. FINALLY.
ONLY TOOK SMASHING ME THROUGH TWO WALLS, BUT THE SPIDER-TRACERS ARE GONE.
BUT WHERE DID THEY GO?

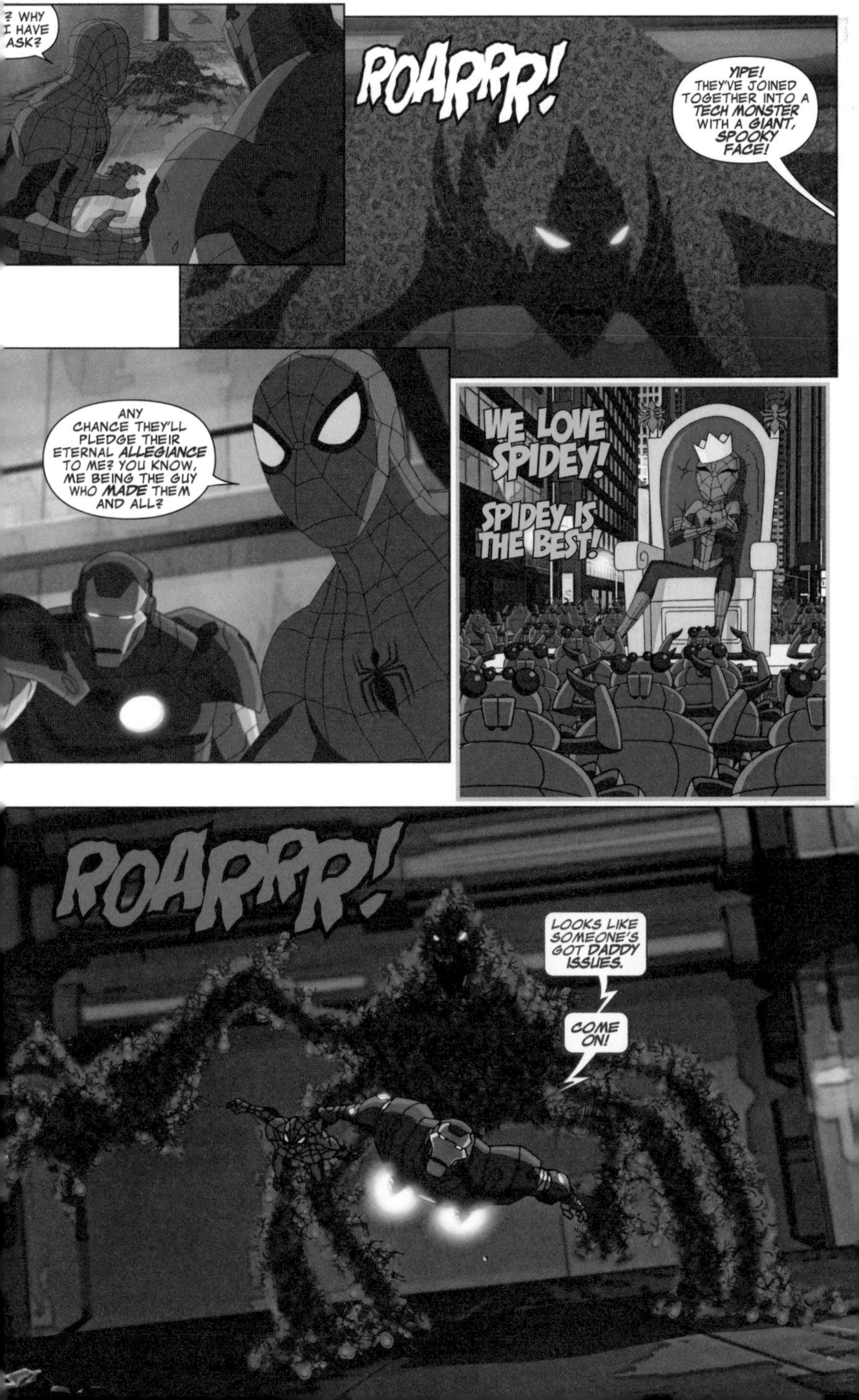
? WHY I HAVE ASK?
ROARRR!
YIPE! THEY'VE JOINED TOGETHER INTO A TECH MONSTER WITH A GIANT, SPOOKY FACE!
ANY CHANCE THEY'LL PLEDGE THEIR ETERNAL ALLEGIANCE TO ME? YOU KNOW, ME BEING THE GUY WHO MADE THEM AND ALL?
WE LOVE SPIDEY!
SPIDEY IS THE BEST!
ROARRR!
LOOKS LIKE SOMEONE'S GOT DADDY ISSUES.
COME ON!

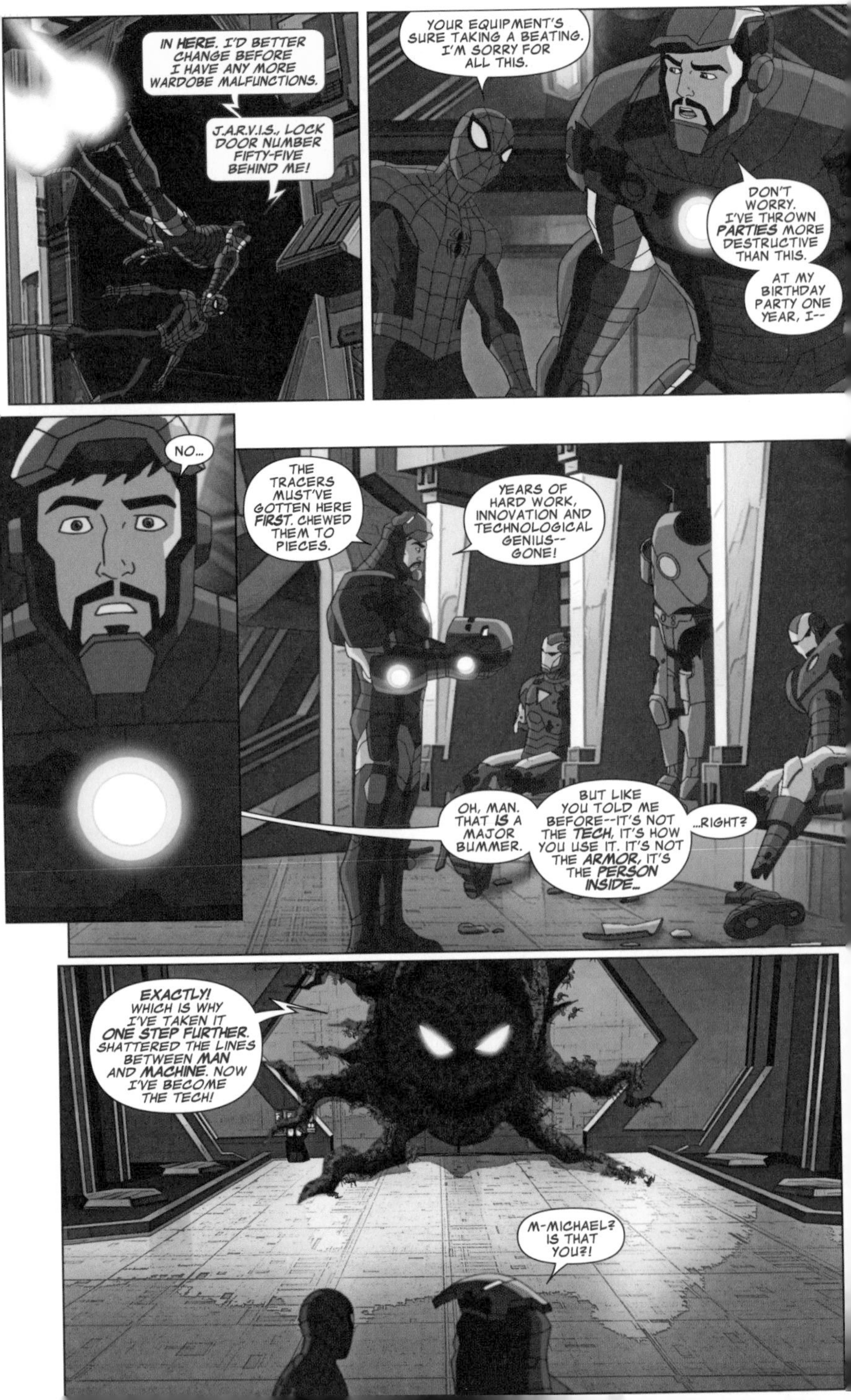
IN HERE. I'D BETTER CHANGE BEFORE I HAVE ANY MORE WARDOBE MALFUNCTIONS.
J.A.R.V.I.S., LOCK DOOR NUMBER FIFTY-FIVE BEHIND ME!
YOUR EQUIPMENT'S SURE TAKING A BEATING. I'M SORRY FOR ALL THIS.
DON'T WORRY. I'VE THROWN PARTIES MORE DESTRUCTIVE THAN THIS.
AT MY BIRTHDAY PARTY ONE YEAR, I--
NO...
THE TRACERS MUST'VE GOTTEN HERE FIRST. CHEWED THEM TO PIECES.
YEARS OF HARD WORK, INNOVATION AND TECHNOLOGICAL GENIUS-- GONE!
OH, MAN. THAT IS A MAJOR BUMMER.
BUT LIKE YOU TOLD ME BEFORE--IT'S NOT THE TECH, IT'S HOW YOU USE IT. IT'S NOT THE ARMOR, IT'S THE PERSON INSIDE...
...RIGHT?
EXACTLY! WHICH IS WHY I'VE TAKEN IT ONE STEP FURTHER. SHATTERED THE LINES BETWEEN MAN AND MACHINE. NOW I'VE BECOME THE TECH!
M-MICHAEL? IS THAT YOU?!

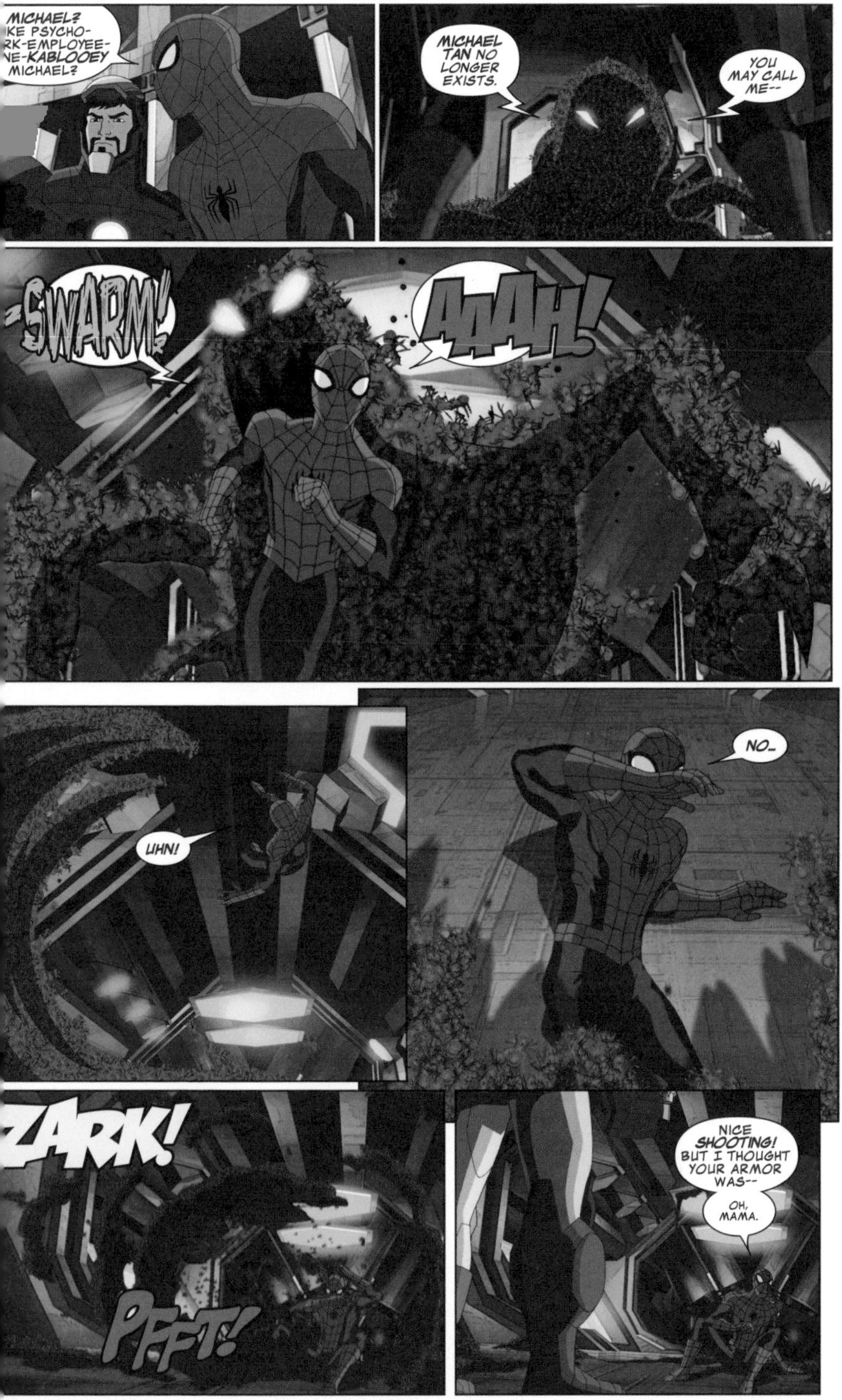
MICHAEL? KE PSYCHO-RK-EMPLOYEE-NE-KABLOOEY MICHAEL?
MICHAEL TAN NO LONGER EXISTS.
YOU MAY CALL ME--
SWARM!
AAAH!
UHN!
NO...
ZARK!
PFFT!
NICE SHOOTING! BUT I THOUGHT YOUR ARMOR WAS--
OH, MAMA.

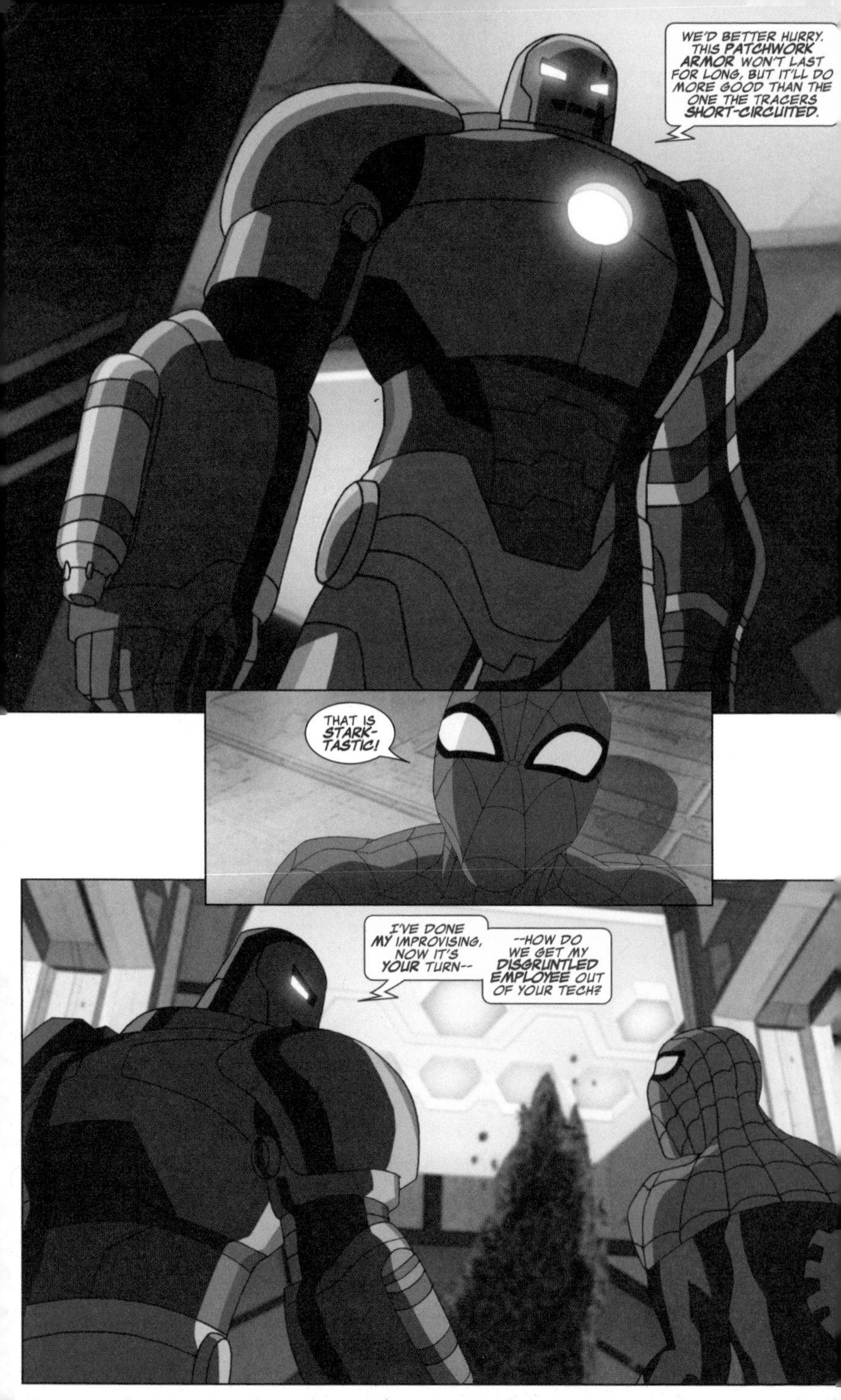
WE'D BETTER HURRY. THIS PATCHWORK ARMOR WON'T LAST FOR LONG, BUT IT'LL DO MORE GOOD THAN THE ONE THE TRACERS SHORT-CIRCUITED.
THAT IS STARK-TASTIC!
I'VE DONE MY IMPROVISING, NOW IT'S YOUR TURN--
--HOW DO WE GET MY DISGRUNTLED EMPLOYEE OUT OF YOUR TECH?

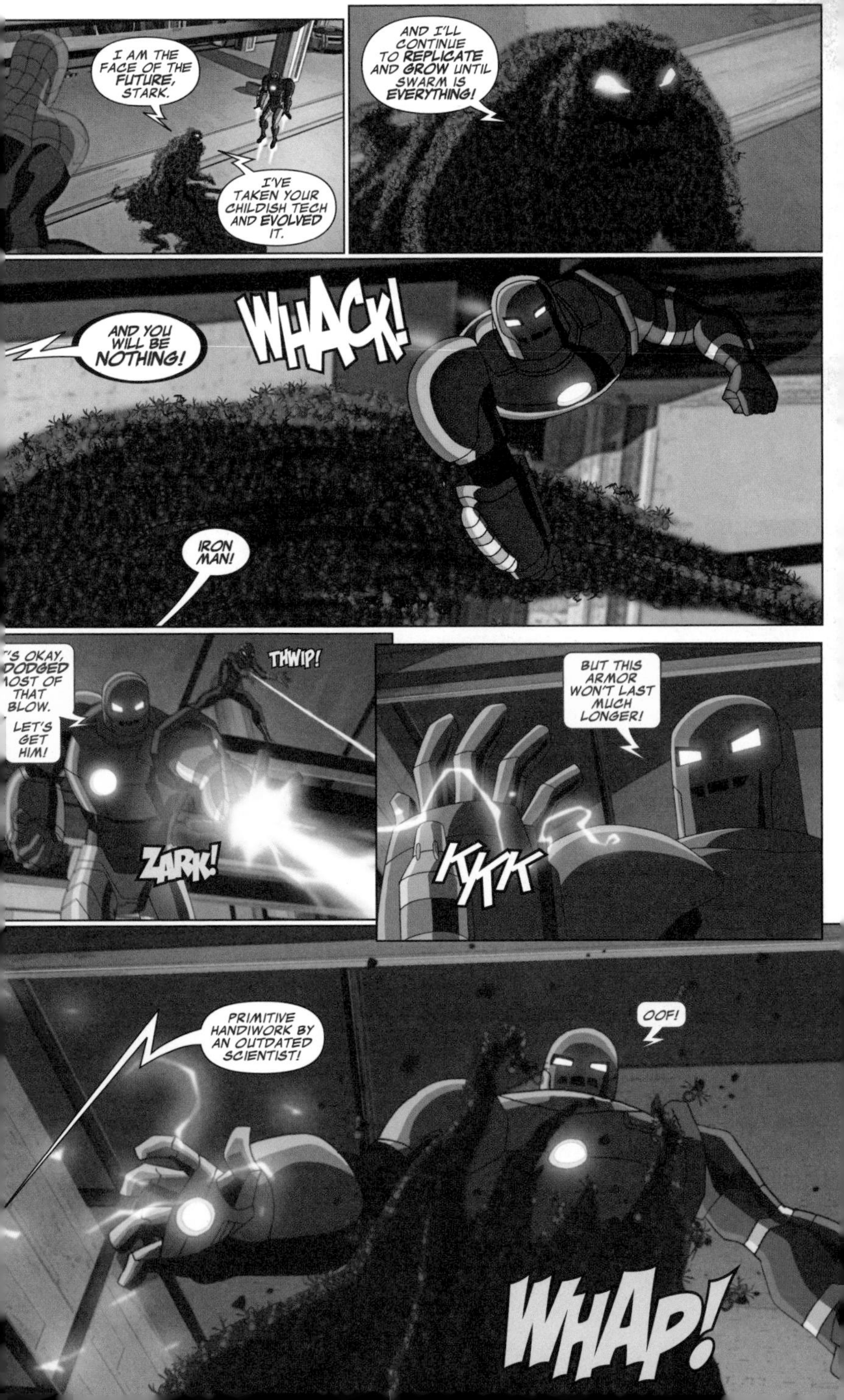
I AM THE FACE OF THE FUTURE, STARK.
I'VE TAKEN YOUR CHILDISH TECH AND EVOLVED IT.
AND I'LL CONTINUE TO REPLICATE AND GROW UNTIL SWARM IS EVERYTHING!
AND YOU WILL BE NOTHING!
WHACK!
IRON MAN!
'S OKAY, DODGED MOST OF THAT BLOW.
LET'S GET HIM!
THWIP!
ZARK!
BUT THIS ARMOR WON'T LAST MUCH LONGER!
KKKK
PRIMITIVE HANDIWORK BY AN OUTDATED SCIENTIST!
OOF!
WHAP!

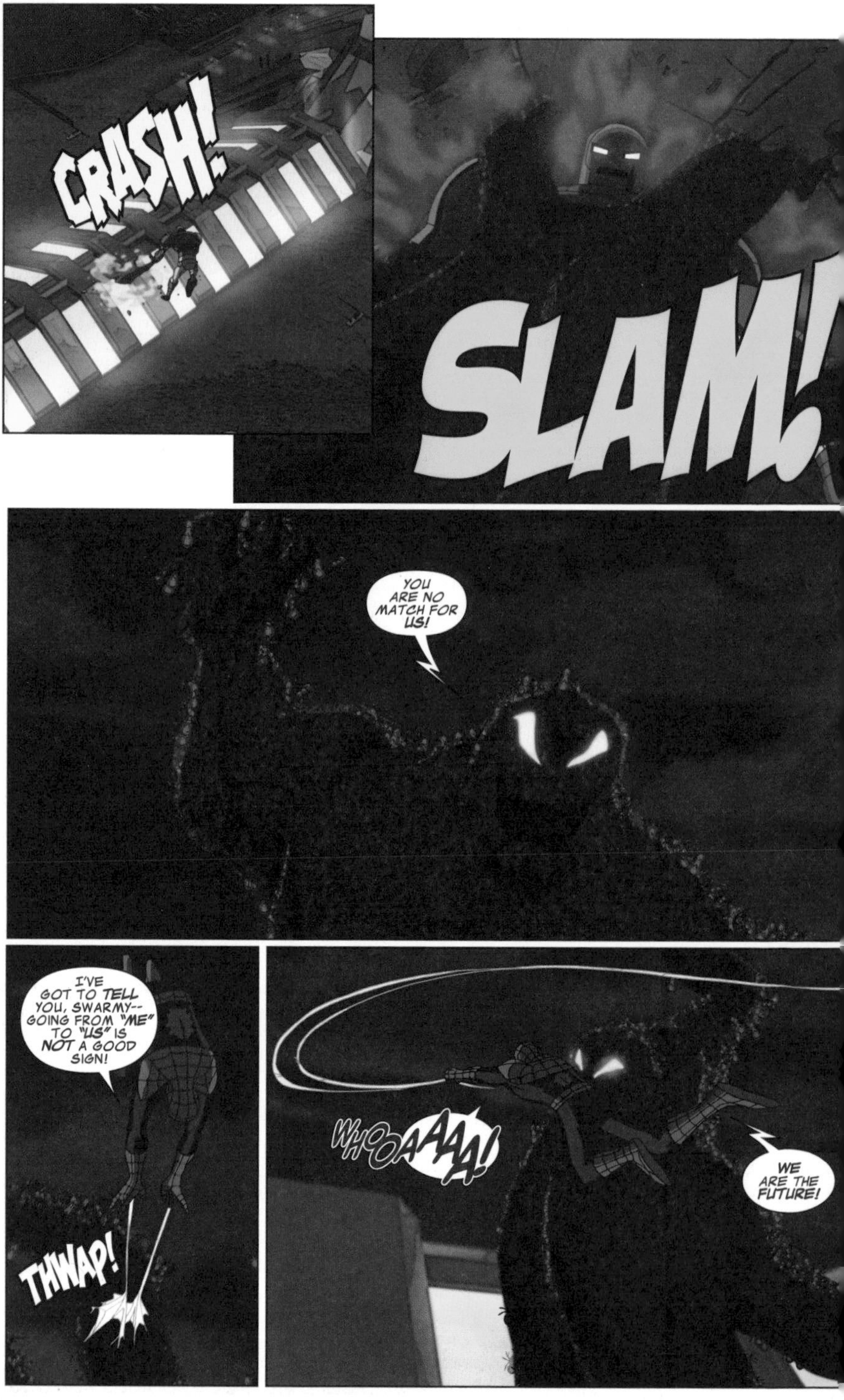

CRASH!
SLAM!
YOU ARE NO MATCH FOR US!
I'VE GOT TO TELL YOU, SWARMY-- GOING FROM "ME" TO "US" IS NOT A GOOD SIGN!
THWAP!
WHOAAAAA!
WE ARE THE FUTURE!

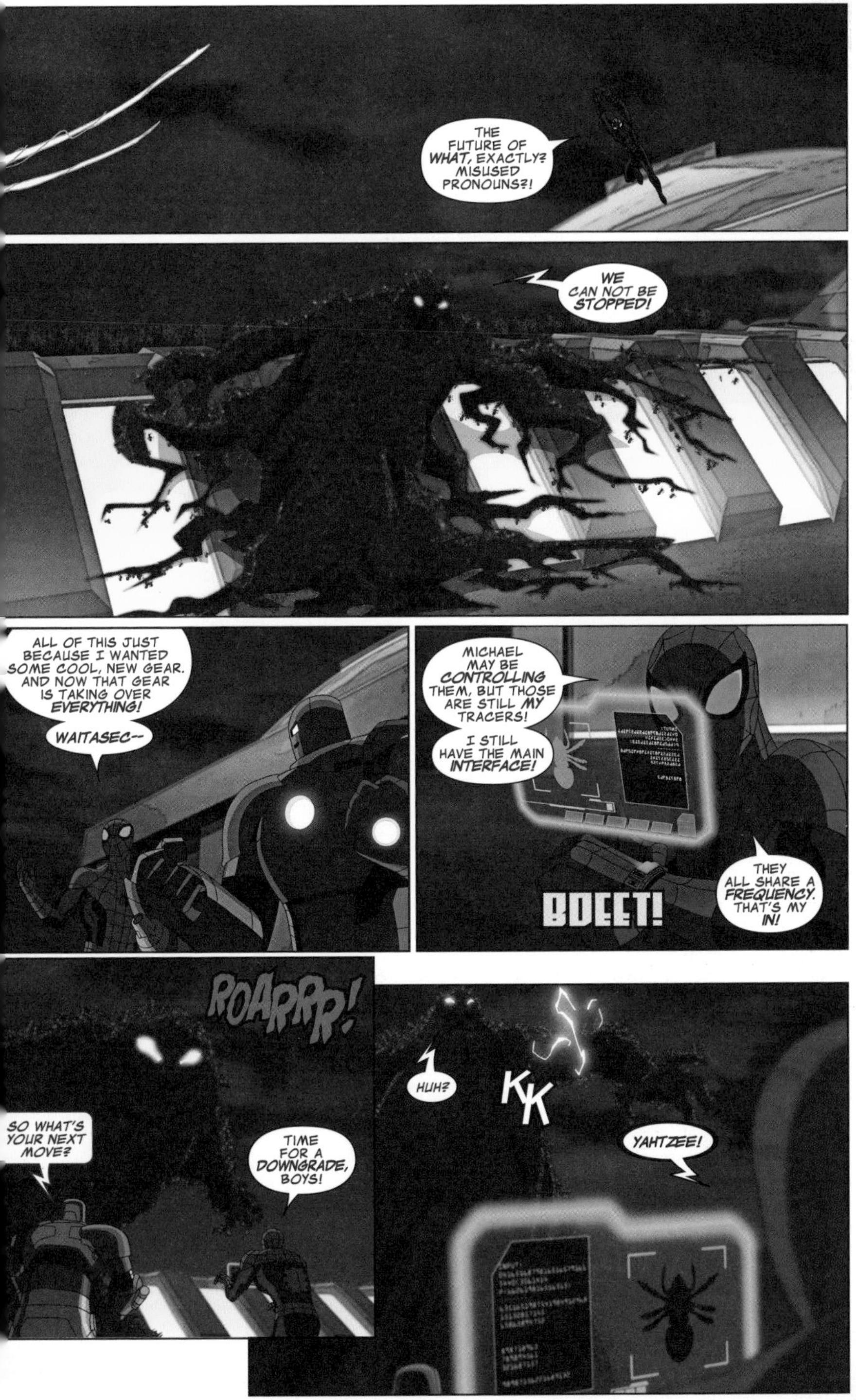
THE FUTURE OF WHAT, EXACTLY? MISUSED PRONOUNS?!
WE CAN NOT BE STOPPED!
ALL OF THIS JUST BECAUSE I WANTED SOME COOL, NEW GEAR. AND NOW THAT GEAR IS TAKING OVER EVERYTHING!
WAITASEC--
MICHAEL MAY BE CONTROLLING THEM, BUT THOSE ARE STILL MY TRACERS!
I STILL HAVE THE MAIN INTERFACE!
BDEET!
THEY ALL SHARE A FREQUENCY. THAT'S MY IN!
ROARRR!
SO WHAT'S YOUR NEXT MOVE?
TIME FOR A DOWNGRADE, BOYS!
HUH?
KK
YAHTZEE!

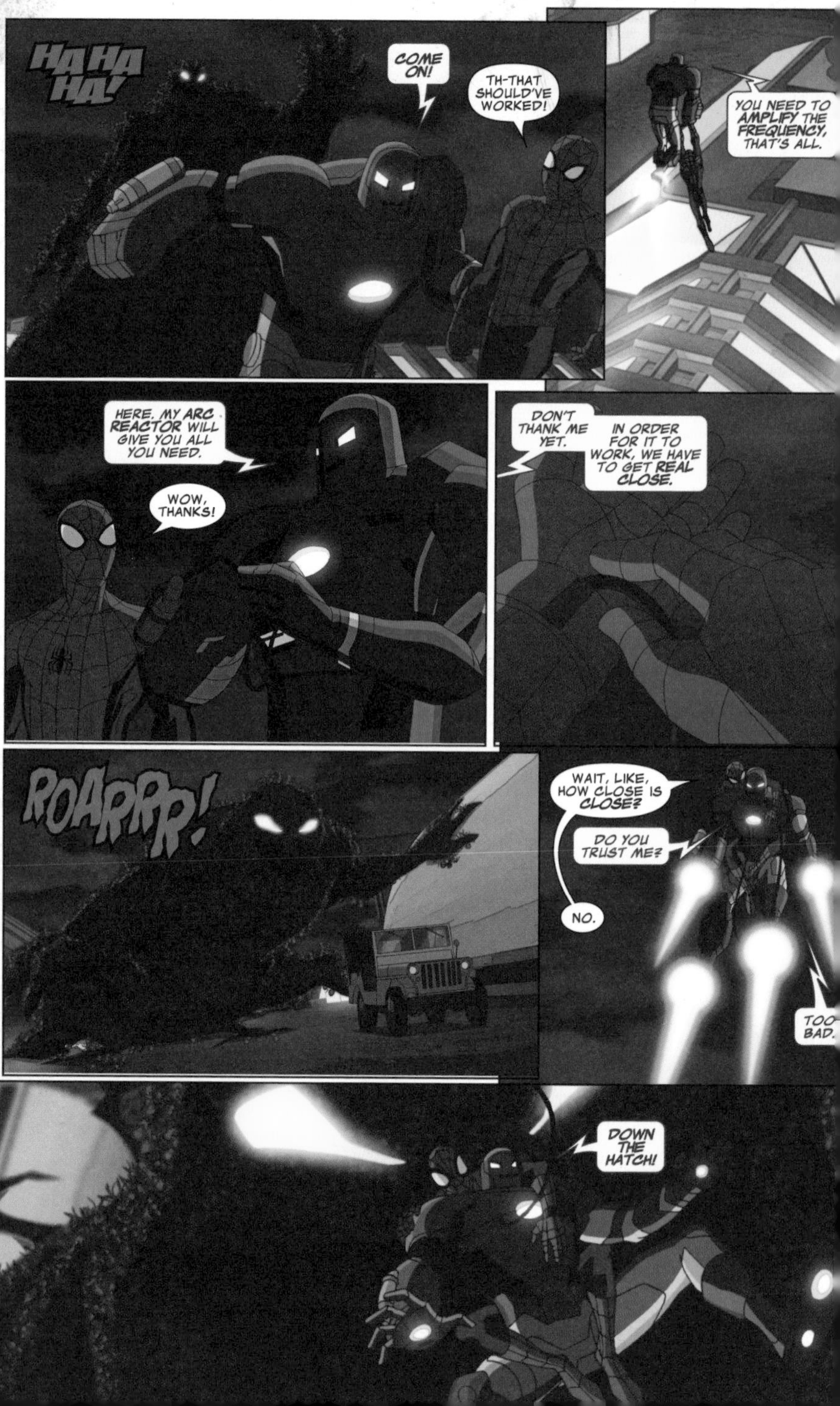
HA HA HA!
COME ON!
TH-THAT SHOULD'VE WORKED!
YOU NEED TO AMPLIFY THE FREQUENCY, THAT'S ALL.
HERE. MY ARC REACTOR WILL GIVE YOU ALL YOU NEED.
WOW, THANKS!
DON'T THANK ME YET.
IN ORDER FOR IT TO WORK, WE HAVE TO GET REAL CLOSE.
ROARRR!
WAIT, LIKE, HOW CLOSE IS CLOSE?
DO YOU TRUST ME?
NO.
TOO BAD.
DOWN THE HATCH!

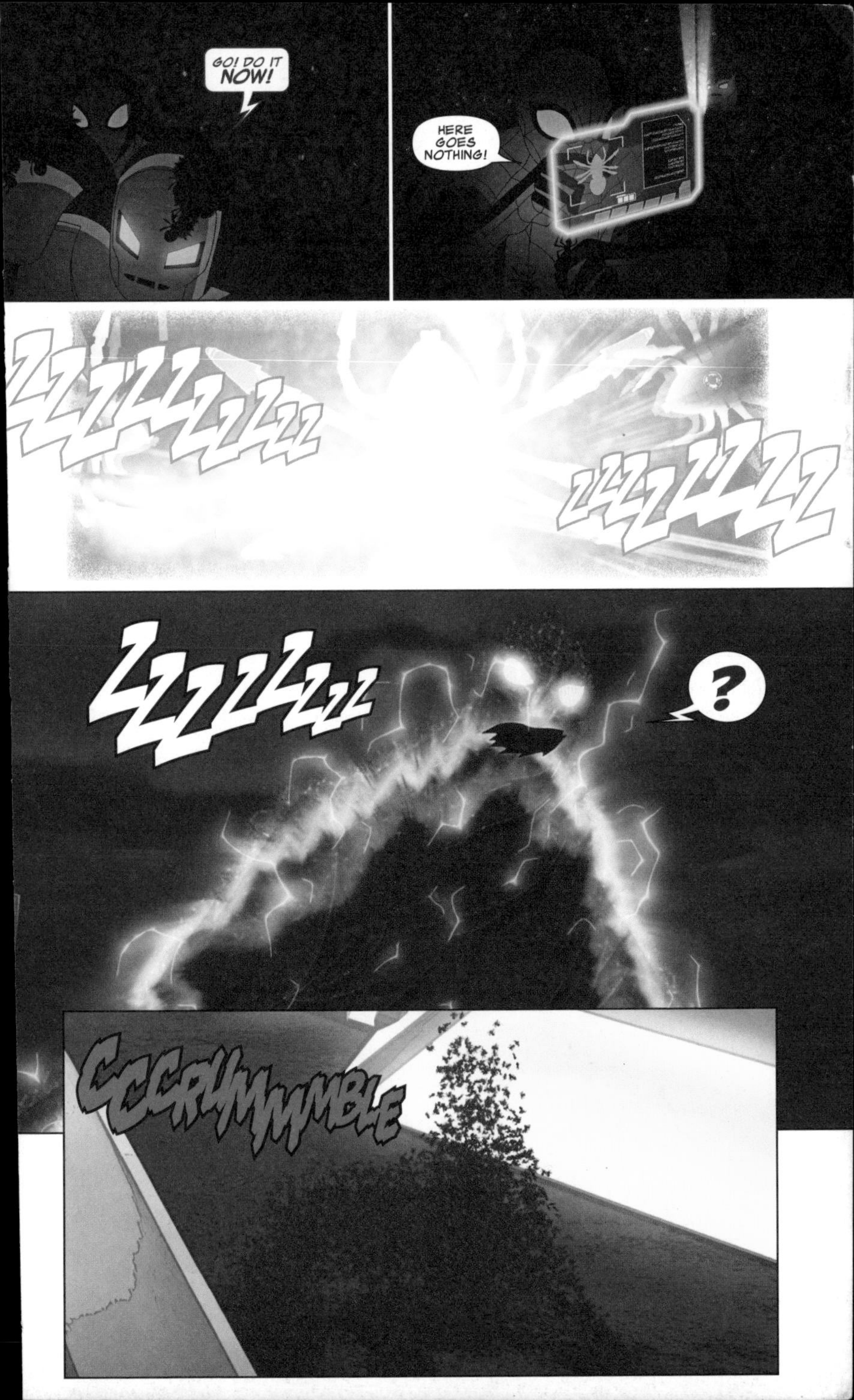
GO! DO IT NOW!
HERE GOES NOTHING!
ZZZZZZZZZZZ
ZZZZZZZZZ
ZZZZZZZZZ
?
CCCRUMMMBLE

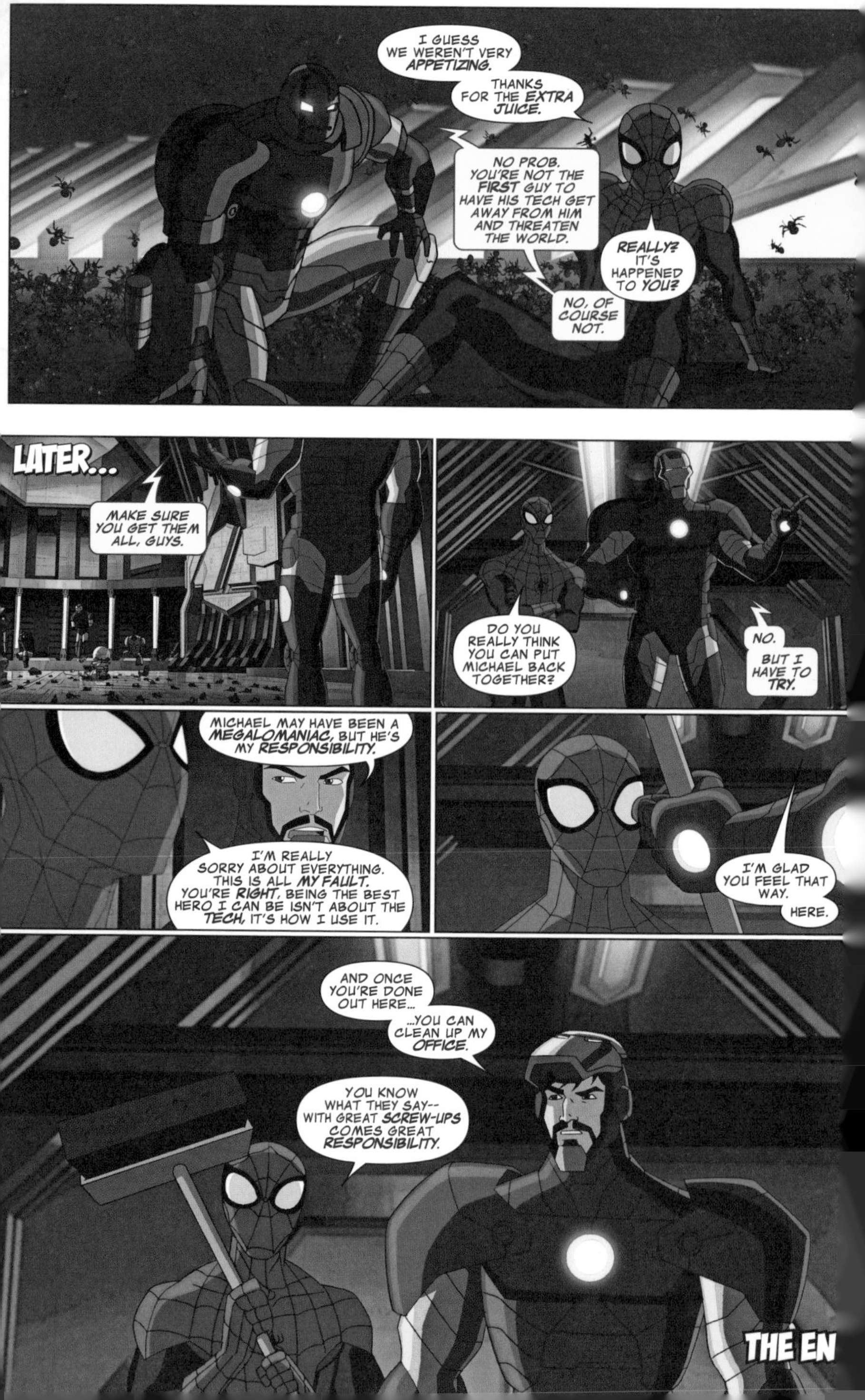
I GUESS WE WEREN'T VERY APPETIZING.
THANKS FOR THE EXTRA JUICE.
NO PROB. YOU'RE NOT THE FIRST GUY TO HAVE HIS TECH GET AWAY FROM HIM AND THREATEN THE WORLD.
REALLY? IT'S HAPPENED TO YOU?
NO, OF COURSE NOT.
LATER...
MAKE SURE YOU GET THEM ALL, GUYS.
DO YOU REALLY THINK YOU CAN PUT MICHAEL BACK TOGETHER?
NO.
BUT I HAVE TO TRY.
MICHAEL MAY HAVE BEEN A MEGALOMANIAC, BUT HE'S MY RESPONSIBILITY.
I'M REALLY SORRY ABOUT EVERYTHING. THIS IS ALL MY FAULT. YOU'RE RIGHT. BEING THE BEST HERO I CAN BE ISN'T ABOUT THE TECH, IT'S HOW I USE IT.
I'M GLAD YOU FEEL THAT WAY.
HERE.
AND ONCE YOU'RE DONE OUT HERE...
...YOU CAN CLEAN UP MY OFFICE.
YOU KNOW WHAT THEY SAY-- WITH GREAT SCREW-UPS COMES GREAT RESPONSIBILITY.
THE EN

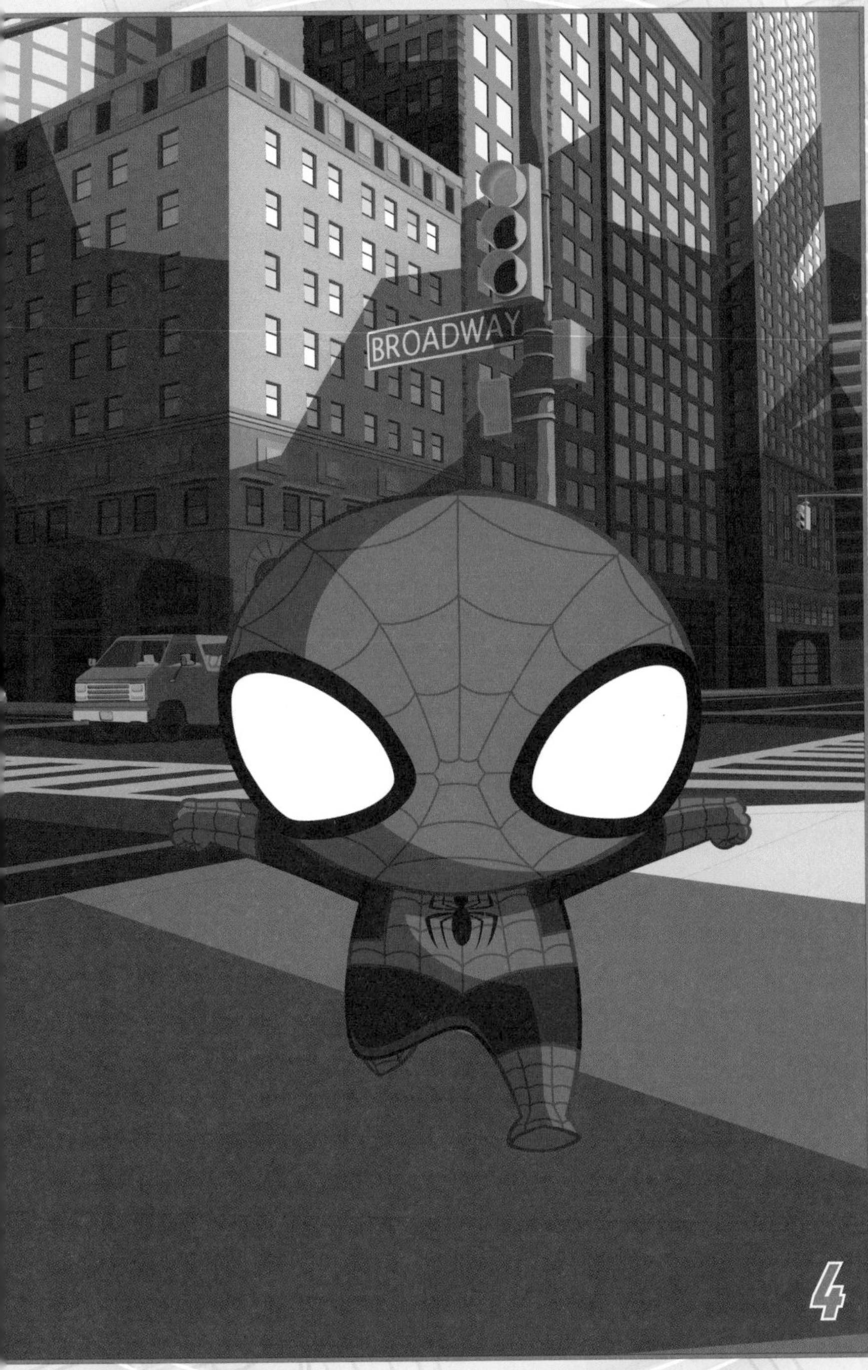
BROADWAY
4

Based on “Itsy Bitsy Spider-Man”

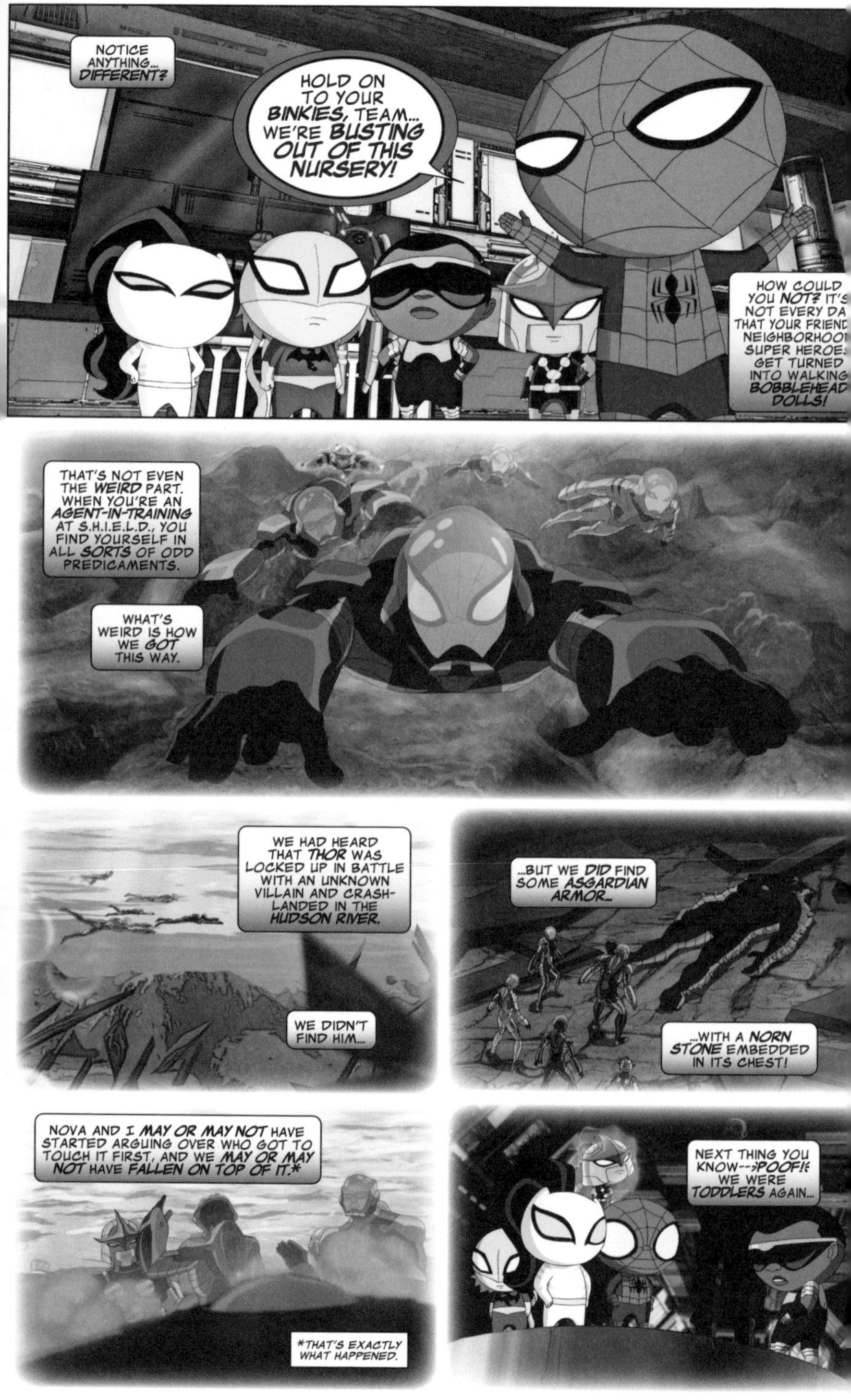

NOTICE ANYTHING... DIFFERENT?
HOLD ON TO YOUR BINKIES, TEAM... WE'RE BUSTING OUT OF THIS NURSERY!
HOW COULD YOU NOT? IT'S NOT EVERY DA THAT YOUR FRIEND NEIGHBORHOO SUPER HEROE GET TURNED INTO WALKING BOBBLEHEAD DOLLS!
THAT'S NOT EVEN THE WEIRD PART. WHEN YOU'RE AN AGENT-IN-TRAINING AT S.H.I.E.L.D., YOU FIND YOURSELF IN ALL SORTS OF ODD PREDICAMENTS.
WHAT'S WEIRD IS HOW WE GOT THIS WAY.
WE HAD HEARD THAT THOR WAS LOCKED UP IN BATTLE WITH AN UNKNOWN VILLAIN AND CRASH-LANDED IN THE HUDSON RIVER.
WE DIDN'T FIND HIM...
...BUT WE DID FIND SOME ASGARDIAN ARMOR...
...WITH A NORN STONE EMBEDDED IN ITS CHEST!
NOVA AND I MAY OR MAY NOT HAVE STARTED ARGUING OVER WHO GOT TO TOUCH IT FIRST, AND WE MAY OR MAY NOT HAVE FALLEN ON TOP OF IT.*
*THAT'S EXACTLY WHAT HAPPENED.
NEXT THING YOU KNOW-->POOF!< WE WERE TODDLERS AGAIN...

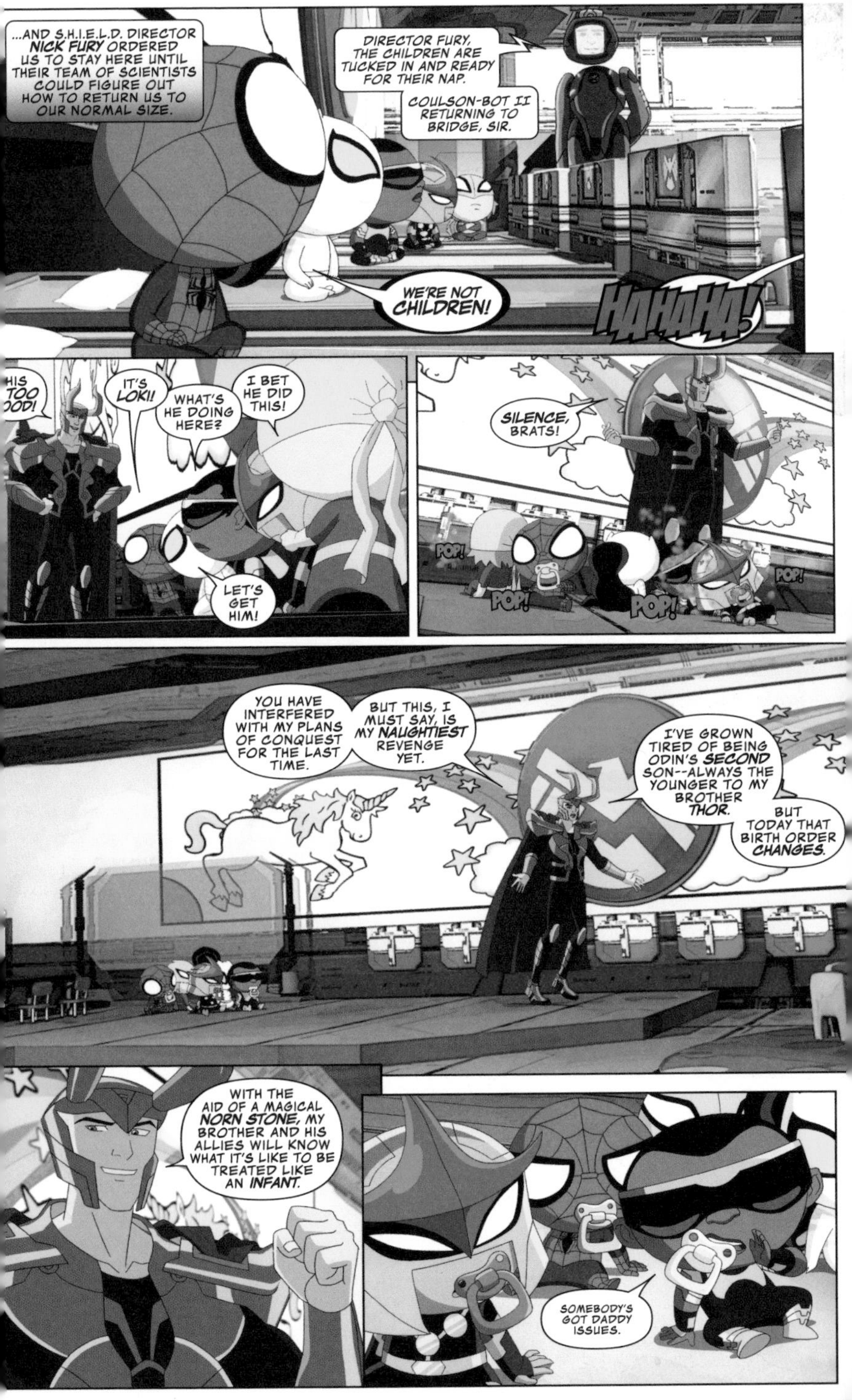

...AND S.H.I.E.L.D. DIRECTOR NICK FURY ORDERED US TO STAY HERE UNTIL THEIR TEAM OF SCIENTISTS COULD FIGURE OUT HOW TO RETURN US TO OUR NORMAL SIZE.
DIRECTOR FURY, THE CHILDREN ARE TUCKED IN AND READY FOR THEIR NAP.
COULSON-BOT II RETURNING TO BRIDGE, SIR.
WE'RE NOT CHILDREN!
HAHAHA!
HIS TOO OOD!
IT'S LOKI!
WHAT'S HE DOING HERE?
I BET HE DID THIS!
LET'S GET HIM!
SILENCE, BRATS!
POP!
POP!
POP!
POP!
YOU HAVE INTERFERED WITH MY PLANS OF CONQUEST FOR THE LAST TIME.
BUT THIS, I MUST SAY, IS MY NAUGHTIEST REVENGE YET.
I'VE GROWN TIRED OF BEING ODIN'S SECOND SON--ALWAYS THE YOUNGER TO MY BROTHER THOR.
BUT TODAY THAT BIRTH ORDER CHANGES.
WITH THE AID OF A MAGICAL NORN STONE, MY BROTHER AND HIS ALLIES WILL KNOW WHAT IT'S LIKE TO BE TREATED LIKE AN INFANT.
SOMEBODY'S GOT DADDY ISSUES.

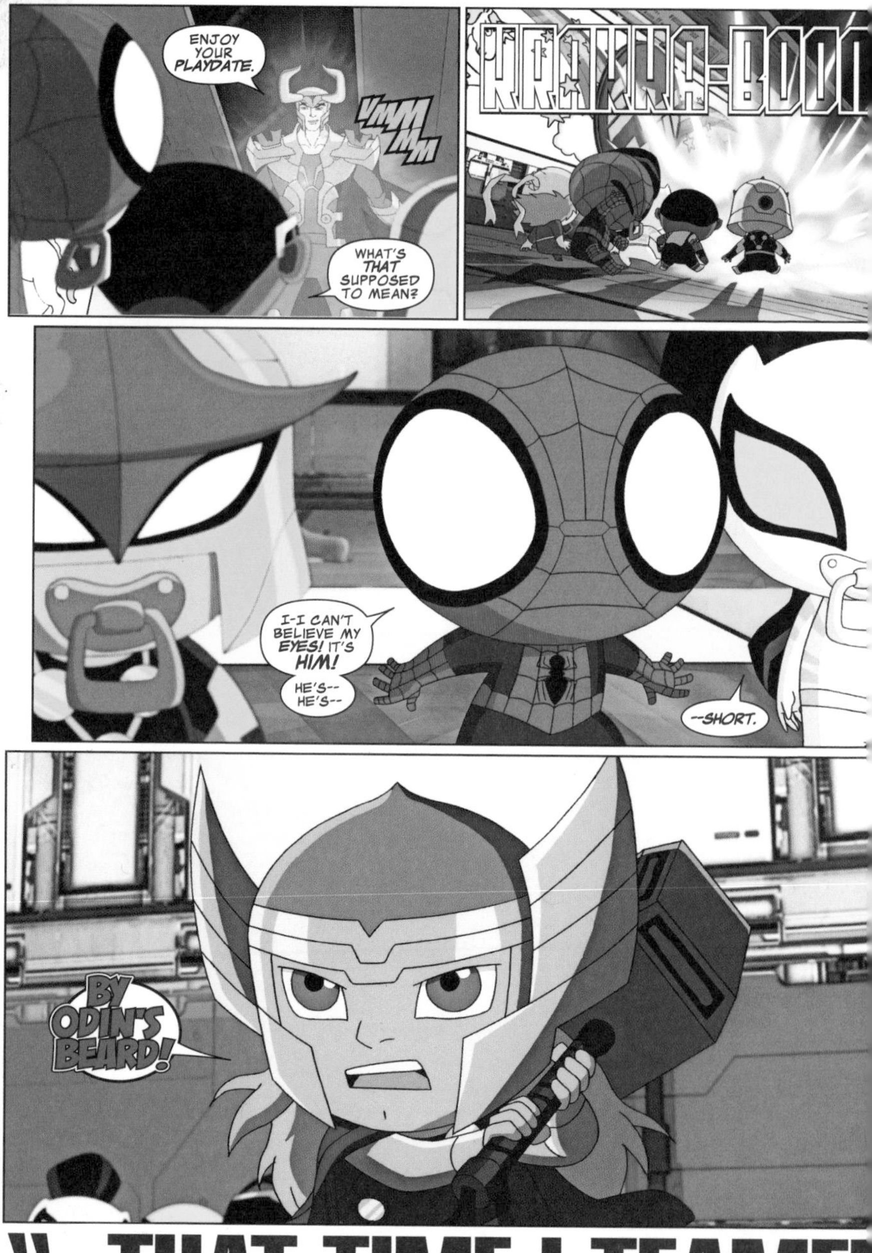

ENJOY YOUR PLAYDATE.
VMMM MMM
WHAT'S THAT SUPPOSED TO MEAN?
KRAKKA-BOOM
I-I CAN'T BELIEVE MY EYES! IT'S HIM!
HE'S-- HE'S--
--SHORT.
BY ODIN'S BEARD!

"...THAT TIME I TEAMED UP WITH Li'l THOR!"

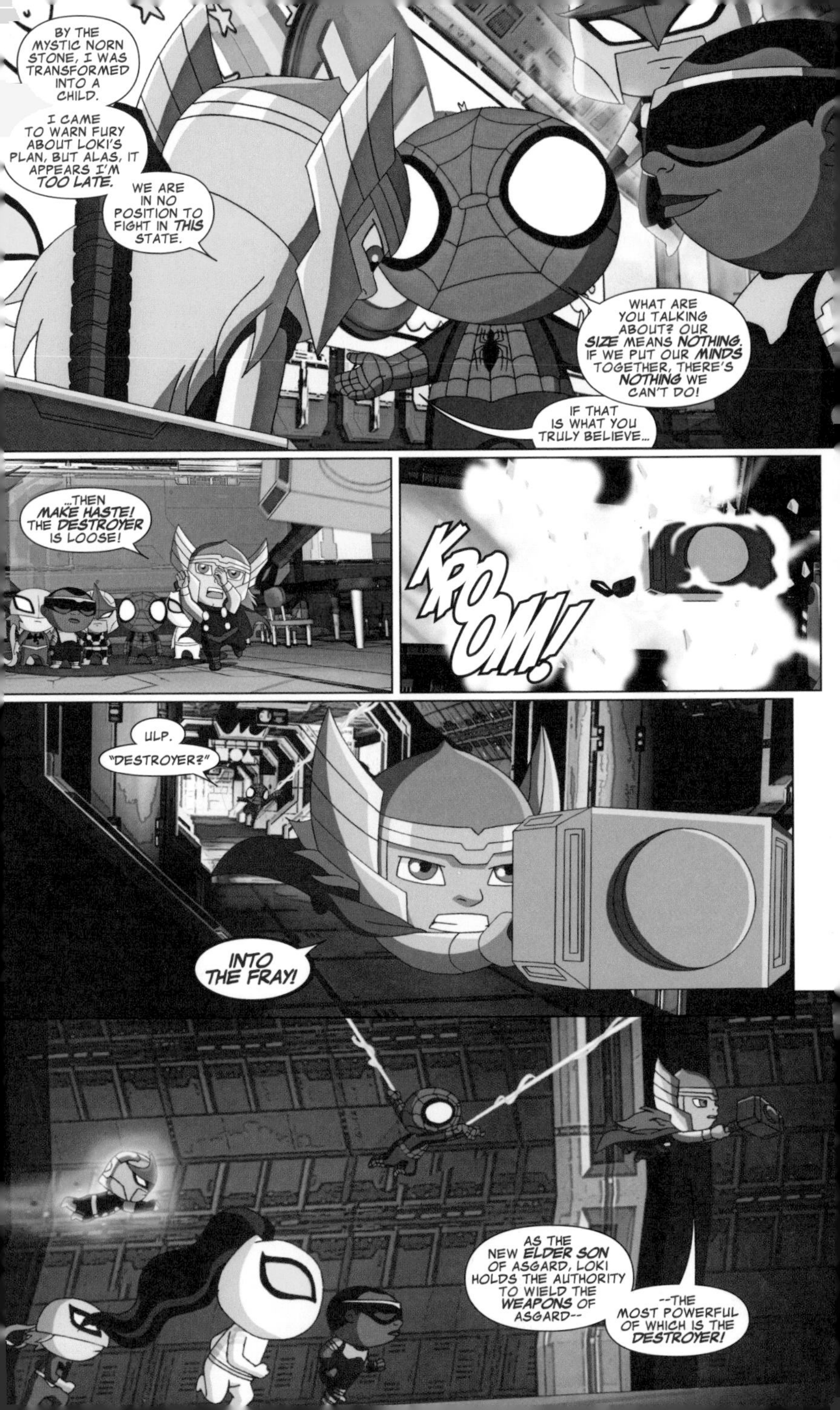
BY THE MYSTIC NORN STONE, I WAS TRANSFORMED INTO A CHILD.
I CAME TO WARN FURY ABOUT LOKI'S PLAN, BUT ALAS, IT APPEARS I'M TOO LATE.
WE ARE IN NO POSITION TO FIGHT IN THIS STATE.
WHAT ARE YOU TALKING ABOUT? OUR SIZE MEANS NOTHING. IF WE PUT OUR MINDS TOGETHER, THERE'S NOTHING WE CAN'T DO!
IF THAT IS WHAT YOU TRULY BELIEVE...
...THEN MAKE HASTE! THE DESTROYER IS LOOSE!
KROOOM!
ULP.
"DESTROYER?"
INTO THE FRAY!
AS THE NEW ELDER SON OF ASGARD, LOKI HOLDS THE AUTHORITY TO WIELD THE WEAPONS OF ASGARD--
--THE MOST POWERFUL OF WHICH IS THE DESTROYER!

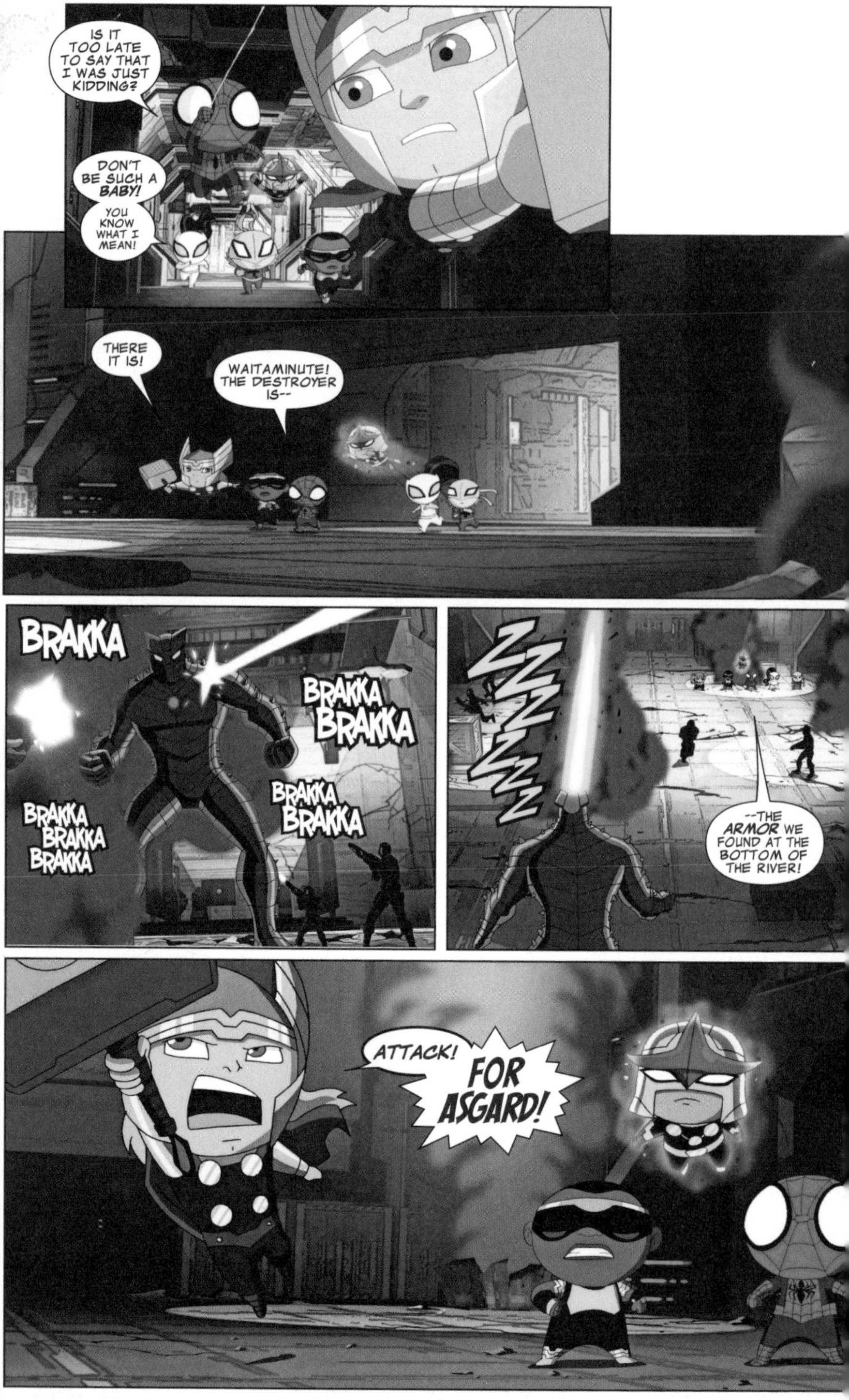
IS IT TOO LATE TO SAY THAT I WAS JUST KIDDING?
DON'T BE SUCH A BABY!
YOU KNOW WHAT I MEAN!
THERE IT IS!
WAITAMINUTE! THE DESTROYER IS--
BRAKKA
BRAKKA BRAKKA
BRAKKA BRAKKA
BRAKKA BRAKKA BRAKKA
--THE ARMOR WE FOUND AT THE BOTTOM OF THE RIVER!
ATTACK!
FOR ASGARD!

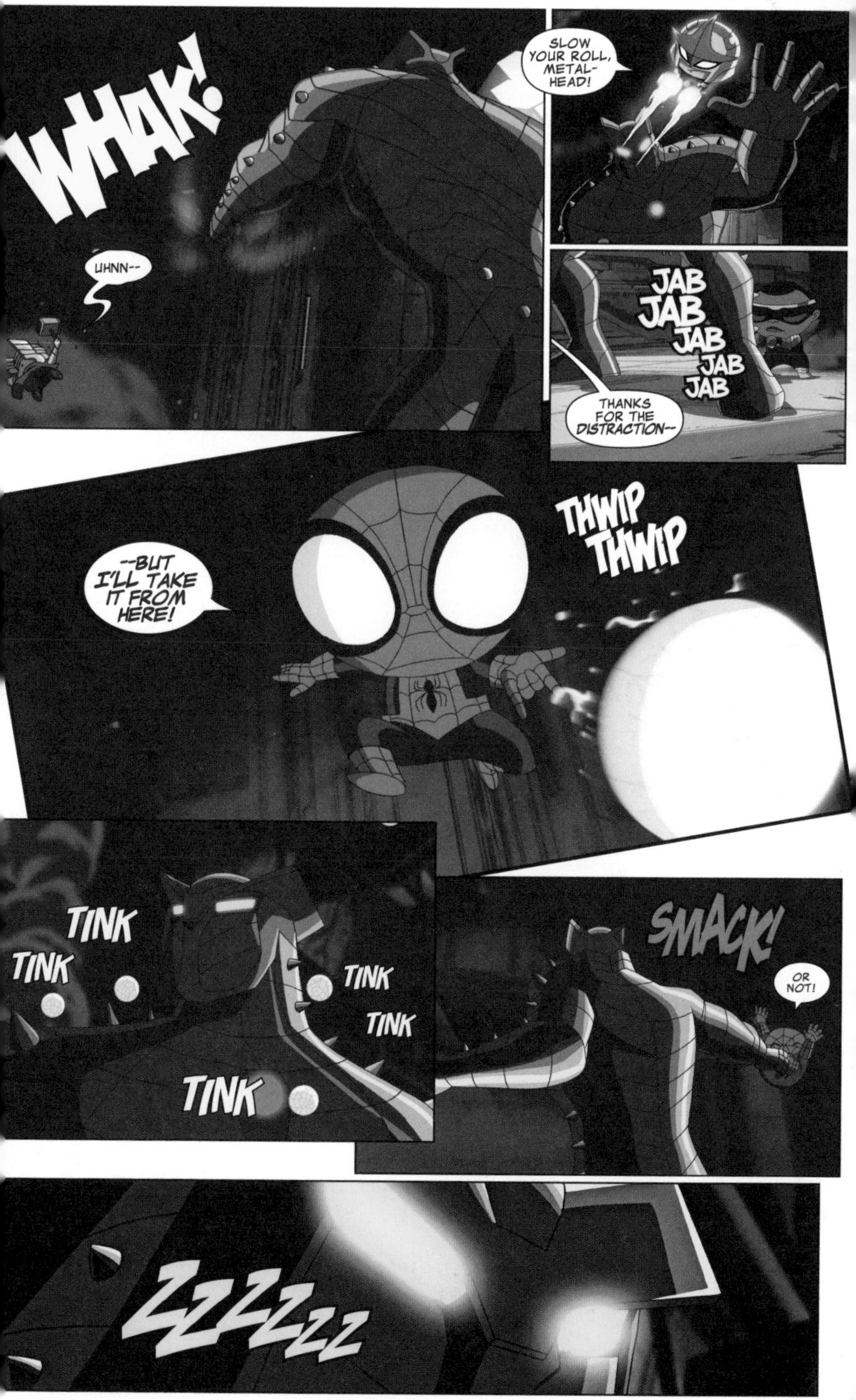
WHAK!
UHNN--
SLOW YOUR ROLL, METAL-HEAD!
JAB JAB JAB JAB JAB
THANKS FOR THE DISTRACTION--
THWIP THWIP
--BUT I'LL TAKE IT FROM HERE!
TINK
TINK
TINK
TINK
TINK
SMACK!
OR NOT!
ZZZZZZ

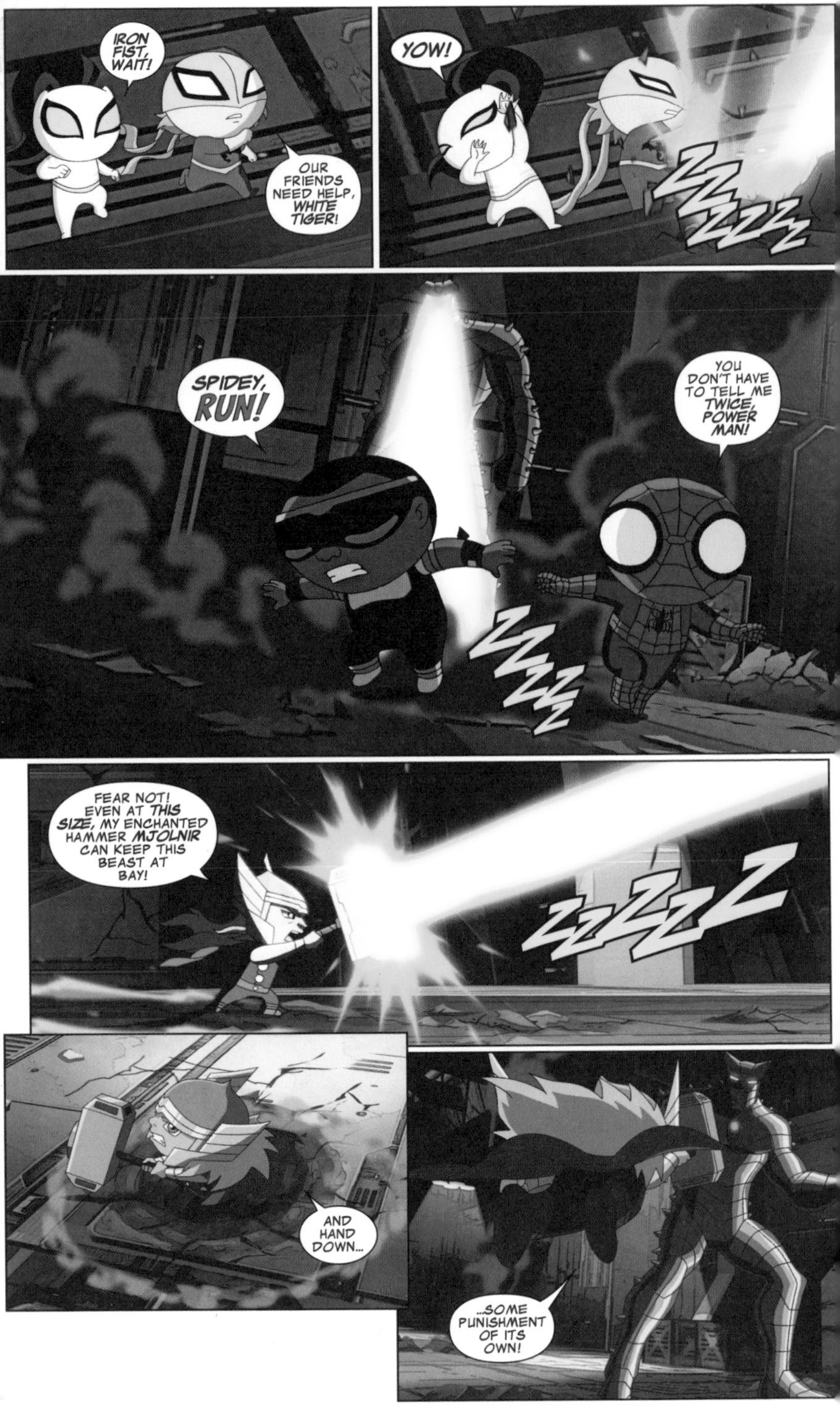
IRON FIST, WAIT!
OUR FRIENDS NEED HELP, WHITE TIGER!
YOW!
ZZZZZZ
SPIDEY, RUN!
YOU DON'T HAVE TO TELL ME TWICE, POWER MAN!
ZZZZZ
FEAR NOT! EVEN AT THIS SIZE, MY ENCHANTED HAMMER MJOLNIR CAN KEEP THIS BEAST AT BAY!
ZZZZZ
AND HAND DOWN...
...SOME PUNISHMENT OF ITS OWN!

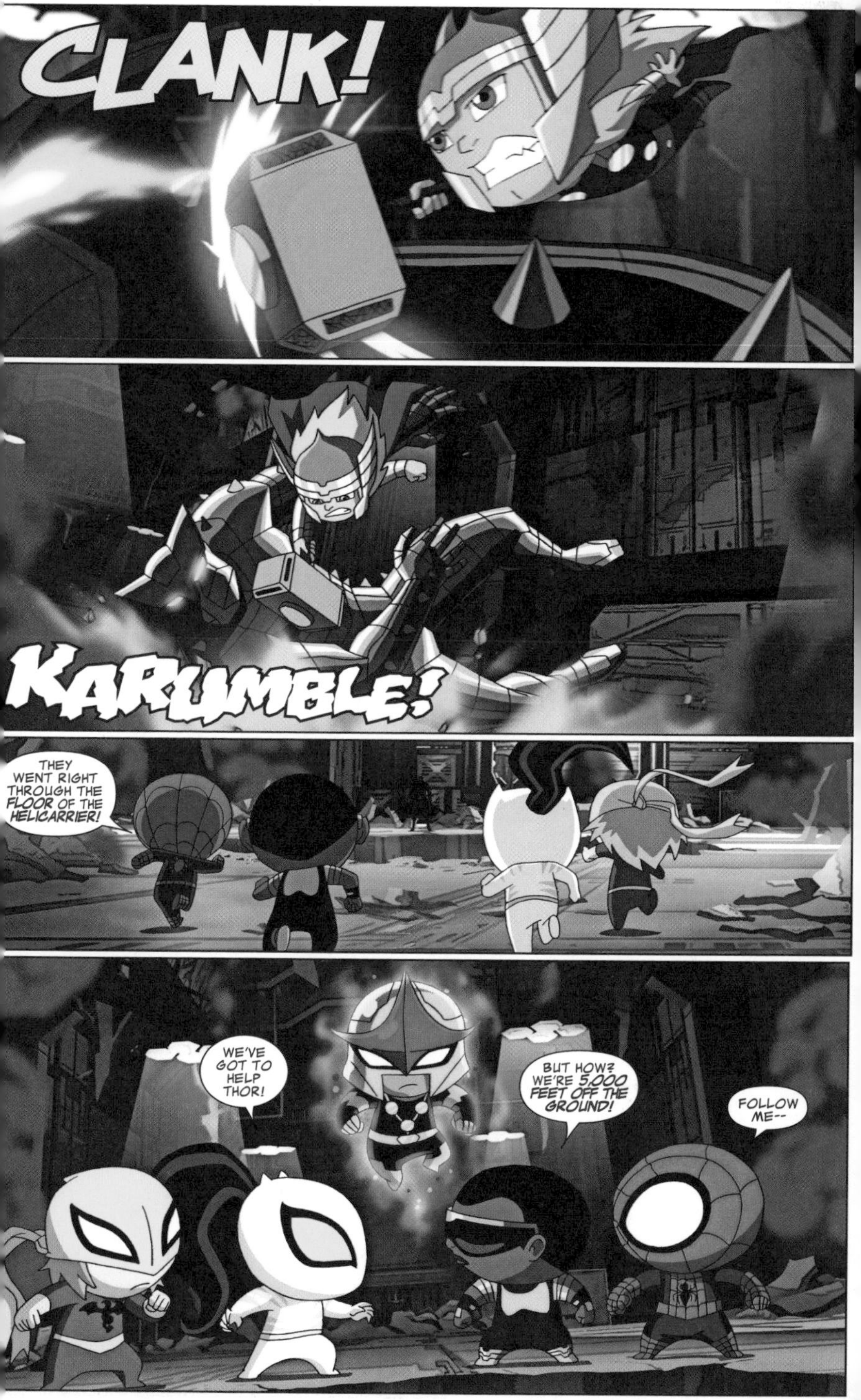

CLANK!
KARUMBLE!
THEY WENT RIGHT THROUGH THE FLOOR OF THE HELICARRIER!
WE'VE GOT TO HELP THOR!
BUT HOW? WE'RE 5,000 FEET OFF THE GROUND!
FOLLOW ME--

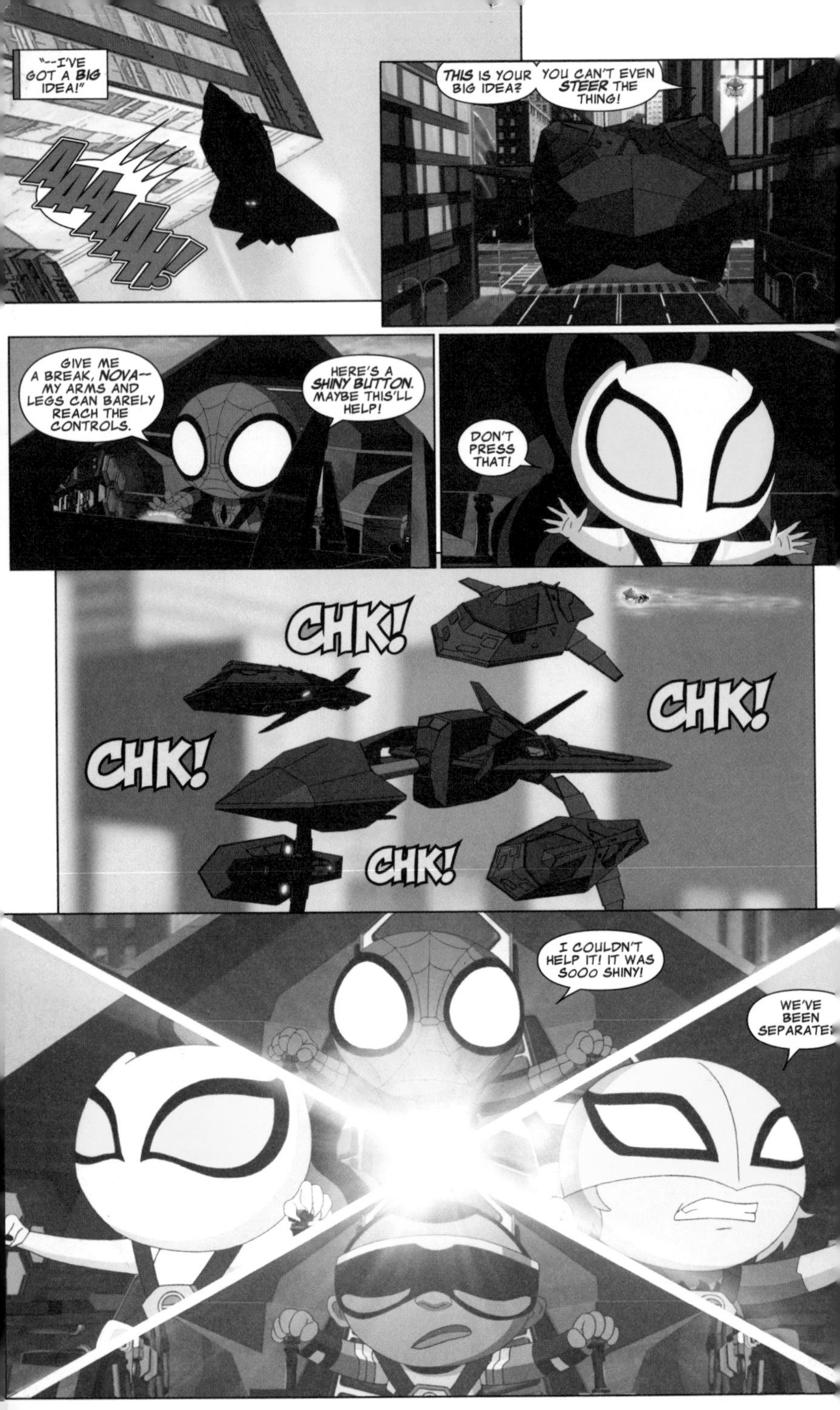
"--I'VE GOT A BIG IDEA!"
AAAAAAH!
THIS IS YOUR BIG IDEA?
YOU CAN'T EVEN STEER THE THING!
GIVE ME A BREAK, NOVA-- MY ARMS AND LEGS CAN BARELY REACH THE CONTROLS.
HERE'S A SHINY BUTTON. MAYBE THIS'LL HELP!
DON'T PRESS THAT!
CHK!
CHK!
CHK!
CHK!
I COULDN'T HELP IT! IT WAS SOOO SHINY!
WE'VE BEEN SEPARATE

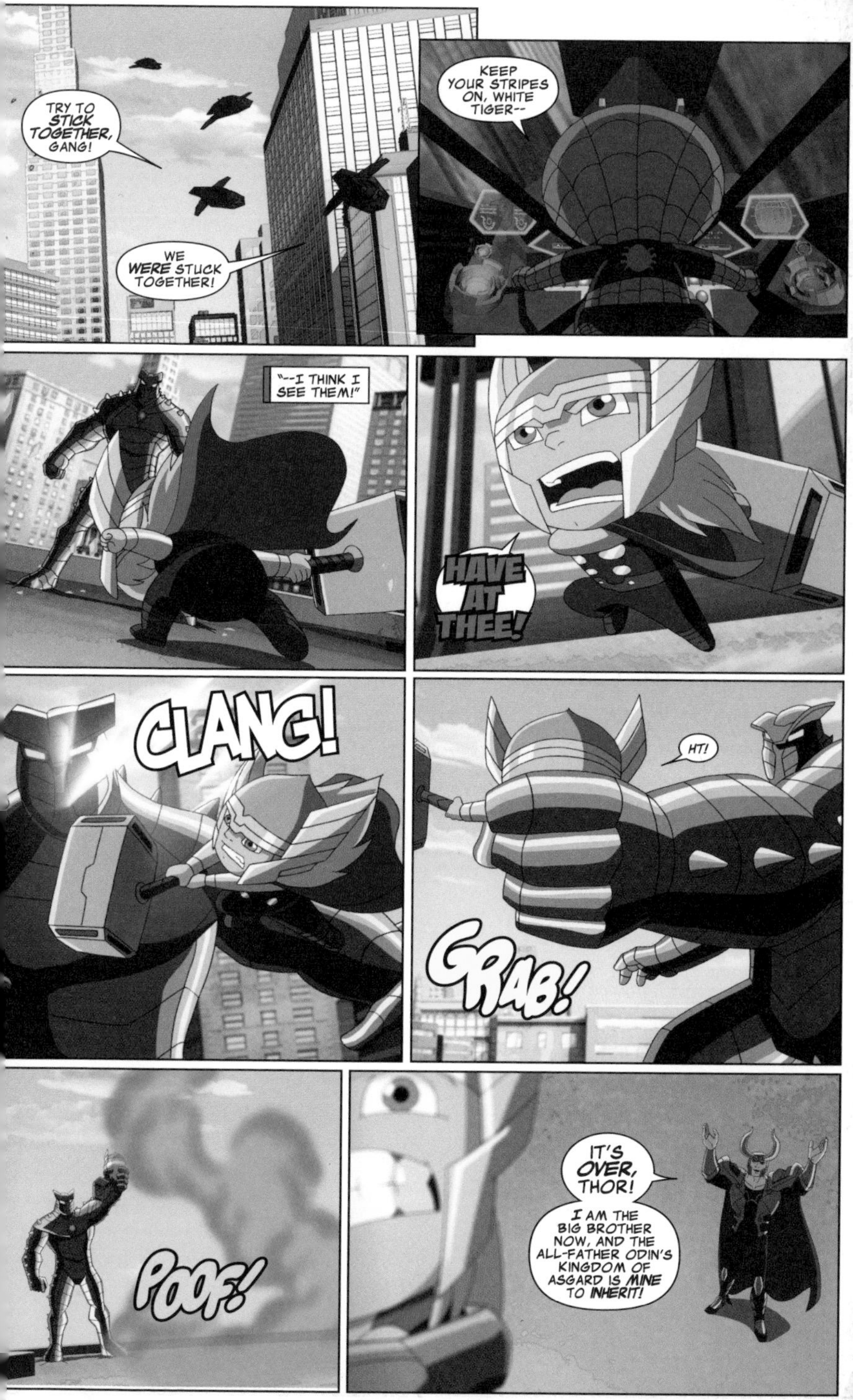

TRY TO STICK TOGETHER, GANG!
WE WERE STUCK TOGETHER!
KEEP YOUR STRIPES ON, WHITE TIGER--
"--I THINK I SEE THEM!"
HAVE AT THEE!
CLANG!
HT!
GRAB!
POOF!
IT'S OVER, THOR!
I AM THE BIG BROTHER NOW, AND THE ALL-FATHER ODIN'S KINGDOM OF ASGARD IS MINE TO INHERIT!

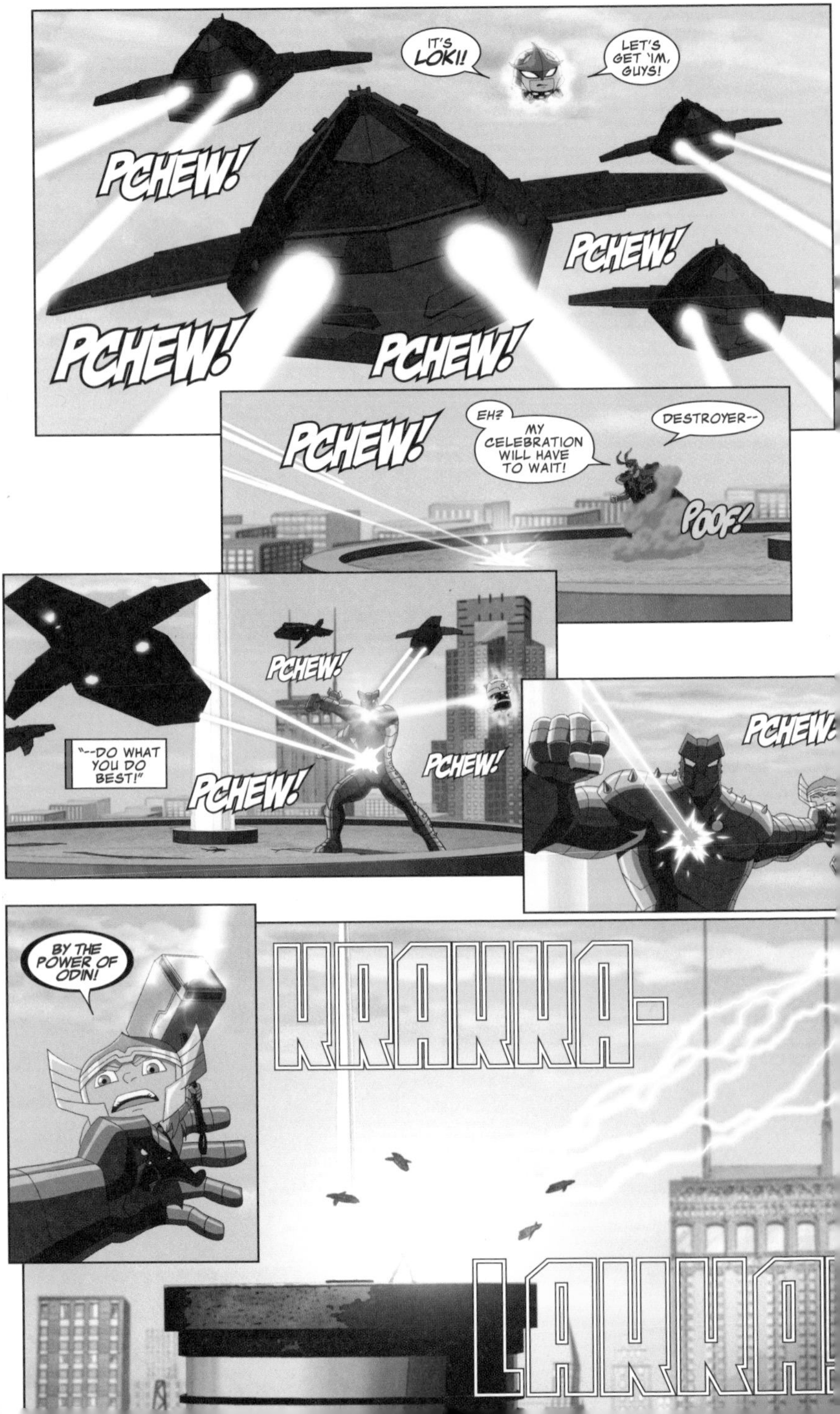
IT'S LOKI!
LET'S GET 'IM, GUYS!
PCHEW!
PCHEW!
PCHEW!
PCHEW!
PCHEW!
EH? MY CELEBRATION WILL HAVE TO WAIT!
DESTROYER--
POOF!
PCHEW!
"--DO WHAT YOU DO BEST!"
PCHEW!
PCHEW!
PCHEW!
BY THE POWER OF ODIN!
KRAKKA-
LAKKA!

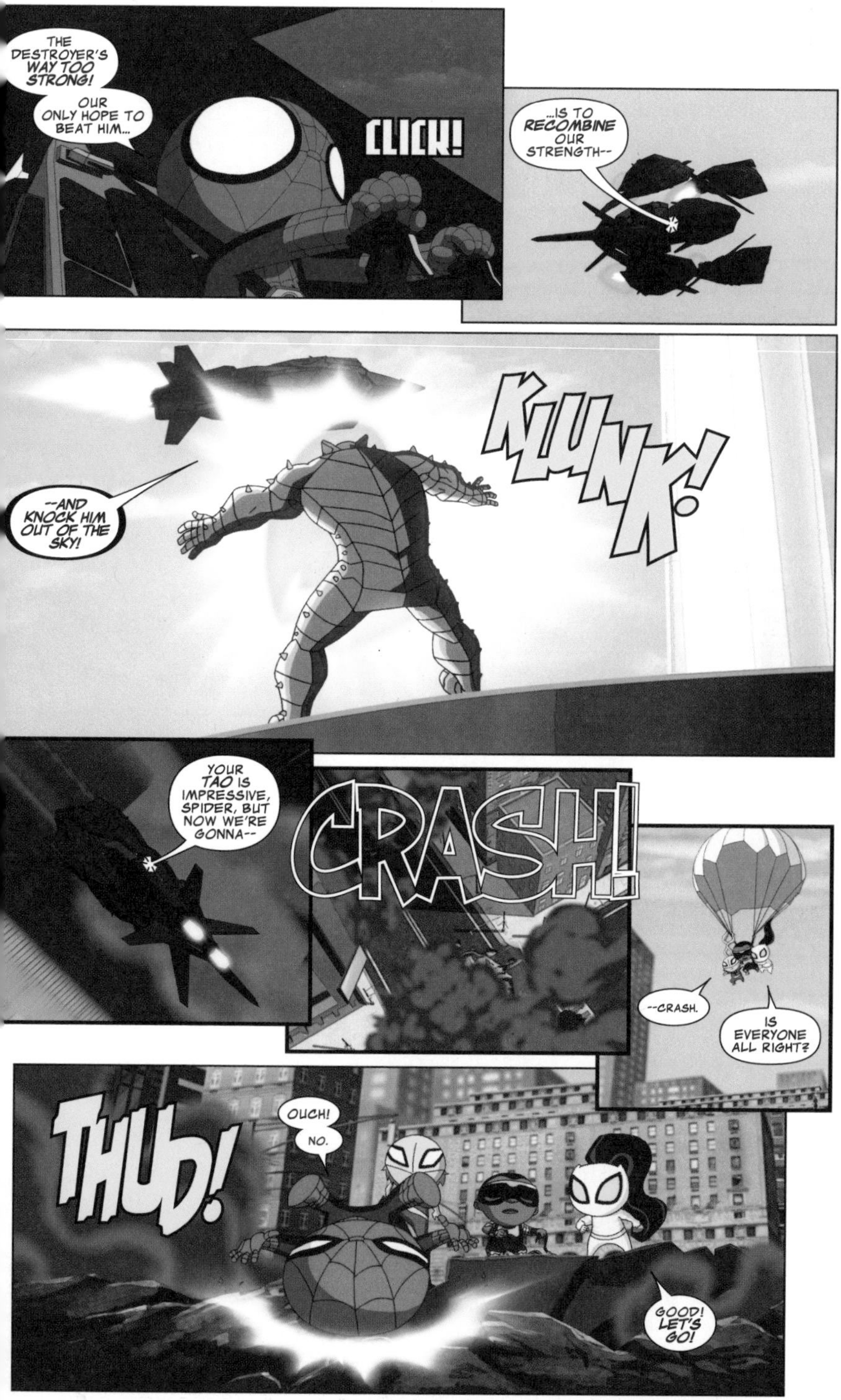
THE DESTROYER'S WAY TOO STRONG!
OUR ONLY HOPE TO BEAT HIM...
CLICK!
...IS TO RECOMBINE OUR STRENGTH--
KLUNK!
--AND KNOCK HIM OUT OF THE SKY!
YOUR TAO IS IMPRESSIVE, SPIDER, BUT NOW WE'RE GONNA--
CRASH!
--CRASH.
IS EVERYONE ALL RIGHT?
THUD!
OUCH!
NO.
GOOD! LET'S GO!

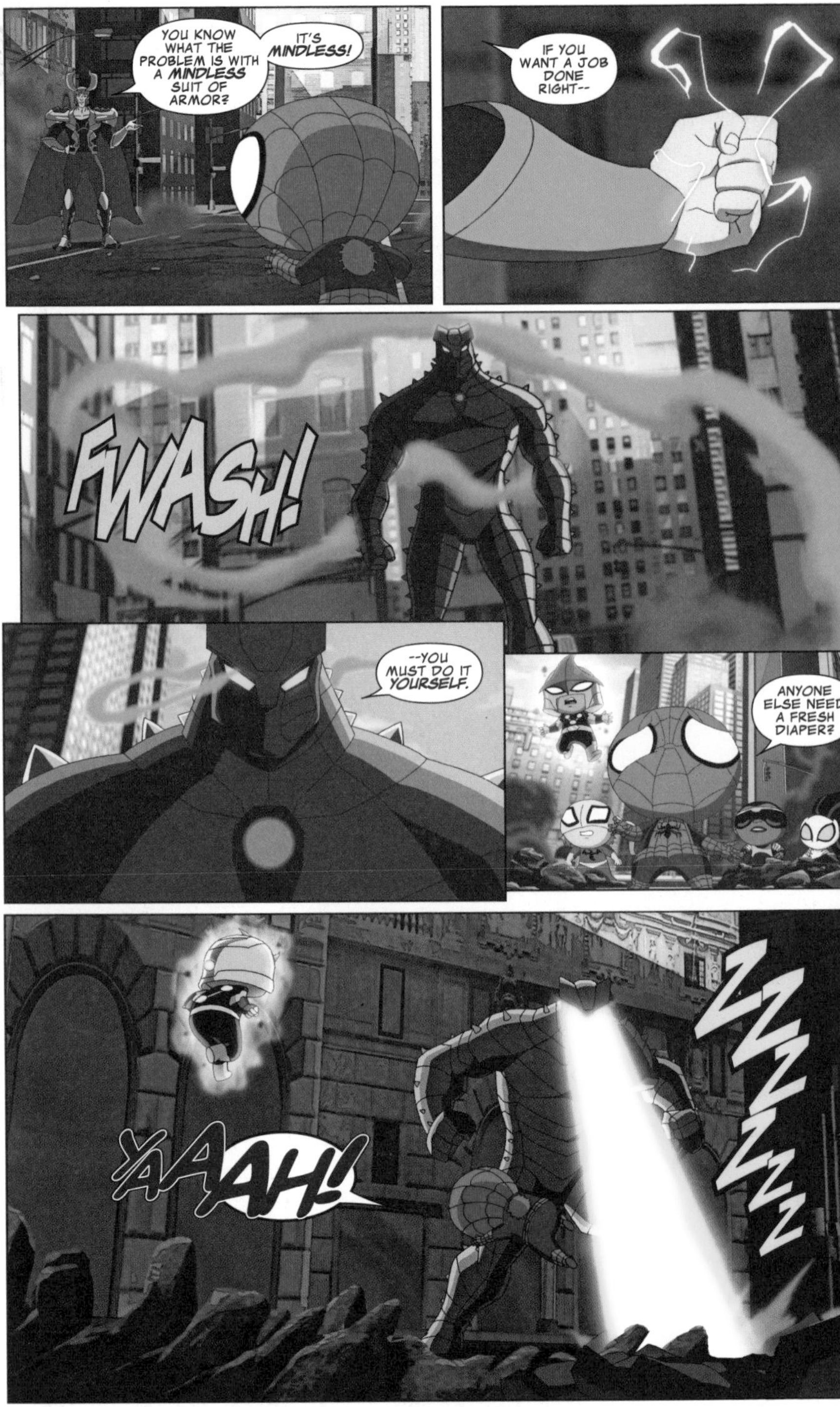
YOU KNOW WHAT THE PROBLEM IS WITH A MINDLESS SUIT OF ARMOR?
IT'S MINDLESS!
IF YOU WANT A JOB DONE RIGHT--
FWASH!
--YOU MUST DO IT YOURSELF.
ANYONE ELSE NEED A FRESH DIAPER?
YAAAH!
ZZZZZZ

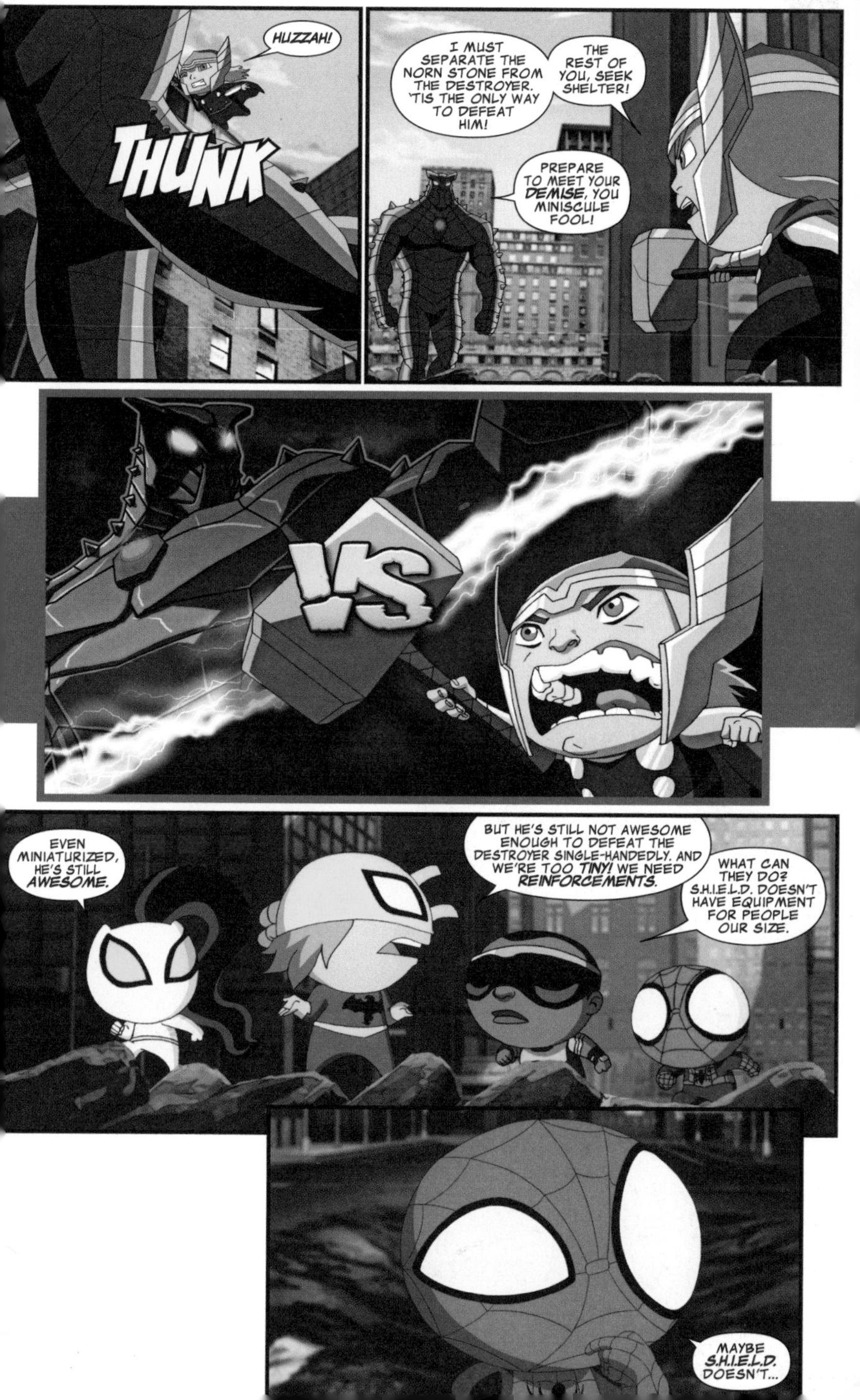
HUZZAH!
THUNK
I MUST SEPARATE THE NORN STONE FROM THE DESTROYER. 'TIS THE ONLY WAY TO DEFEAT HIM!
THE REST OF YOU, SEEK SHELTER!
PREPARE TO MEET YOUR DEMISE, YOU MINISCULE FOOL!
VS
EVEN MINIATURIZED, HE'S STILL AWESOME.
BUT HE'S STILL NOT AWESOME ENOUGH TO DEFEAT THE DESTROYER SINGLE-HANDEDLY. AND WE'RE TOO TINY! WE NEED REINFORCEMENTS.
WHAT CAN THEY DO? S.H.I.E.L.D. DOESN'T HAVE EQUIPMENT FOR PEOPLE OUR SIZE.
MAYBE S.H.I.E.L.D. DOESN'T...

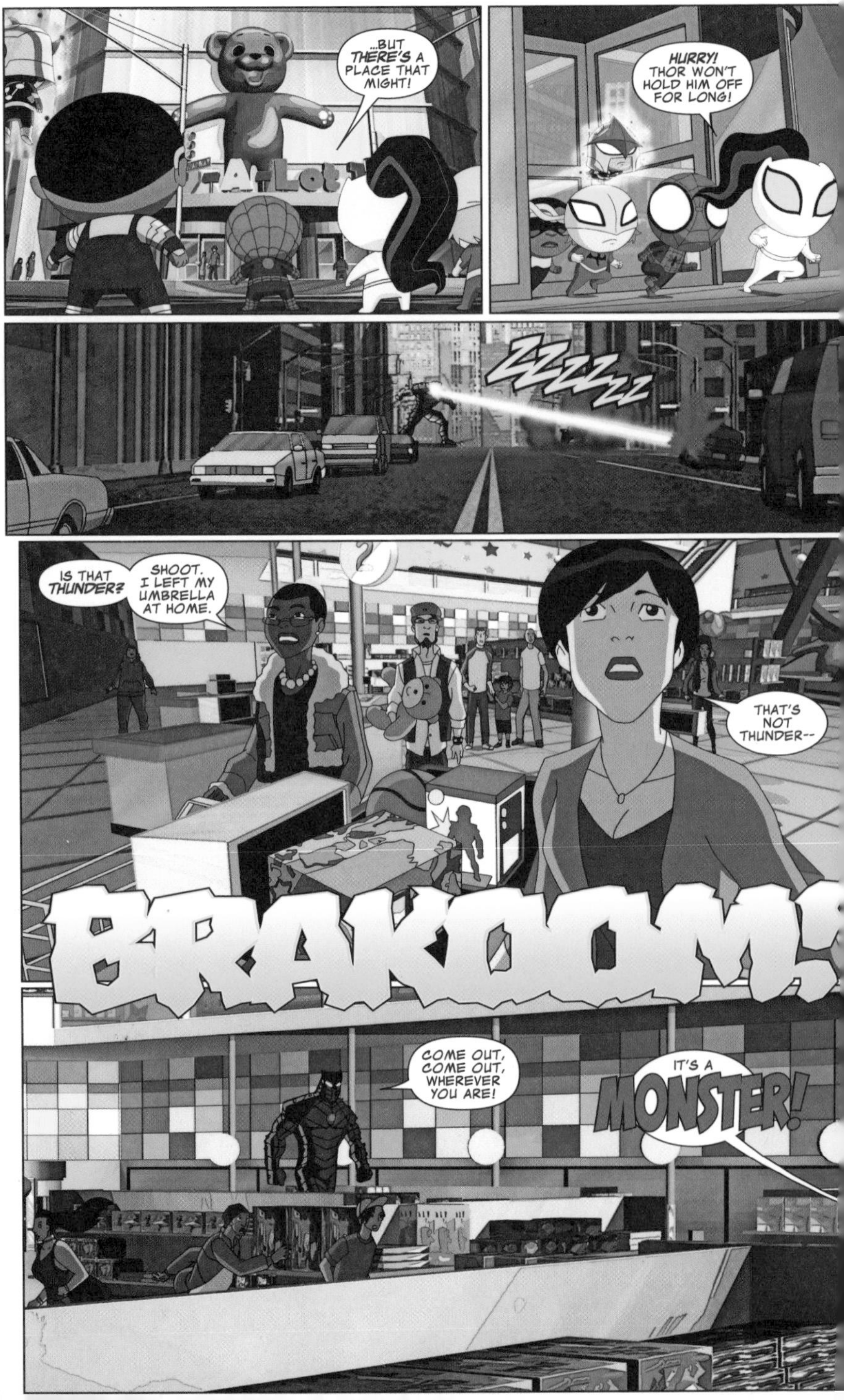

...BUT THERE'S A PLACE THAT MIGHT!
A-Lot
HURRY! THOR WON'T HOLD HIM OFF FOR LONG!
ZZZZZZ
IS THAT THUNDER?
SHOOT. I LEFT MY UMBRELLA AT HOME.
THAT'S NOT THUNDER--
BRAKOOM!
COME OUT, COME OUT, WHEREVER YOU ARE!
IT'S A MONSTER!

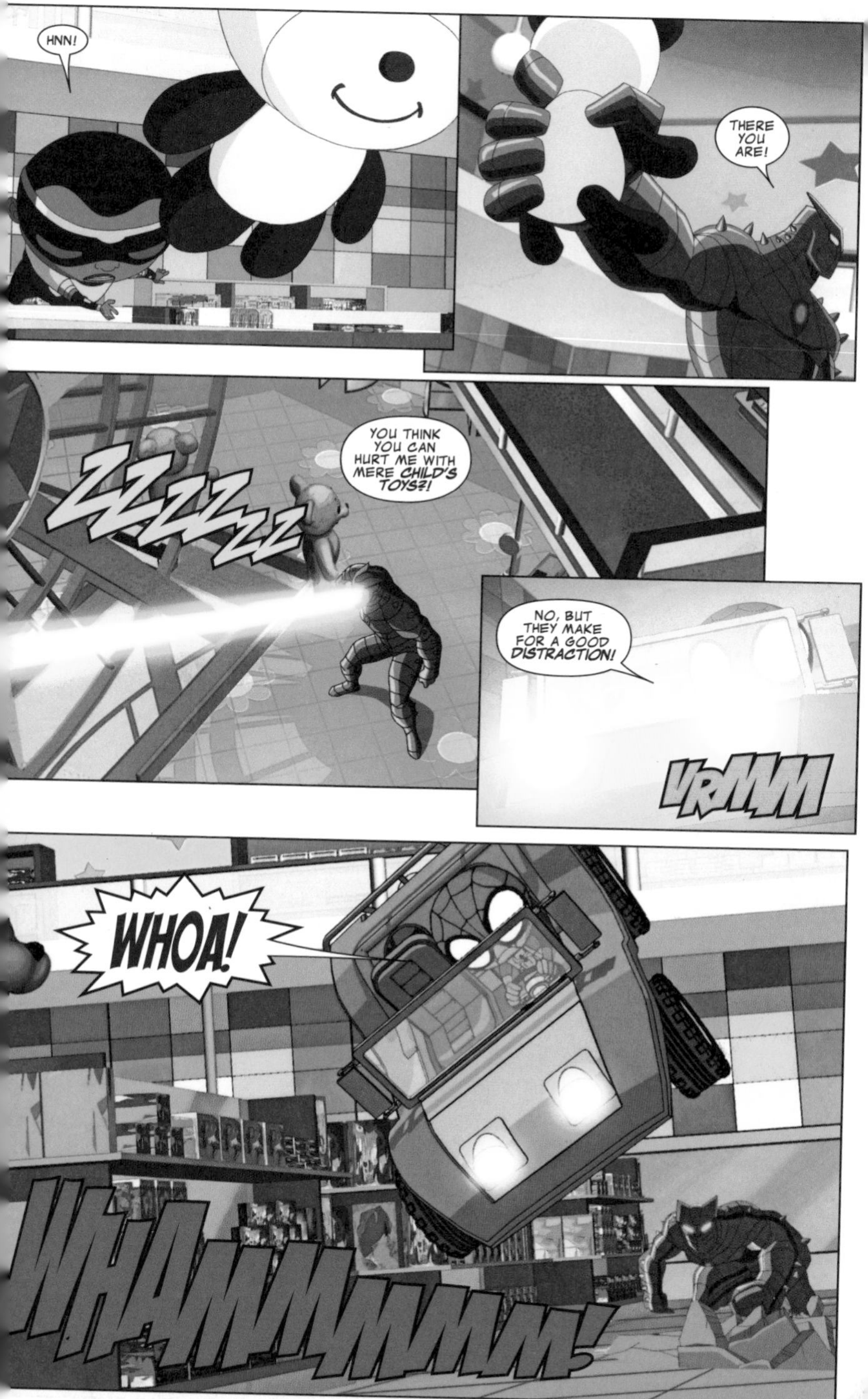
HNN!
THERE YOU ARE!
YOU THINK YOU CAN HURT ME WITH MERE CHILD'S TOYS?!
ZZZZZZ
NO, BUT THEY MAKE FOR A GOOD DISTRACTION!
VRMMM
WHOA!
WHAMMMMMMM!

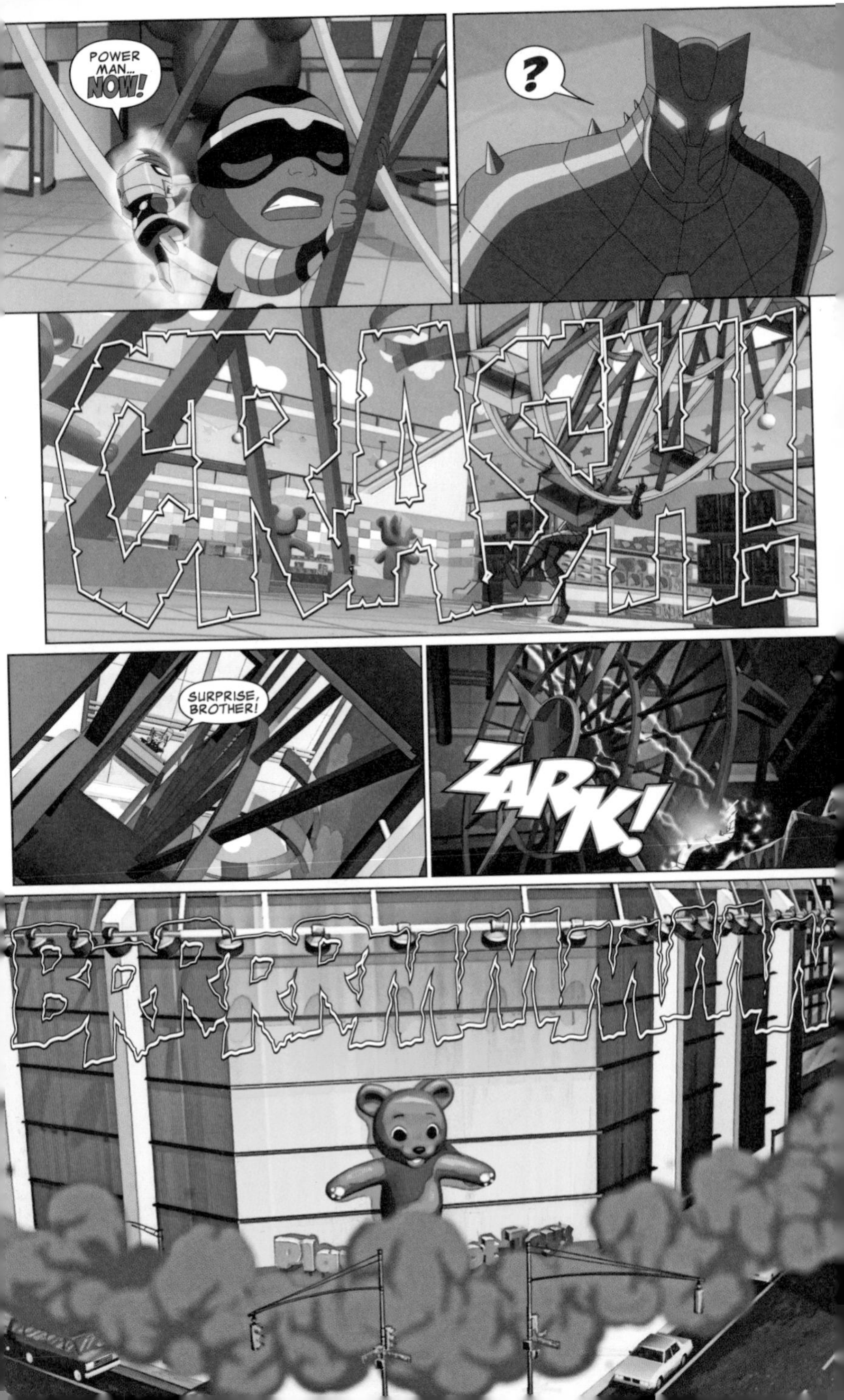

POWER MAN... NOW!
?
CRASH!
SURPRISE, BROTHER!
ZARK!
BRRRMMMMM

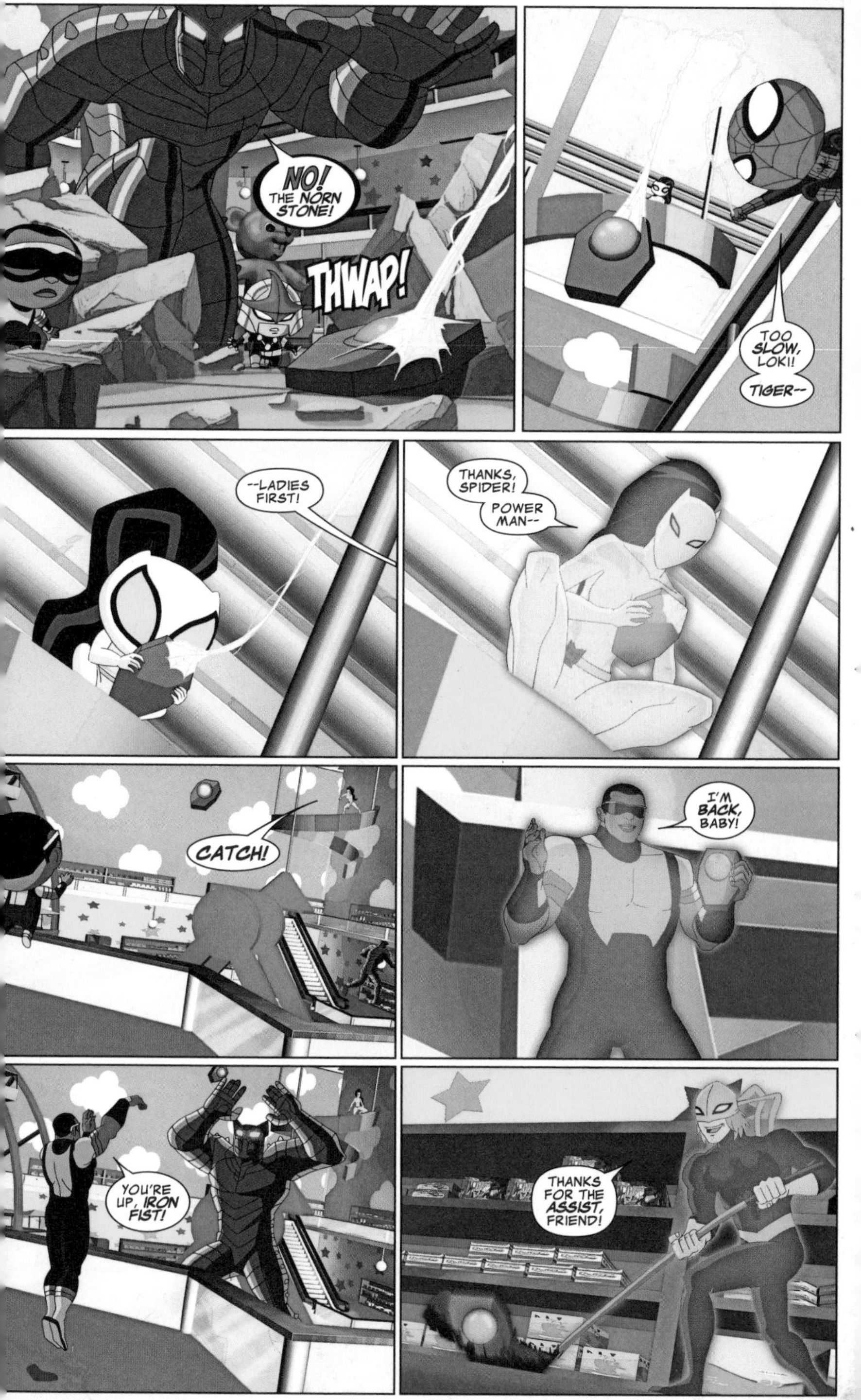
NO! THE NORN STONE!
THWAP!
TOO SLOW, LOKI!
TIGER--
--LADIES FIRST!
THANKS, SPIDER!
POWER MAN--
CATCH!
I'M BACK, BABY!
YOU'RE UP, IRON FIST!
THANKS FOR THE ASSIST, FRIEND!

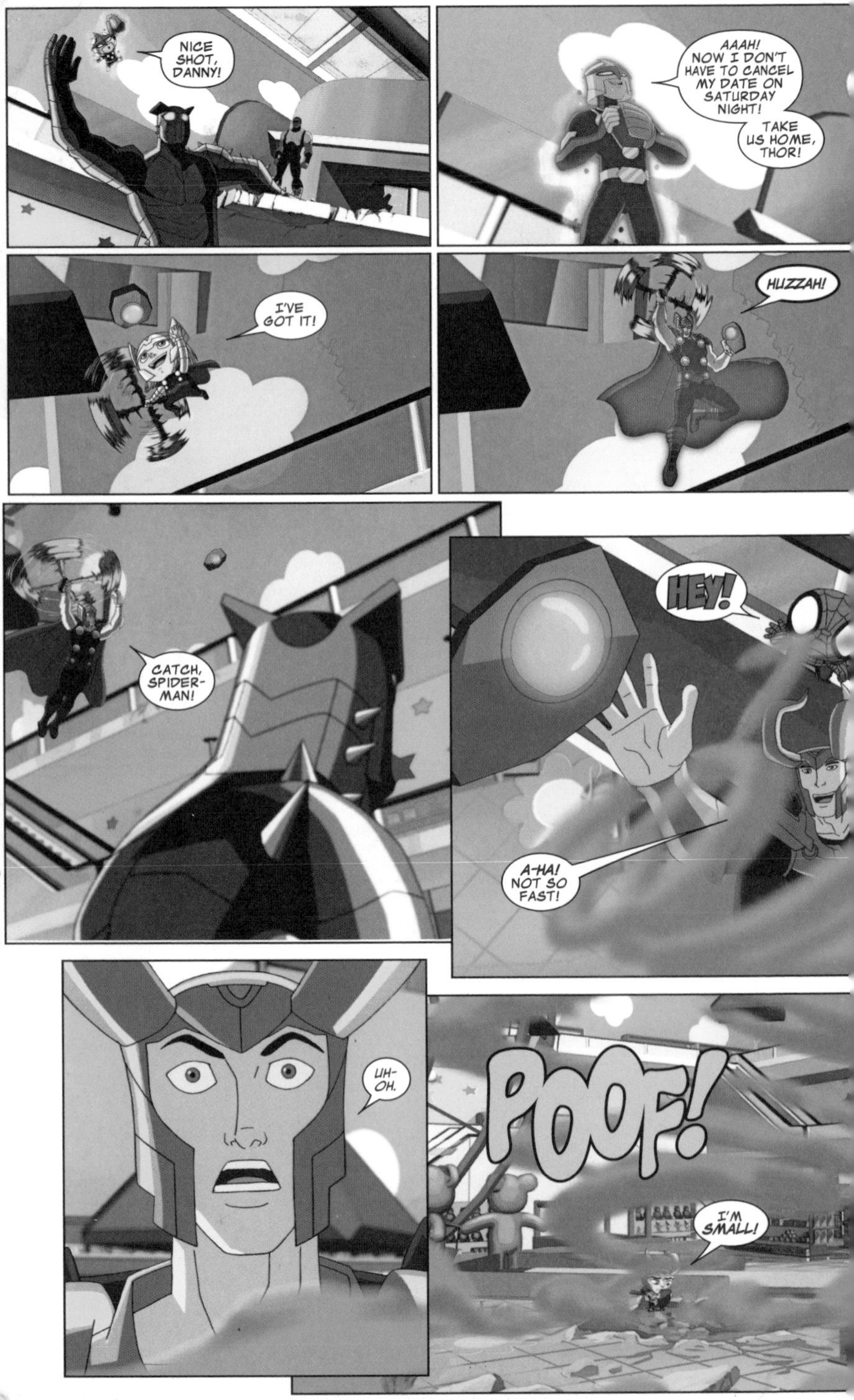
NICE SHOT, DANNY!
AAAH! NOW I DON'T HAVE TO CANCEL MY DATE ON SATURDAY NIGHT!
TAKE US HOME, THOR!
I'VE GOT IT!
HUZZAH!
CATCH, SPIDER-MAN!
HEY!
A-HA! NOT SO FAST!
UH-OH.
POOF!
I'M SMALL!

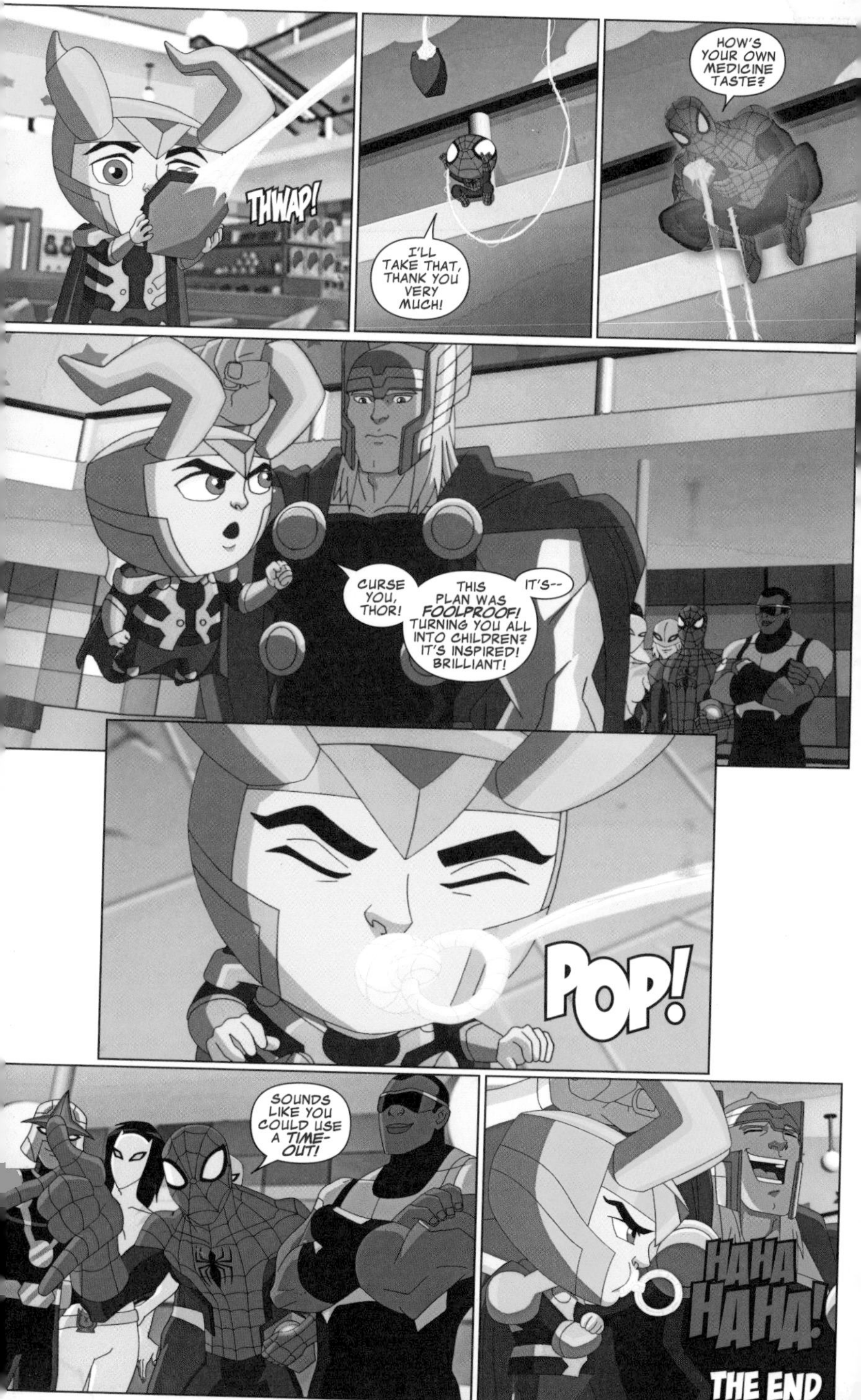
THWAP!
I'LL TAKE THAT, THANK YOU VERY MUCH!
HOW'S YOUR OWN MEDICINE TASTE?
CURSE YOU, THOR!
THIS PLAN WAS FOOLPROOF! TURNING YOU ALL INTO CHILDREN? IT'S INSPIRED! BRILLIANT!
IT'S--
POP!
SOUNDS LIKE YOU COULD USE A TIME-OUT!
HAHA HAHA!
THE END